LESSER KNOWN MONSTERS

RORY MICHAELSON

rorymichaelson.com

LESSER KNOWN MONSTERS

Book One

LESSER KNOWN MONSTERS

E-book edition ISBN: 978 1 8381660 0 7
Paperback ISBN: 978 1 8381660 1 4
Hardback ISBN: 978 1 8381660 2 1

Cover design by Dean Cole ©
Illustrations by Urban Knight Art ©
Coin art by Vincent Corsano ©
Cover images © istockphoto.com

CONTENT NOTE

This book uses British English conventions, spelling, and grammar.

Please be aware that this work contains depictions of anxiety, implied physical abuse, emotional abuse, violence, and death/dying.

For those who feel like they are not part of this world, are not so sure they wish to be, and one who makes me feel like I should be.

EXCITARE

I t is the eleventh of October, at four twenty-three in the morning. The weather in **London** is overcast with a temperature of nine degrees Celsius (forty-eight point two degrees Fahrenheit if you're into that sort of thing.) There has been mild precipitation; this *is* **England**, after all.

Oh, and **the world is ending**.

The world is ending, and it is due to the choices of a young man named **Oscar Tundale**. He is entirely average in many ways and less than average in more. This is the story of why the world is ending.

And how Oscar let it happen.

I

THE EDGE OF SHADOWS

THE BLANKET MONSTER

"Oh, Oscar," Paige groaned. "You're about as much use as tits on a teapot."

A hedgehog in a condom factory.

A fart in a colander.

A cock flavoured lollipop.

If Oscar had learned one thing from Paige, it was how many interesting but not very useful things he was the human equivalent of. Though the last one didn't sound bad at all in his opinion.

"I'm sorry," Oscar rubbed at his eyes with his free hand. "I'll do it when I get back. Promise."

His sister sighed, her breath rasping in the earpiece of his phone. "Make sure you do. If they cut the electricity off, I'm not there to warm a bath up for you with the fucking kettle again."

"Sorry, Paige."

"Don't be sorry. You're always sorry! Just sort it out this time," she snapped. The hum of voices in the background was making it difficult to hear her now; he heard someone call her name. "Listen, Oscar, I've got to go. Some shit's kicking off. I'll call you later. We need to talk about something."

"Okay."

"And Oscar?"

"Yes?"

"Pay the bloody electricity bill."

"I will." The words were still leaving his mouth when the line disconnected with a blip in his ear. Oscar sighed, pushing his phone into his pocket, and looked up at the night sky.

So far as the London autumn sky was willing to disclose, it could have been seven at night or in the morning. As far as Oscar's bones and brain were willing to share, it was definitely around four o'clock in the morning. That was the point when the night shift always started to drag into monotonous delirium.

He took a moment, burying cold fingers into the hungry pockets of his threadbare pea coat. His old jacket had seen better days, but Oscar had a habit of wearing things until they fell apart. Besides, this jacket was perfect year-round if he added or subtracted layers underneath. What more could he ask for?

His breath misted the night.

Paige had been gone for three months. Finally living the life she'd always dreamed of. He was happy for her, she'd worked hard, and when the offer for an internship at a big magazine in New York came through, her bags were half-packed before she even put the phone down. It meant Oscar had the apartment they shared all to himself. It was a little lonely sometimes, but he did have much more time to spend with Zara and Marcus, and he definitely spent a lot less time being scolded.

His phone buzzed in his pocket, and he inched it out carefully, just enough to peer at the screen but still protect his now warming fingers from the night's nipping chill.

Come back in Booboo. We got a new patient.

— ZARA

Oscar smiled tiredly and cast a glance up at the half-eaten moon, before making his way back into the hospital.

THURSDAY NIGHTS WERE USUALLY PRETTY slow, aside from the occasional toddler who found something exciting and dangerous to eat whilst their parents weren't looking. The Children's Assessment Unit had an otherwise steady stream of irritating coughs, nasty vomiting, or troubling fevers that kept it ticking along. When he got back to the Nurse's Station, the look on Zara's face told Oscar that the new patient in bed seven hadn't been admitted for eating their building blocks.

This time of night was usually the worst time for new admissions. Ripe for sighs, stoic and exhausted half-smiles, and the occasional sloppy mistake. Zara, however, was practically bouncing on her toes.

"What happened?" he asked.

Zara's eyes flashed, the colour of freshly fallen autumn leaves. Her round face and golden-brown skin practically glowed under the dimmed lighting, usually bright and hostile on the day shift.

This is not how someone should look at this hour.

"A new patient just came in." She tucked her hair behind her ear. Finishing at her jaw, it was streaked with a vivid teal at the moment and was shaved short at her right temple to show a row of gold piercings in her ear. "No parents with her...and she's been *cut*."

Oscar frowned. "Like...she cut herself on something?"

"No, like someone cut her. Pretty bad, apparently. The on-call surgeon patched her up in Emergency, but she might have to be operated on tonight."

"Oh my God." Oscar's eyes widened. "Who would do that to a child?"

"Some sicko. Probably one of the parents." Zara's eyes sparkled angrily.

Oscar flinched. Zara's heart was kind, but as one of the most senior nurses on the unit, she was a force to be reckoned with if a child needed her. She would stop at nothing to help her patients. Oscar had nowhere near her qualifications or responsibilities and often found himself watching her with awe. He'd seen her face down more arrogant junior doctors than he could count.

"Who's on call tonight?" Oscar swallowed, dreading the reply.

A flash of concern passed across Zara's face, but she quickly replaced it with a forced smile. "Ocampo." She tried to make the name sound as gentle as she could manage, but Oscar's face twitched anyway. "Don't worry," Zara said quickly. "I'll try and keep her away from you."

"How are you going to do that? By flirting?" Oscar grumbled.

Zara raised her hands innocently. "It's totally a professional crush. I mean she's an amazing doctor. And yeah, Ocampo is hot. That little pouty thing her mouth does when she's thinking. And how she always looks kind of...*mean*. That's weirdly hot, too." Zara smiled, staring into space wistfully, then caught sight of Oscar's scowl. "Okay it's a professional crush first and a sexy crush second. But definitely in that order." She cleared her throat. "Anyway, we should, umm..."

"Should I go and do observations on the other patients?"

"Ah. Well..." Zara scrunched her eyes and shifted on her feet uncomfortably. "I actually kind of need you to go and sit with the new kid. She must be scared, and we don't have the staff to send a nurse to do it. She's all alone, Os."

Oscar's stomach dropped. *All alone?* "Really? But...what about social work?"

Zara sighed. "They won't be here until the morning. The police called them when they dropped her off. They'll be back again tomorrow to try and take a statement. The girl wouldn't talk apparently, and they couldn't find her parents anywhere." Her eyes caught his for a moment, and he saw a flash of emotion.

Oh.

Oscar ran his hand through the messy chestnut mop that was his hair. *They left her. Just like…*

He pushed the thought away firmly. "Are you sure it's okay?" Usually, his duties involved taking routine observations and serving out meals. Supervising a child who'd just been assaulted wasn't something he'd done before.

"Just press the buzzer if you need me, Booboo." Zara reached over and squeezed his shoulder, giving him an encouraging smile. "I know you'll do great."

OSCAR'S FINGERS traced the door handle as he worried his lip.

What should I say? Is there something that might help? Something that might have helped…me?

Finally steeling himself, he decided to give a gentle knock before pushing the door open. "Uh…hello?" He made his voice as soft as possible as he peeked around the edge.

The small en suite's fluorescent light glared through the half-closed door casting a dull glow over the attached bedroom. On the bed, a pair of large dark eyes peered at him from amongst a bundle of hospital linen. The sheets were pulled up to nearly completely cover the new patient, only owlish eyes and a tangle of raven hair standing out in the darkness.

"Hi," Oscar said nervously, aware of the tremor in his voice as he slid through the narrowly opened doorway. "I'm Oscar Tundale, one of the Health Care Assistants. Zara asked me to come and sit with you. Is that okay?"

The girl stared back at him in muted silence for a long moment, then finally gave him a single uncertain nod.

"Your name's Nina?" Oscar made his way toward the tall backed chair at the bedside.

The bundle of blankets, hair, and large dark eyes jiggled again in the affirmative.

Oscar sat down, his knee knocking painfully against the side of the bed as he did. The clatter and Oscar's gasp of pain made the little girl recoil inside her swaddle of sheets.

"I'm sorry. Are you okay?" The words tumbled out of Oscar's mouth. "Does it hurt? I can ask Zara if you need some medicine."

The bundle shook side to side in a motion that he guessed was a no.

Oscar relaxed a little and felt some of the tension leave his smile. "It's very late. Aren't you sleepy?"

There was another shake side to side for 'no.'

"Well...I suppose blanket monsters don't get tired easily. This is the first time I've really met one myself, though." Oscar tried to grin encouragingly.

The blankets inched back, revealing the girl inside. The first thing Oscar thought was that she looked much younger than he had expected, maybe only eight or nine years old. This thought was chased by the horror that anyone would ever raise a hand to harm her. Her skin was a sandy brown, and her eyes almost as black as her hair, with round, cherubic cheeks and the sweetest bashful smile.

Oscar formed his mouth into a perfect 'O' and widened his eyes. "But you're not a blanket monster at all!" He raised his voice in mock surprise. "You're a little girl!"

The girl nodded, firmly folding her arms and trying to pull a serious face that was somewhat ruined by the grin she was unable to smother.

"That's probably why I wasn't scared. I'm not very brave, so if I met a real blanket monster, I'd probably just run away."

Nina gave him a shy smile and started to wriggle back into her blankets. As she moved to pull them about her, she suddenly stiffened in pain and let out a low squeak.

"Oh." Oscar reached out, but the girl flinched away from his touch, looking at him fearfully. Quickly, Oscar pulled his hand back, placing it on the edge of the bed instead. "Are you okay?"

Nina looked at him with dark teary eyes, her bottom lip trembling.

"I'm sure you are...you're not like me," Oscar tried to make his voice light and playful again. "You're super brave. I bet if you saw a blanket monster, you wouldn't even run away. I bet if you saw *any* monsters, you wouldn't run away, would you?!"

Her large dark eyes shone like pools of bitter chocolate, and Oscar felt like his heart was being squeezed. *This girl...*

The door creaked open slowly, and Nina jumped. Her small, cool fingers shot out and latched onto Oscar's hand.

"Hey there. How are you two getting on?" Zara beamed, peering around the door.

Nina's grip relaxed slightly.

"I came to bring you some medicine. Doctor Ocampo just called to let me know she's nearly here." Her eyes took in Nina's hand clutching at Oscar's, and she gave him an encouraging smile. "Do you think I could check your dressings while I'm in here?"

Nina shot an anxious look at Oscar.

"Oscar can stay. You can squeeze his hand if it hurts." Zara winked, setting the tray of medicines down.

The little girl looked back at Zara and nodded tentatively.

Zara held out a translucent purple syringe cloudy with thick sticky medicine. The girl surprised Oscar by leaning forward and quietly taking the medication from Zara and popping it between her teeth, gulping down the substance inside without any fuss.

Instead of being surprised, Zara used the opportunity to ease the blankets wrapped around the girl from her back and gently pull her long hair over her shoulder. The back of her gown was misshapen with the swell of bandages beneath. Oscar couldn't help but let out a gasp when Zara unknotted the ties and let the fabric slide free. Most of the girl's back was covered in thick pressure dressings. Several patches were dark with dried blood. *Who would do this to a little girl?*

Oscar caught a glimpse of Nina's large, dark eyes fixed on his face, and realised the expression she must have seen. He forced the shock down into his guts and plastered on what he hoped was a reassuring smile. "Those bandages look really cool, Nina," he said weakly.

The girl gave him a doubtful look.

"They're all intact and dry," Zara said, shifting the gown back into place. "Hopefully we will be able to let you rest for the rest of the night."

There was a rhythmic clopping from the hallway outside, gradually getting louder.

The hairs on Oscar's arms raised, and ice ran down his spine. He recognised that sound well, and nothing good ever came of it. Not for him anyway.

"Oh. It sounds like Doctor Ocampo is here," Zara said with a forced airiness, avoiding Oscar's gaze. Oscar wondered if this is how his own fake smile to Nina looked just moments ago.

The feeling of unease settled into an unpleasant dread wriggling in his stomach.

Well, he thought resignedly, *it's too late to escape now.*

THE BAD MAN

There was an ever so delicate rap of knuckles against the door before it opened to admit Doctor Ocampo. She had only been at the hospital for a year but already owned a formidable reputation. Zara explained to him that Doctor Ocampo was highly regarded across the medical community and could have chosen almost anywhere to work and named her price. She had published a myriad of contentious and cutting-edge studies, and her employment caused an excited buzz amongst the existing medical team. After her arrival, that buzz had quickly escalated to a screeching cacophony of protests and dismay.

Excellence. She always expected excellence. Only her own standards seemed agonisingly far above everyone else's, and she had no qualms about letting them know it. Her reputation wasn't hurt by the fact that she cut such a striking figure either. Angular features, porcelain skin, and black hair like silk gathered in a bun at the nape of her neck. Tonight, she wore a sumptuous plum blazer over a sleek black dress. Her high-heeled pumps were such a pristine white, Oscar couldn't help but wonder if she took them off to go outside.

"Doctor Ocampo, thank you for coming so fast. I was just looking at Nina's dressings," Zara said smoothly.

Doctor Ocampo's dark eyes took in both the girl and Zara, before drifting toward Oscar, Nina's hand still clutched in his own. One immaculate eyebrow twitched, her thin lips pursed, and she smoothed her blazer as if the thing could fit her any better. She pulled short of open disdain, a pleasant surprise for Oscar. Doctor Ocampo never made any secret of how underwhelmed she was by his existence.

When Doctor Ocampo spoke, it was short, sharp, and precise. Decisive cuts of a surgical blade. "Hello Nina, I'm Doctor Ocampo." She flashed a smile just brief enough to serve its purpose. "I'd just like to have a look at your back if that's okay?"

The girl seemed hypnotised by Doctor Ocampo and gave her an awed nod.

"Excellent," Doctor Ocampo said crisply. "I'm going to need a dressing pack." Her dark eyes drifted to Oscar with expectancy.

"I can get it," Zara chirped.

"I'd prefer you to stay and take down the dressing, Zara." Doctor Ocampo's sharp voice softened for Zara. A honeyed scalpel for her.

"I'll fetch it," Oscar squeaked. He disentangled his fingers from Nina's and concentrated on not tripping over his own feet as he rushed to the door.

Oscar let out a tense breath as he let it close behind him.

He wasn't sure exactly what he had done wrong so far as Doctor Ocampo was concerned. He was convinced that, in her opinion, he just never did anything right.

His charting was messy.

His answers were slow.

His hands were clumsy whenever she asked him for help.

There was such a thing as a self-fulfilling prophecy, and this one was fuelled by the fact that Doctor Ocampo seemingly saw no value in him at all.

Oscar chided himself as he rushed down the dimmed corridor. *Just keep your head down and work harder.* Zara said he worried too much about what other people thought, and that's was what made him so anxious and indecisive. It was kind of a difficult obstacle to overcome, particularly when someone made their negative thoughts so clear. He could imagine Doctor Ocampo now, patting her freshly washed hands dry with a paper towel, the corner of her mouth curling with thinly veiled disdain that Oscar was taking so long for a simple task. He spun around the corner to the storeroom and collided bodily with something. Or rather, someone.

Something between an instinctive apology and a shocked yelp burst out of Oscar's mouth even as he belatedly tried to slow down, step back, and stop all at once. His feet caught against one another, and he tumbled backwards. He would have fallen flat out on the dingy speckled laminate floor, but a pair of hands shot out and clutched him, one by the shoulder and one at his waist.

"Oh, God. I'm so sorry," Oscar blustered, struggling to regain his footing. "I'm...oh."

Pale grey eyes regarded him with concern. "Are you okay?"

Of course.

Of all the people, it had to be him.

"I'm fine, thank you, Dmitri," Oscar managed breathily.

Dmitri ran a hand through his dark hair, tucking a few stray strands back behind his ear. He wasn't much taller than Oscar, but something just seemed more *solid* about him. A plump bottom lip weighed down a perfect cupid's bow, a nearly delicate nose, and a sharply angled jaw that seemed to have a permanent shadow of stubble. His intense stormy grey eyes fixed on Oscar from beneath thick dark brows in a way that made Oscar's knees feel like jelly.

"Good, I'm glad. I didn't mean to surprise you." His lips quirked in a charming half-smile.

Too handsome, Oscar thought numbly. *And the accent*. His words curled like he was kissing them out of his mouth and they just wanted to go right back in. Oscar never felt quite so awkward as he did when he was speaking to this man. Not just because of what *happened*, but because standing beside him made Oscar all the more aware of his own flaws. The way he stood all gangly-limbed like one of those tufty haired *Troll* toys. His long arms and legs never quite seemed to get the memo of exactly what he wanted them to do, and he was so clumsy he usually had at least one good bruise on him at all times. That was why Zara had taken to calling him *Booboo*. He almost felt the urge to cover his face and hide his long, freckled nose and the small gap between his front teeth.

Instead, Oscar laughed awkwardly, willing the pink he knew would be blossoming around his ears to subside. "It's my fault, I was in a rush. Are you okay?"

Dmitri crinkled his eyes like he was confused by the question and shook his head. "Of course, I'm fine."

Why did he always have to smell so good? Clean, like citrus, but with a deep and smoky note. Like charred cedarwood.

Oscar tensed, realising that Dmitri's hand was still on his shoulder, and was immediately conscious of every finger. He was suddenly sure they were burning through the thick fabric of his pale green uniform. He was still standing far too close; he could practically feel Dmitri's breath on his face.

Dmitri tilted his head curiously, eyes searching.

Oscar's stomach leapt, and he took a stumbling step away, almost tripping over his own feet again. "So, can I help?" he slurred, his tongue seemingly too large for his own mouth.

For God's sake.

It was one date.

One coffee.

They hadn't even *kissed*, though Oscar had spent the whole hour watching Dmitri's lips move as he spoke, wondering how they would feel against his own. It ended quite abruptly, a glance at a phone and an apology for the need to rush off.

Then Dmitri never contacted him again.

Zara had been full of advice for that, as if she hadn't been the one to encourage him to go on the date in the first place. She didn't want to hear about how awkward Oscar felt now whenever the far too handsome doctor from the labs made an appearance on the ward. *Why is someone so intelligent allowed to look like that anyway?*

"I'm here to see the new patient. To take photographs and swabs," Dmitri said softly.

"Oh, yes." Colour flooded Oscar's face. *Now? Why?!* Was every part of his body going to betray him? He needed to get away from here before blood started pouring from his nose, or his eyes popped out like a ridiculous cartoon character.

"She's in cubicle seven." He waved emphatically back in the direction he came from.

Dmitri gave a small smile and stepped past him.

Oscar, feeling like his bones were now half dissolved, practically slithered to the storeroom door a few feet away.

"Do you need any help?" Dmitri asked. Oscar turned to see him still watching, brow slightly furrowed.

"No," Oscar replied far too quickly to be polite. "No, thank you," he added with a nervous grin. Dmitri chuckled, raising a hand in a motionless wave, before rounding the corner.

Oscar let the storeroom swallow him up, hoping that the ground might open up beneath him too if he wished hard enough. The door closed behind him, and he leaned back on it, feeling it cool against his back through his uniform. His heart rushed in his chest like it had somewhere to go and needed to get out. From the way his skin tingled, he was quite sure that if he took off his shirt now, he would see two handprints—one on his arm and one over his ribs.

He let out a deep breath and dropped his head back against the door with a loud hollow *thunk*.

～

IT TOOK a few moments more than it should have for Oscar to find the dressing packs in the cluttered storeroom. He checked them every day and should have been able to find them with his eyes closed. Still, the combination of Doctor Ocampo and Dmitri had undoubtedly caused some kind of short circuit in his brain. When he was nearly back to the room, he wondered if he'd been gone for much longer than he anticipated.

Doctor Ocampo was coming out of the cubicle when he approached. Her pale skin had taken on a slightly mottled tone, and her eyes flashed with bubbling rage.

"Sorry, Doctor Ocampo, I—" Oscar began.

Doctor Ocampo reared back like a snake about to strike, an expression of alarm on her face. Or maybe surprise that he had the nerve to continue to exist. "What?" she spat, eyes flashing to the dressing pack in his hands. "Oh. Zara will see to that. I've had quite enough for one night." She waved a lithe hand in dismissal and stalked past him with an angry clicking of heels.

Curious and confused, Oscar pushed into the cubicle, where Zara was fussing over Nina, who wriggled and whimpered on the bed.

"What happened?" Oscar looked around the room, feeling both relief and disappointment that Dmitri was not there.

Zara shot him a significant look. "Labs came up to take a sample from the wound. Nina was frightened, and Doctor Ocampo got really mad and sent him away."

Oscar placed the dressing pack on the foot of the bed.

"Wow."

He was glad that he managed to avoid *that* situation at least, but it was difficult to imagine someone lashing out at Dmitri. He was always so placid and amiable. But then, Doctor Ocampo did seem to have excess venom that needed to be drained regularly.

Nina was coiling the blankets around her again, sobbing quietly. Sighing, Zara stepped back, looking at the shaking bundle with worried eyes. "Listen, can you stay with her, Os? I'll go and get something to help her settle down."

"Okay." Oscar bit his lip, realising he sounded more confident than he felt, and made his way back to the chair by her bed.

The door banged shut behind Zara.

Oscar sat, tensely watching the whimpering blankets, struggling to find the right words.

She must be so scared. No one here to comfort her...I...what can I...

"Hey there, blanket monster," he said softly. "I thought you weren't really a blanket monster at all?" The words sounded limp even to him.

The bundle let out a little mewl.

"I'm sorry you were scared," Oscar said sadly. "The man that came...he just wanted to help you. He wanted to make sure whoever did this to you didn't get away with it, and—"

A small cold hand darted out of the sheets and grabbed onto Oscar's wrist, short nails digging in and making him gasp in surprise. The bundle of covers slid down, and Nina's face appeared, large black eyes terrified and welling with tears.

"That man. It was him." Her small voice was strangled and full of woe.

"What?"

"That...that was the bad man."

3

THE SHADOW THAT LIVES

Oscar dropped his bag on the countertop with a thud. It vaguely occurred to him that it was *precisely* the spot that Paige always scolded him for putting it. He could almost hear her now. *Why would you put your dirty bag where you prepare food, you absolute fuck-ninny?*

Tired and stubborn, he left it where it was and moved across the small kitchenette to fill the steam kettle and set it on the grubby hob. He silently reminded himself he needed to get some housework done. It wasn't that he was dirty exactly, but he had other things to worry about more important than cleaning.

Right now, Oscar had four urgent matters on his action plan: *Shower, tea, book, bed.* That was his usual post-night-shift routine. But today, rather than jumping in the shower while the kettle heated, he dropped limply onto the large, squashy leather armchair. The leather was torn in more than one place, but the doughy padding was still thick enough that it threatened to swallow his tired body whole. He tilted his head back and closed his eyes, shutting out the pale morning sunshine that broke through the curtains. Shutting out the walls that he and Paige had gleefully painted a sunshine yellow a few years ago and the thick black-framed photographs scattered across them. Pictures of holi-days he barely remembered with their parents. Pictures that were the only thing that kept their faces clear in his memory.

The events of the night hung heavily on Oscar. He knew they would buzz angrily in his head at him until they tired themselves out. Paige often pointed out that it was the time Oscar spent worrying about things he couldn't do anything about that meant he messed up the things that he *did* have control over. She was smart like that. Sharp in a way Oscar wasn't.

Oscar wasn't really good at *anything*. He couldn't really blame his gene pool for his lack of talents. By all accounts, his parents had been brilliant. An art historian and a botanist, both highly respected in their field, at least until…

Oscar pushed *those* thoughts away. He tried not to think about them, but now he was finding it impossible. All because of the little girl.

He started to wonder what Zara made of last night. He told her what the little girl said, of course, the first chance he got.

It was him.

Oscar's eyes opened like he had been dunked in ice water. He could practically see the haunted anguish in Nina's dark eyes. So full of innocence and fear. A chill ran up his spine, and he sat forward, rubbing his eyes.

Zara said that the girl was probably hysterical and overtired. Talking nonsense in the final throes of exhaustion. She said that maybe the person who did it *looked like* Dmitri, and it really was a clue of some kind. Then she came back with a dose of diazepam that made Nina sleep for the rest of their shift.

Oscar hadn't missed it. He knew Zara too well.

He'd seen the thoughtful twist in the corner of her lips. The distant flicker of doubt in her eyes. The question, like a lingering ominous ghost of a thought. Impossible not to wonder.

What if he did do it?

The thought put a prickle between Oscar's shoulder blades.

It wasn't like he *knew* Dmitri. It had only been one date and a couple of short, polite conversations before. Well, that, and a few awkward encounters after. It would never have worked out anyway. Oscar put him at his early thirties—only a few years older than he was himself, but something about Dmitri just seemed so...*together*. His eyes shone with knowledge that Oscar would never attain, his mouth always hinting a smile from a joke that Oscar could never understand. He was successful, smart...almost irritatingly handsome. He probably had a string of men sniffing after him. Probably even warming his bed on a rotation. Imagine if something *had* happened. Then things would have been really awkward. Oscar didn't know if his nerves could have taken it.

What if he did do it?

The girl seemed so sure.

Maybe Zara was right. The person who did it could have looked like Dmitri. Perhaps they too had pale knowing eyes and a sullen smile. Maybe the girl *was* on the edge of exhaustion and speaking nonsense. He remembered the look of terror on her face, the frightened quiver of her voice.

That was the bad man.

Oscar's phone buzzed in his pocket, startling him out of thought. He pulled it out, blinking at the screen.

We need to meet up later.

— ZARA

He keyed in his response with clumsy thumbs.

Why? What's up?

— OSCAR

Only a few seconds passed before her reply.

I was talking to Marcus before he went to work. About what happened last night. Let's meet up for coffee later?

— ZARA

The knot of worry in Oscar's chest throbbed. *Of course, she'd told Marcus; they lived together after all.* Marcus had dubbed their trio the 'Three Lusty Queers' though Oscar wasn't sure he'd ever been qualified to be called 'lusty.'

Marcus was pretty much a genius, or as close to it as Oscar had ever known. He worked in the hospital's IT department and excelled with minimal effort. His inquisitive mind and boundless energy were usually a huge asset, but it also tended to make him...*overly suspicious*. Oscar might go so far as to say paranoid. He would *definitely* make a huge deal out of *this*. Oscar's phone buzzed again.

Coffee this afternoon?

— ZARA

He chewed his lip, thumbing 'ok,' before setting his phone

back down and pulling off his shirt, the cold air licking at his lean, pale body as he tossed it on the back of his couch. A cursory sniff confirmed that there was no avoiding the shower this morning.

He was halfway through tackling his jeans when the kettle started to whistle. He hopped over to the stove until his foot was free then tossed the jeans to join his shirt before switching off the hob. The best thing about Paige being away is definitely clothes being optional. He dropped his underwear, leaving it where he stepped out of it, and made his way toward the bathroom.

A dark shape flashed at the edge of his vision, to the right, by his bedroom door.

Oscar's heart jolted in his chest. His head snapped around, searching for the shadowy intruder.

The bedroom door hung open. Bed unmade, and yesterday's T-shirt and shorts that he'd slept in on the floor. Nothing unusual there.

Heart fluttering in his chest, Oscar closed his eyes and took a slow, shaky breath. When he opened them, he walked steadily into his bedroom and looked around. Of course, there was nothing there.

Well.

Nothing but a pile of clothes, unknown in their cleanliness, and a few books scattered on his desk.

It had just been a *fleck*.

As a child, he'd seen three opticians, an ophthalmologist, and several other doctors before they decided that the shadows that he sometimes saw had more to do with *him* than his eyes. Visual hypersensitivity triggered by severe anxiety. That's what they called it. His panic attacks didn't present with many other symptoms, unless it was a particularly bad day, and the counselling never seemed to make much difference. His counsellor had encouraged him to name them, an exercise to control the fear she claimed. He came up with flecks. Innocent enough, almost like the floaters you saw when you blinked in the sunlight. He still was not sure how successful *that* had been. It got worse when he was stressed, and after last night with Ocampo and what the little girl said...well, he'd be lucky if he could get any sleep at all.

He padded into the bathroom, trying to ignore the tight thrumming in his chest, and flicked on the light, twisting the shower and bringing it to life with a hiss. It would run cold for a good minute before it heated up enough to stand under. Plenty of time to nip back to the kitchen and pour the hot water into a cup with a teabag to let it stew. As he passed the coffee table, his phone buzzed again.

We need to talk.

— PAIGE

Oscar sighed. It may be better to leave that conversation until he got some rest. She was probably checking that he paid the electricity bill. *I'd better actually remember to do that.* Oscar was about to set his phone down when it buzzed once more in his hand.

Marcus just looked at the duties for last night. Dmitri wasn't scheduled to be at work.

— ZARA

A chill ran up Oscar's spine, and his skin broke out in goose-bumps. Another fleck danced in the edge of his vision, closer this time, near the kitchen. Oscar flinched, eyes flashing around to see...nothing. *Nothing. It's always nothing.*

A wave of nausea rolled over him, and he put down his phone with a heavy thud. Dmitri wasn't even supposed to be there? Maybe he had been covering for someone. Maybe the roster was wrong...maybe...

Maybe he did it.

Oscar's stomach twisted at the thought.

He checked that the door was locked four times before he got into the shower.

TAXONOMY OF MONSTERS: THE DITHERFOX
(VULPES TEMPES)

Fur sleek and full, like fine-brushed cloud,
Eyes meek and mild, tail thick and proud.
The Ditherfox at midnight came.
Her claws are soft, her teeth won't pierce,
She's safe from all, even those fierce.
The Ditherfox, her manner tame.
To see her is to know your fears,
Moments, seconds, bleed to years.
The Ditherfox, your time will claim.

— RONALD JAN, 1911-1985

4

THE GHOSTEE

Marcus sat, legs crossed in the faded plaid chair, his straight back accentuating his long body. He held his iced coffee in both hands, russet brown eyes wide and bright. "All I'm saying is that you don't really know anything about him at all. None of us do."

"But that doesn't mean that he had anything to do with...*that*." The last word left Oscar's mouth quietly, worried a passerby might hear. "I mean, why would he?"

"Why does anyone do anything?" Zara said sagely, sipping her cappuccino. "To make them feel good? Powerful? This wouldn't exactly be the first instance of someone hurting others for no good reason other than to get their jollies. A rich white guy to boot."

Oscar deflated slightly. He knew she was right. *Sometimes people do horrible things just because they can. Especially if they think they can get away with it.*

"It's okay. We feel you, Os. It must be hard finding out that your sexy doctor fancy-man is an evil sprog slicer." Marcus grinned darkly, popping his straw between his teeth. "What should we call him? McStabby? Oh, oh, how about McScreamy?"

Oscar shot him a miserable look, which Marcus returned with an overabundance of wide-eyed innocence. The door behind him swung open and closed to admit a couple of women speaking to each other and giggling.

The coffee shop was just busy enough that the general din drowned out the grizzlier parts of their conversation. Oscar was still conscious, particularly with where they were sitting, that people might overhear. They often sought out the alcove with large comfortable sofas, but today it had been snagged by a fashionable looking group of teens, leaving them with the drafty table by the door. Marcus had, of course, managed to procure himself the comfiest chair, resulting in Oscar and Zara having to make do with the stiff pleather bucket seats around the tiny table.

Setting his half-drained coffee on the table, Marcus leaned back, put hands behind his head, and stretched. His hair, as always, looked freshly buzzed at the sides, so close that his deep umber skin was visible through it. Stylish gold-rimmed glasses sat on his broad nose, and a neat moustache crowned his faint smirk proudly. Marcus had the most animated face of anyone that Oscar had ever known, and right now, he looked...*excited*.

"I called the labs. Told them I was doing a key card audit. Asked around his colleagues to see why he might have been in overnight, and none of them had any idea." Marcus leaned forward, waggling his eyebrows significantly.

"Maybe he was just working on a project. Or decided to help out?" Oscar said.

"Maybe. Or maybe he was looking to make sure the little girl didn't ID him and came to finish her off." Marcus' grim expression matched his tone.

Oscar sighed, picking up his green tea and taking a sip. "I don't know, Marcus."

"The criminal always comes back to the scene of the crime," Marcus said proudly, crossing his arms.

"The hospital wasn't the scene of the crime," Oscar pointed out.

"Her back was," Zara mumbled.

Marcus pointed at Zara, nodding fiercely.

"So what?" Oscar said. "The girl will tell the police today, and they can investigate. Figure out if it's him or just someone that looks like him."

"Maybe." Marcus shrugged, his eyes meeting Oscar's, "or maybe they won't get to her quick enough. Maybe he hurts someone else in the time it takes them to investigate."

"So?" Oscar shook his head, at a loss. He looked from Marcus and Zara. "What are you looking for? You want to make a citizen's arrest or something?"

"EVIDENCE!" Marcus crowed so loudly, several people in the coffee shop turned around. Oblivious, Marcus grinned, a wild look in his eyes.

A pretty waitress with a heart-shaped face covered in freckles framed by frizzy red hair darted over, looking concerned. "Is everything alright? Can I get you anything else?"

"No, thanks, everything's great!" Zara gave her an exaggerated smile, eyes flashing angrily at Marcus.

The girl stuffed her hands into her green corduroy dungarees pockets awkwardly, mouth a straight line of consternation. Oscar cringed; *she's probably going to throw us out*.

Marcus grinned at the waitress, one eyebrow lifting as he adjusted his glasses. "Hey." His voice was even richer than usual.

"Hey." She giggled, blushing nearly the same colour as her hair, before returning to her duties with a slight spring in her step.

A few moments later, the steady hum of conversation in the coffee shop had picked up again.

"Jesus, Marcus. Can you keep it in your pants?" Zara said drily.

"Not even a little bit." Marcus smirked, eyes still on the pretty redhead. "So," he began, finally pulling his eyes away, "I looked in the staff personnel files and found his address..."

"Marcus!" Oscar gasped. "I'm pretty sure that's illegal."

Marcus gave him a level look. "Not as illegal as cutting little girls Oscar. Besides, shut up and listen for a minute. I have a...contact. Online. They pulled up police records for me, and I looked into crimes in the area of his registered address."

Zara leaned forward, face stern. "Marcus...police records? That sounds *really* illegal."

Marcus pressed on, ignoring the interruption. "Over the last ten years, there have been seven killings by multiple stab wounds within a one-mile radius of his address."

"That you found out about by being a criminal," Zara chided.

Marcus rolled his eyes. "It wasn't me," he said impatiently. "It was my online contact."

"Which they did with confidential information you provided. So, what, you count as an accessory?" Zara shot back.

"A fabulous one," Marcus said flatly, with a slow blink. "Now can I finish telling you what I found out, or do you plan to keep interrupting me? Because this is getting very boring for me."

Zara's eyes narrowed, and she scowled. "Well, I suppose done is done."

"Most of the cases, no one was prosecuted," Marcus continued. "Apparently that's an uncommon concentration of unsolved murders in such a small area."

"I suppose it depends on the area," Zara said.

"Highgate," Marcus replied.

Zara whistled through her teeth. "So not only might he be a killer, but if he is, he's a killer that's a fancy bitch."

"So it would seem." Marcus took another sip of his iced coffee.

"And?" Oscar said incredulously. "You want to go to the police and tell them you had someone break into their systems? That you think that some guy from work is a murderer who hurt a little girl?"

"Of course not," Marcus scoffed, slurping at his straw until the dregs rattled the leftover ice. "I want to hop on the tube and go and have a look."

Oscar stared blankly for a moment then laughed. Marcus held his flat, patient stare. "You're serious?!" Oscar groaned. "No way! Marcus. A look at what?"

"The area." Marcus shrugged suspiciously.

"Just hear him out." Zara shifted forward in her chair. "I mean, there's no harm in going to see the area, right? It might be fun."

"Fun?" Oscar echoed. "We're a person and a dog short for this kind of adventure, Velma."

Zara slowly turned her head, raising her hands and eyes wide with exaggerated horror. "I know you did not just Velma me. You'd better take that back and recognise that I'm a Daphne right now."

"Zara, you are way better than Daphne, girl. You're off the Gellar scale." Marcus waved a dismissive hand in Oscar's direction. "Ignore him, he knows not of what he speaks."

"Seriously. This is too much," Oscar moaned. "I mean, if you really think there's something to this, then we need to tell someone. The police would probably already be looking into it if any of this were even remotely true."

Marcus blew a raspberry. "Os, stop trying to protect your little boyfriend. We know you want to have him butter your crumpets, but this is business."

"Leave him alone," Zara warned softly. "They only met up once, then the asshole ghosted him."

"That sounds like a normal date. A normal Oscar date, at least." Marcus shrugged. "Well, aside from some heavy breathing and whispered promises with no intentions of being kept. Actually, that sounds kind of like my dates too..."

"But aren't you usually the ghoster rather than the ghostee?" Zara prodded.

"That's beside the point." Marcus waggled his finger. "Anyway, let's get this show on the road." He raised his hands to his mouth and boomed, "Gayvengers, assemble!"

Oscar sunk low in his chair as seemingly everyone in the coffee shop turned to look.

"Settle down," Zara smiled. "We only got the LG and T. We do have oodles of Q, but we're a few letters short of the full squad."

Marcus was already pulling on his coat, too excited to hear her.

"Come on," Zara squeezed Oscar's arm, "let's go for a nice little walk. An adventure. I promise we will try not to get ourselves stabbed too much."

THE HIDDEN HOUSE

Oscar had never been to this part of London before. The houses were beautiful in a foreboding gothic sort of way, looming on either side of the street, powerful with history and grandeur. The autumn afternoon sun drooped in the overcast sky, and the mild cool was turning to an uncomfortable cold. Mixed leaves, light and dark, crunched pleasantly under his feet as he followed Zara, who walked a few steps ahead in her smart mustard-coloured trench coat. Marcus prowled further ahead, dark-furred parka hood pulled up, marching with a determined stride despite having no idea where he was going.

"It's good to get some fresh air," Zara said with thin cheer.

"I'd rather be in bed than on another one of Marcus' 'missions.'" Oscar sighed. As predicted, his short sleep had been slow to come, then broken and fitful at best when it arrived. He hadn't been able to stop thinking. Thinking about Dmitri. Thinking about Nina, scared and alone.

"Any leads, Detective?" Zara called out toward where Marcus wandered ahead. "Time to head home?"

Marcus turned to give her an irritable, distracted look in return.

"Give him a little bit longer. He'll tire himself out soon," she promised in a hushed voice.

Oscar nodded, not so sure as he returned to watching his feet mill through the leaves. Zara dropped back to match his pace.

"He didn't mean to hurt your feelings; he was just being silly. Are you okay?"

Oscar cocked his head, pretending not to know what she was talking about, and forced a grin. "Of course, I'm fine. Have to be, don't I?" Paige told him that Mum always said that. Oscar didn't remember her saying it—barely remembered her voice even—but somehow, he seemed to have osmosed it.

"The whole ghosting thing."

"Oh." Oscar felt his cheeks colour. "Yeah, it's fine. I guess that's what happened anyway. And it *has* kind of happened more than once."

"That was months ago," Zara said sympathetically, "and it was only a coffee. Surely it's not even weird anymore."

Oscar sighed. "I don't know. Not really, I guess. Just weird when I run into him at work."

"Are we even sure he's gay?" Zara retreated to the familiar excuse she tried to use to make Oscar feel better about the rejection. "I mean, I still think he might have just wanted to hang out, then figured out it was very...*datey* and bailed."

Oscar shrugged. There was a chance she was right. It wouldn't be the first time that Oscar had catastrophically misread someone's signals. But with Dmitri, he thought he sensed something. Something different, like a deep familiarity that didn't really make sense.

Up ahead, Marcus wandered into a narrow inlet, wading through a thick layer of leaves on the ground surrounded by thickets of unkept grass. He trudged forward, an intrepid suburban explorer, trying to peer over the untidy hedges.

"No one in the picture at the moment?" Zara asked tentatively.

Oscar shook his head.

"Really? Not since Rami?"

Rami was Zara's cousin. He and Oscar had dated for a few months, and it had...not ended well. It was only a few weeks after that the Dmitri incident occurred. "Nothing. I mean, no one," Oscar admitted quietly.

"Oh Oscar," Zara chided. "You can't have your last boyfriend be *Rami*. There are apps for that. Give me your phone, we'll download them." A mischievous grin lit up her face.

Oscar laughed. "I don't think those apps are boyfriend apps."

"Well, you have needs, Booboo. Maybe we should go on the prowl this weekend. You shouldn't give up; you've just had a bad run."

Oscar forced a smile. *Have I ever had a good run?* The guys he got with always seemed to lose interest in him pretty quickly. His appetite for men was at an all-time low after Rami. Being told that you were *boring* and *don't have prospects or ambition* was a bit of an eye-opener. Then the whole Dmitri thing happened and...Oscar hadn't particularly felt any urge to put himself out there again since.

Marcus was wandering further up the overgrown pathway. Zara and Oscar meandered behind him on the uneven ground, only car tracks and potholes suggesting any level of function.

There was a splash beside Oscar, and Zara wobbled, angrily checking her feet. "For Christ's sake, Marcus, where are you taking us?" she barked. "My boots are getting ruined!"

"Just a minute!" Marcus snapped impatiently from ahead.

Zara harrumphed and turned her attention back to Oscar. "Seriously though, Os, we should find you a man. You don't want Rami as the last guy on your CV; he's an absolute bell end."

"He's your cousin!"

"Exactly! So, I know what I'm talking about!" Zara grinned. "I mean, I'm not sure why it was even a thing. Yes, he's kind of cute.

Yes, he has arms as thick as your neck, but I knew he was no good when he killed half of my dolls."

"Well, he's handsome. Successful. Funny. And the arms are...good." Oscar raised his eyebrow. "Didn't the doll thing happen when you were like seven?"

Zara shrugged. "I hold a grudge. And he's not funny."

Oscar tilted his head thoughtfully. "Yeah. I guess he's not. I mean, definitely not as funny as he thinks he is."

"Also, I don't know if he's really *that* successful either," Zara added. "Yes, he's in the police, but I'm pretty sure he just fetches all the more important officers' coffee. And here I am, running a unit for sick and dying kids, and my parents fully give zero shits." She sighed.

Oscar gave her a sympathetic look.

"But you bought into the hype," Zara said. "I get it. My Mum's pretty obsessed with him. Nani can't stand him, though."

"Nani always knows best," Oscar said thoughtfully.

"Always," Zara agreed. "She can spot an asshole a mile off. That's why I'll never take the girls I date to meet my family. Just in case she bursts my bubble. Well, that and it might finish my dad off..."

Oscar bit his lip. "Yeah...how is that?" he ventured.

Zara's face stiffened. "No change. My dad still says he wishes I'd never told him I liked girls. Every chance he gets. Mum just does that sad little smile and shakes her head, staring at me. Like she can see my future husband and children, and I'm just drubbing them with a giant stick that says 'Lesbian' on it."

Oscar cringed. "What does Nani say?"

A smile crept onto Zara's face. "Nani is fresh out of fucks to give, as usual. Keeps telling me about some of the great sapphic women of power in history. Says Florence Nightingale was a lesbian, too."

"Hey!" Marcus yelled, picking his way back down the muddy path, his long legs taking comedically careful steps. Somehow, he had managed to avoid getting dirty at all. "I think...I think it's here!" He practically vibrated with excitement.

"What?" Oscar replied.

"Come on, follow me. At the end of this path."

"Seriously, Marcus. You are trash, and I hate you," Zara grumbled.

Marcus gave a wolfish grin and hopscotched around the muddy potholes, disappearing out of sight around the overgrown bushes.

"Leave him," Zara said dispassionately. "He can become the eighth unsolved murder."

Oscar grinned. "He'd love that! To be right in the middle of all the excitement and mystery, forever recorded in the annals of history."

"You're right," Zara said. "Quick, let's rescue him before anything he might like happens."

Oscar laughed as they picked their way through the muddy hazards in the direction Marcus had gone. They didn't have to go far; he was just around the corner, where the gnarled hedges had reached out to obscure him.

"What are you doing, Marcus?" Zara released Oscar's arm to give Marcus a good shove in the back.

Marcus' body swayed from her push, but he ignored her, fixated on the house before them.

"Oh, wow," Oscar gasped.

It was probably extremely beautiful once, but now it was just...sinister. Its grand Victorian stature whispered of a past of dinner parties and carriages, but was now snarled with overgrown moss and vines. The red brick walls were filthy, and though the large windows were intact, they looked rotten. A fence just as worn as the windows and at least ten feet tall surrounded the edge of the old house, only a few dried scraps of chipped bottle green paint left on its slats.

"Dmitri's file says he lives at one hundred and thirty-eight

Kinmount Street." Marcus grinned. "I couldn't find it anywhere on the main street, so this must be it!"

"Oh, well, that solves it." Zara grabbed Oscar's arm and pulled him close. "This is definitely a place where murder is routinely committed. He did it. Let's go now."

Oscar's stomach was like a fist inside him. "We need to get out of here," he murmured. "What if he sees us?"

"It's cool." Marcus was bouncing on the spot with overflowing energy. "Like I said, I spoke to the lab staff. Dmitri was not on duty last night, but he definitely *is* on duty today. He'll be at the hospital for a few more hours yet."

"So what?" Zara's voice was growing impatient. "You're going to see if his family's home?"

Marcus sparked a wicked grin and pointed with both index fingers at Oscar with an elaborate flourishing gesture.

Oscar groaned. *It was one of the few things that Dmitri had told him on their brief coffee date.* "He lives alone. His family is in Romania."

"And *that* is why I listen to my friends." Marcus basked.

"You listen to your friends' bad date anecdotes in case the guy turns out to be a murderer so that you can go creep on his secret murder house?" Zara asked dryly.

"Yup!" Marcus chirped, spinning on his heel and marching toward the house.

Zara sighed. "You know, the Illuminati stories I can take. The Government putting drugs in the water to control people's behaviour, fine. But I think *this* is going a little too far now."

"You were all for it before," Oscar said glumly. "You were the deciding vote."

Zara raised her hands, defeated. "It seemed like a good idea at the time?"

There was a clatter, and Marcus was up ahead, rummaging through a pile of half-rotten wood and debris that looked ready for a bonfire.

"Okay, Marcus, let's go," Zara called out hopefully, but he had already moved on and was inspecting the rotting old fence by the side of the house. "Marcus, come away. You have too much melanin for this nonsense. This place is spooky as shit, and the odds aren't our friend based on horror movie history."

Marcus started to pull at the fence.

"I'll buy you a cookie!" she cried.

The panel moved.

"Two cookies?"

Marcus didn't stop to look back before clambering through the gap, his long limbs and narrow body making it easy for him to slip between the slats.

"Oh, God." Zara groaned.

"Marcus!" Oscar hissed, leaving Zara behind and dashing to the battered old fence. "Come back!"

A moment passed, and then the rotten slat moved aside with a squeak of rusty nails. Marcus' grinning face appeared. "You *have* to come and see this."

6

THE HUNGERING EARTH

Oscar wrapped his arms around himself. The dusky horizon was rapidly claiming the skies as the sun fell, his breath becoming ever more visible.

"I'm not lying for you if you get arrested for trespassing." Zara's voice was acidic but somewhat muffled from the other side of the fence.

Oscar *definitely* regretted his decision to follow Marcus, but ultimately, he had been pushed over the edge with the overwhelming need to see what Marcus was up to.

The area behind the tall fence made for something of a sad garden. It was even more overgrown and ruined than the house itself. The bricks were barely visible for moss, and the dilapidated back porch looked close to falling down. Dewy cobwebs sparkled in the final throes of failing sunlight. The side of the house was slightly sunken, with ramshackle repairs in the form of wooden boarding beneath a grubby window a few inches higher than the top of Oscar's head. The bottom of the garden was completely closed off by a wall of tall, wild-looking trees. Three large storage containers dominated the space, metallic, like the ones you would find in an industrial zone or shipping yard. Battered and worn.

Thick brown rust crawled up their sides, decorating the peeling blue paint.

"Maybe he keeps his victims in those," Marcus whispered, somehow sounding haunted and hopeful at the same time. He cast a look at Oscar, licking his lips and pointing toward the closest one. Oscar could see why. Its hinged door hung ajar.

"Marcus, it's getting late, we should go," Oscar whined. "There's no way this is Dmitri's house. There's no way *anyone* lives here."

Marcus ignored him, instead making his way to the container and leaning over to peer inside. "What the..." he muttered, leaning chest-deep.

"If you get tetanus, I'm going to laugh," Zara barked. Oscar was so startled that both his feet left the ground at once. He turned around and saw that she had moved the fence panel aside and was peering through, her mouth a grim line and eyes glittering with irritation.

Marcus pulled back out of the container, tugging awkwardly at something.

"Marcus, stop!" Oscar begged.

Marcus did, but only because he had already achieved his goal. A large plastic sack hung halfway out of the rusted door. Marcus rummaged for a moment, then leaned back, looking puzzled. "Sodium Bicarbonate?" He turned, face twisted with confusion.

"What?" Zara asked.

"Sodium Bicarbonate? Like...for baking?" Oscar frowned.

"Maybe he...uses it to dissolve his victims?" Marcus guessed.

"Unlikely," Zara said. "I mean...there would be multiple better things to use in terms of chemical body disposal."

"I'm going to pretend I'm not a part of this conversation," Oscar whined weakly, feeling sick.

"Well, he must *really* like baking," Marcus muttered, straightening his glasses. "This thing is full of these sacks. Tell me *that's* not suspicious."

"Weird, maybe," Zara admitted. "Suspicious may be a push. Now, come on, we need to leave. It's getting dark, and this place gives me the creeps." Her face disappeared, and the fence panel dropped back into place with a brittle clatter.

Oscar plodded back to the fence, trying to avoid his shoes getting any dirtier. He was just pulling back the fence panel when he heard a hollow thump.

Marcus was beside the house, standing on the wooden boarding. "I can see inside!" he shouted excitedly, leaping again to try and peer through the small window.

"Come on, Marcus," Oscar said tiredly. "You were right, this was definitely super weird." He pushed the fence slat aside and began to clamber through the gap, which was not quite so easy as Marcus had made it look. He swung a leg over, straddling the beam that sat across the middle.

"One sec!" Marcus insisted, followed by another hollow thud.

Oscar bobbed his head through the gap in the fence where Zara stood, grimacing and stamping her feet against the growing cold. "Seriously," she snarled, "if we get in shit for this, it's all on him."

Then there was a loud CRUNCH followed by an unintelligible yowl of surprise.

Oscar's heart stopped dead in his chest, and he twisted toward the sound, bashing his head against the fence clumsily. Through the gap, he just caught a flash of Marcus' flailing arms sliding into the ground. Then he was...gone.

Gone.

Oscar's stomach dropped like it wanted to follow his friend into the earth.

"What the fuck just happened?!" Zara shouted, panicked.

Oscar pushed his way back through the gap, scraping his shin painfully; he felt his jeans rip. "Ah shit!" He gasped, tumbling onto his hands and knees, scuffing them on the damp gritty earth. He scrambled awkwardly to where he had seen Marcus disappear, his heart hammering in his chest to make up for the missed beats before.

The wooden panelling on the ground was half intact, the rest was bowed with a large portion splintered and collapsed. "Marcus," Oscar breathed. He leaned forward, trying to see where his friend had gone but too afraid to put much weight on the panelling. Oscar fumbled in his pocket, trying to get his phone out. Clumsily activating the built-in torch, he held it up to try peer down the gap.

Damp sloping earth, a few bits of broken wood, and then...just darkness. *It looks so deep.* A few stubborn weeds grew out of the ground, angling steeply under the house. "Marcus?" he called, daring to lean forward a little more.

Oscar heard the fence rattle beside him and turned to see Zara's leg sticking through. "What happened?" she cried.

"Marcus was trying to look through the window and fell down a hole," Oscar said, near the edge of hysteria.

"Oh, God. Oh, shit." Zara struggled at the fence fiercely. "For fuck's sake, I can't get through."

"MARCUS!" Oscar yelled down the hole.

Hopelessly miserable silence filled the air for several ragged breaths, and then a voice echoed back. "Yooooo!"

Oscar fell back on his knees, breath escaping him all at once. He closed his eyes for a moment, gathering himself, willing his heart to slow down. "Are you okay?"

There was a moment of ominous silence before Marcus' voice echoed back up the hole. "Yeah, I'm just a little scraped up. On the plus side," he added brightly, "I'm in the house now!"

"What did he say?" Zara asked, from where she still straddled the fence.

"He said on the plus side he's in the house now," Oscar repeated dully.

Zara groaned, then yelled back, voice harsh from the effort,

"YEAH AND ON THE MINUS SIDE YOU FELL DOWN A HOLE, WANKER!"

Oscar watched as Zara struggled to get her leg back out from the gap in the fence, losing her balance as the slat swung back into place. She stumbled free with a curse.

"Oscar?" Marcus' voice echoed from the hole.

"I'm here," Oscar shouted, quickly deciding not to share Zara's words of wisdom. "Can you get back up?"

There was a long pause. Oscar thought he heard some scrabbling and the sound of loose earth falling, then a yelp of surprise before Marcus called back, "No." His voice sounded only slightly less excited than before. "It's way too steep. I think I'm in the basement; it's really dark. Maybe I can come up through the house. Wait a minute."

Oscar dropped back, ignoring the cold and damp slowly wicking into the seat of his jeans. He tried to focus on his breathing and recount the terrible choices that had led up to this moment. He was just reconsidering his decision to follow Marcus into the garden when his voice echoed up from the hole again. "So, bad news or good news?"

"What's happening?" Zara snapped from the fence, the slat pulled aside again so she could peer through.

"Marcus says do we want the bad news or good news."

Zara growled. "We don't have time for this."

"Good news?" Oscar said, hoping it would be quicker to humour Marcus.

"The basement's locked. But I think you could throw down some rope or something?"

"What?" Oscar called back, feeling his nerves unravelling again. "What's the bad news?"

"I need to pee."

Oscar sighed, wondering if he was going to throw up. "He's stuck," he moaned.

"Oscar." Zara's voice was rigid. Oscar looked up and met her eyes. She had that *look* she got. When things got bad on shift, if a kid was really sick or someone was causing trouble, Zara sometimes got this scary look on her face. Flat, hard, and resolute. Her voice was steady and smooth. "Check the back door."

Oscar's stomach lurched, his eyes darting to the half-ruined porch. "Really?"

"We have no other choice." Zara stared daggers at the hole in the ground. "And tell *him* if anything happens, I'm leaving his skinny arse down that hole."

Oscar was sure she didn't mean that last part. *Probably*.

Oscar climbed to his feet, quickly scanning the area. Maybe there was something they could use? Marcus said rope might work. Perhaps some old sheets they could tie together. *Anything*. But there was nothing aside from an old broken apart window and a rusty hubcap.

"Oscar," Zara said firmly. "The back door."

Oscar gave her a fearful look.

"Just go and check, and I'll go check the front."

With dull resignation, Oscar slowly began a death march to the old decaying steps leading up the porch. They felt hollow and brittle under his feet, and for a second, he imagined falling through them just like Marcus had the planks beneath the window.

"Oscar, quickly," Zara urged.

Oscar swallowed, reaching the top and lifting his hand. His fingers wrapped around the old door handle, cold as ice in his grip. He twisted, and the old door popped open readily in its frame. His heart sunk.

"Oscar?" Zara's called.

Oscar sighed. "It's open."

"Oh, shit. Then get inside, go."

"Marcus," Oscar shouted, hoping his shaking voice would carry. "I'm coming to get you."

TAXONOMY OF MONSTERS: THE SOOTERKIN
(UMBRA INFANS)

"There are places and times that the veil grows thin; this is when its influence is most apparent. The Sooterkin is spawned after a short gestative period from humans who have come into close contact with the breach, indiscriminate of sex. Sooterkins often mimic their influencing sire's characteristics, and typically flee and rapidly perish on this barely habitable planet."

— EXCERPT: THE REVENANT'S ARCANUM

7

THE MURDER HOLE

The inside of the house felt somehow colder than outside. It did, however, seem to be in marginally better condition than outer appearances suggested. The door opened into what Oscar supposed was some kind of old boot room. Vinyl tiles faded and peeled in parts, and the walls were a sickly pale yellow that might once have been white. The room itself was utterly empty of possessions and furniture.

Oscar was becoming more and more certain that not only did Dmitri not live here, but no one did. It was a derelict house. The hollow remains of a large dead creature that had swallowed Marcus up. It was dangerous, and they needed to get out as quickly as possible.

An errant thought surfaced in his mind. Maybe someone *was* living here. He had gotten in easily enough; what's to say that some homeless people hadn't taken up residence? He felt a flash of panic. It was better someone used this place for shelter than it standing empty, but he didn't want to startle any inhabitants and get a hostile reaction.

Gingerly, Oscar made his way through the boot room and into the kitchen. If this was the heart of the home, then this home was definitely dead. The pale walls showed faint patches of mould, and the plastic floor shifted to a retro black and white tile. The cooker was more rust than metal, and the dark marble counters were clear of any accoutrements.

Something tickled the back of Oscar's mind, and it took him a moment to realise. *There isn't anything here...but there is a sound.* He quickly tracked the low hum to the large old refrigerator in the corner. Tall and narrow, the dingy colour of dirty chalk. Oscar had a sudden image of opening the door and finding a decapitated head staring back at him. A stack of disembodied limbs on the shelves, and jars of eyeballs staring out. He forced the image from his head, eyes travelling around, looking for other signs of life instead. The room was relatively clean, a little stale and cobwebby perhaps, but nothing to signify use.

If no one lives here...then why is the power on?

Oscar's teeth clenched until his jaw hurt, but he forced himself to move forward. They didn't have much choice now. He was already here, and he had to get Marcus out.

His limbs moved like they didn't want to comply as he crept across the creaking floor and reached for the handle of the kitchen door, pulling it open with a creak. A hallway stretched before him, a clear passage to the ornate glass windows of the front door, where the pale glow of evening light shone through. There was a flash of darkness in the edge of his vision, and his heart skipped a beat. His head snapped around before he could help himself, chasing the fleck away.

Beside him were two doors, both open. The closest led to what looked to be a dining room. The green walls may have been vibrant once, but now they were dull and moody. The deep green of dried seaweed or dark wet moss. The edge of a large table and chair were visible, crafted from a wood deeper and richer than the old floorboards. A cabinet, only a little shorter than him, stood in the corner. Everything looked visibly dusty in the dull light. Like it had been preserved from another time and left just for show.

Oscar's eyes travelled to the other room, which was darker, nothing visible inside at all. With the way his heart was beating right now, there was no surprise he was seeing flecks. Just as he was about to look away, he saw something in the darkness. Something low to the ground, and shining. *Eyes.*

Oscar watched the darkness.

And the darkness watched back.

Oscar opened his mouth to cry out in surprise, but only a pathetic squeak escaped. He blinked, staring at the form, willing it to flee like all the other flecks. Instead, it moved *toward* him.

Oscar stumbled backwards, sure that his heart was about to give out. He thudded into the wall behind him.

The small shadow came into the dull light of the hallway and gave a soft, curious *bork*.

"Oh, my God," Oscar gasped, his whole body shaking.

There was a rattling bang on the front door, and the shock brought Oscar back to his senses with a jolt that seemed to start his heart again.

"Come on, Oscar!" Zara's blurry shape shouted through the window.

"O...Okay," Oscar's voice cracked as he replied. He crouched down and reached out his hand to what had become of the shadow.

The puppy eyed him curiously, sniffing at his fingertips, and cocking its head. Its fur was dark and fluffy, dark eyes shining with intelligence.

"Hey, little guy," Oscar murmured, reaching out.

The puppy took a couple of clumsy steps back. Oscar didn't know much about dogs and couldn't place the breed. Maybe it was a mutt? Some kind of labrador mix? His paws looked too big for his body.

"Oscar, seriously. Hurry up," Zara shouted impatiently.

The puppy retreated into the shadows nervously, eying the front door.

"Sorry, buddy." Oscar stood up as the small dog disappeared back into the darkness. A chill ran up his spine. *What's in that room? Is it...whoever the puppy belongs to?*

Oscar quickly took stock of the various locks on the front door. There was little chance he was going to be letting Zara in without a key or five. Behind him, the wall that he had backed into had, in fact, been the stairwell. Not far from where he had collided was a narrow door. *That must be it*. He pushed down the handle.

"Marcus?" he shouted, tentatively down the narrow steps inside. The smell of stale air was even stronger from the damp bowels of the dead house.

"Come on, Oscar. I swear, it's spider city down here," Marcus' muffled voice pleaded.

"Coming," Oscar shouted, carefully making his way down the stairs, taking care to avoid the thick cobwebs above.

The narrow stairs twisted around on themselves. As Oscar rounded the corner, stooping his head to avoid the low ceiling, he found that the door at the bottom was not at all like the door at the top. In fact, it wasn't like any door he had ever seen before. Where the others in the house seemed old and rickety, this one looked new. Not only that, it was made of metal. Thick and robust, with several heavy locks on the outside.

Oscar's eyes scanned them. *Just one of them being locked would mean Marcus is trapped.*

The two thick padlocks thankfully appeared not to be fastened, so he quickly set about pulling at one of the three large deadbolts; it gave with a grudging pop. The next was at the bottom of the door driving into the old concrete below. It was stiff, and the cold metal bit into his fingers as he pulled.

"Jesus, what are you doing? Hurry up. I swear there are spiders in here bigger than me. I had to put my hand in a bunch of cobwebs to find my glasses. This is like the worst escape room ever," Marcus whined; his voice sounded close to the other side of the door now.

Finally, the bottom bolt pulled free, and Oscar started tugging at the last.

"Sorry. There are lots of locks, hang on." Oscar grunted, using both hands to pull as hard as he could. With a wriggle, the last bolt came free. He twisted the handle and pushed. The door was heavy, and he had to put his whole body behind it to get it to move.

The potent stench of the basement hit Oscar like a wall as he opened the door. Earthy, and something sourer than mould and closer to rot. A figure lunged out of the darkness and grabbed him, causing Oscar to yelp and release the door.

"Oh, thank you, Oscar. I thought I was going to die down here. I'm sorry I made fun of you earlier. You have my eternal loyalty," Marcus panted, squeezing Oscar tight against him.

"It's okay." Oscar's eyes scanned around the dark basement, expecting more flecks. Marcus had been right. There were a terrifying number of cobwebs down here. The only light was the now faint beam from a gap above, in the edge of the ceiling. That must have been where Marcus fell through.

"What's with this door?" Marcus grumbled, prodding at one of the locks over Oscar's shoulder.

"I don't know. It looks kind of new." Oscar felt his phone buzz in his pocket against his chest.

"It's so thick and *metally*. And the locks..." Marcus said. "This is scary. This guy is definitely bad news. He must keep his victims down here." Marcus didn't sound excited anymore. For the first time, Oscar thought he actually sounded scared.

"Well, maybe." Oscar tried to think reasonably.

Marcus pushed him back, holding Oscar by the shoulders to give him a wide-eyed look of disbelief. "Maybe what? This is some kind of cobwebby sex dungeon? Oscar...this is a murder hole, and we need to go. *Now*."

Oscar's phone buzzed in his pocket again. He freed himself from Marcus' hands, slipping his phone out. It buzzed in his hand, the screen lighting up the darkness. A message was visible on the screen.

GET OUT. HE'S HERE.

— ZARA

8

THE THING THAT LIVES IN THE CUPBOARD

"Shit, shit, shit, shit," Marcus chanted as they stomped up the stairs.

"I thought you said he wouldn't be back for hours!" Oscar whined shrilly. *Surely this isn't happening? Dmitri can't live here. This doesn't make any sense.*

"He wasn't supposed to be! Who cares, just go!"

Oscar burst through the doorway at the top of the stairs, Marcus so close behind him that their bodies were touching as they rounded the corner to the kitchen. The back door still hung open, beckoning them to freedom. But between them and the door was a dog.

It looked like the same breed as the puppy, its fur dark and lustrous. Only this dog was *big*, standing as tall as Oscar's hips. Even worse, this dog was *not* happy to see them.

Dark eyes glittered threateningly as it bared its sharp teeth, hackles raised, and gave a low, threatening growl.

Oscar let out a strangled yelp, reeling back into Marcus.

"Ohshit," Marcus gasped, all in one word. His fingers clawed the back of Oscar's jacket.

The dog took a step forward, forcing Oscar to retreat further back into the hallway, Marcus still clutching his back.

Oscar raised his hands and spoke in what he hoped was a soothing voice. "Easy, doggy, sorry we're in your house. We just need to get by..."

"Oscar, we have to go," Marcus whimpered.

There was a rattle behind them at the front door and the tell-tale sound of keys entering one of the many locks.

The dog growled louder, taking another step toward them. Dark claws scratched on the floorboards.

"Oscar," Marcus warned, his fingers releasing Oscar's jacket.

"Oh, God." Oscar shuffled to one side, stepping back into what he realised was the dining room. It was a move of sheer panic, and a cacophony of thoughts ran through his mind.

Maybe there was a window that they could get out of this way.

They could trap the dog in this room.

Giving the dog two targets might distract it.

Maybe this way, one of them could escape and get help.

There was nothing noble or calculated about his step into the dining room. Still, his thoughts stumbled, trying to handle the situation. Clawing at all the options and possibilities, he came up with nothing but a useless clump of jumbled panic.

There was a rattle and grinding click as another lock on the door opened.

"Bad dog. Bad dog," Marcus hissed, still in the corridor. He waved his arms, trying to make himself look more threatening.

"Marcus," Oscar moaned, backing further into the dining room.

The dog certainly seemed more interested in Marcus now, and Oscar saw his friend's eyes bulge with panic as he realised the same thing.

When the door opened, every muscle in Oscar's body froze.

Marcus bolted, all frightened flailing limbs, moving desperately to get past the dog and follow Oscar into the dining room.

He almost made it.

"ED," a deep voice boomed, "PRINDE!"

Oscar saw Marcus' eyes bulge with panic, as the dog moved in a flash. He heard the tearing of fabric as Marcus' feet were pulled out from beneath him, sending him sprawling onto the wooden floor with a thud. Marcus howled as the dog pulled at him, dragging him back into the hallway.

Oscar staggered back, hitting something hard that rattled. Rapt with horror, he watched Marcus thrashing on the floor and the dog...

The dog. Something was *wrong* with it.

Its skin was *wriggling*. Bubbling even, and it seemed to be swelling. Growing.

It was now bulkier than any dog that Oscar had ever seen, muscles rippling underneath its thick fur. It barely fit in the hallway.

Even as Marcus struggled, it snarled, jaws now bigger than Oscar's arm span, yanking and catching on the hood of Marcus' parka. Its massive dark haunches thudded against the door at the stairwell as it shook Marcus roughly with its enormous maw.

"WAIT," Marcus sobbed loudly, "I'M SORRY."

"Incolo," the voice commanded darkly.

The dog, if it could even be called that anymore, shifted its grip. Oscar felt as if he were watching the scene from outside of his own body as its massive mouth closed around Marcus' head.

His whole head.

Its vast maw engulfed Marcus' head and his shoulders quickly. His arms and legs still thrashed desperately, and Oscar could hear Marcus' muffled cries from inside the beast's dripping mouth.

The dog's powerful haunches bulged as it dragged him back toward the kitchen. Marcus' arms and legs hammered against the walls and floor as he disappeared from view.

Oscar's breath heaved ragged in his chest, each one burning

like it was his first or last. His heartbeat hammered in his ears as Marcus' muffled screams faded.

Then, he heard footsteps in the hall.

Shaken, Oscar desperately looked behind him, finding the dusty ornate cupboard. His fingers scrabbled at the door, pulling it open frantically. *Empty*. He stooped inside and closed the door as softly as he could, hoping against hope that he had moved fast enough. Quietly enough.

Marcus.

He couldn't hear Marcus' screams anymore.

Overwhelming terror flooded Oscar, filling every fibre of his being. His ears rung with it. He wasn't sure if his whole body was shaking or if the world was humming around him, like a tuning fork that had just been struck. All he could hear was the rasp of his own breath in the dark cupboard. Thoughts flashed through his mind, each a semi-lucid flash, a desperate hope too slippery to take hold of, like fish darting beneath the surface of a pond, impossible to catch with his bare hands.

He waited. What was he doing? What else *could* he do?

He thought of his phone in his breast pocket. His limbs felt stiff and dead, and he didn't think he could move to get it out easily in the cramped cupboard. Who would he call? What would he say?

The already crowded walls seemed to close in on him, and he struggled to maintain his shaky breaths. Terrified and trapped.

Oscar knew he was a coward. He had just stood and watched what happened to Marcus.

What happened to Marcus? Is he...? Where is Zara? Is she okay? Did something happen to her too?

None of this was right. None of this made sense. Oscar's inner spiral of fear tightened until he descended into darkness. His hopes took a last circle of the drain before falling deep into a hollow, buzzing pit deep within himself.

And then he heard the voice.

"I am sorry about what happened with your friend." Calm. Like he was discussing the weather.

Oscar's breath caught in his chest, failing him.

"I needed to get the situation under control." The voice sounded...regretful? "So we could talk. Without...distractions."

Oscar's breath writhed within him like a bundle of snakes in his chest, struggling to force its way back out. He managed to let it escape.

"I don't want to hurt you. Only talk."

Oscar waited, closing his eyes. He counted to ten, feeling the sweat beading on his brow, prickling his back uncomfortably.

Then twenty.

Silence.

His breaths came more evenly now.

"Oscar." The tone of voice suggested endless patience. "I know that you are in the cupboard. Please come out and talk to me."

Oscar's heart stopped.

"I don't mind waiting, but it can't be very comfortable for you in there."

Oscar bit his lip painfully, and then with a shaking hand, he reached out and pushed the door open. His feet dragged like ten-tonne weights as he stepped out into the dark dining room.

Dmitri sat on a chair by the table.

He leaned forward, fingers linked, and gaze intent. His crisp white shirt creased across his broad chest. He looked strange here. Like he didn't fit. Clean and put together in *this* place. Dmitri watched him patiently.

"What...what's going on?" Oscar's voice shook.

"I'm sorry," Dmitri said softly, pale eyes fixed on his. "Oscar. Please don't be scared. But perhaps I could ask you the same question?"

Oscar stepped back, his heels hitting the base of the cupboard and nearly sending him tumbling back in.

Dmitri's brow furrowed. "You can go back in there if you want, but it won't help us sort this out." He slowly stood, hands raised. "You should sit down. This must have been a lot for you."

Oscar stared at him, struggling to structure the words that rushed through his mind into what he wanted to say.

"Please. Sit," Dmitri repeated calmly, gesturing to the chair.

It's true. It's all true. He did it.

Oscar edged away instead, keeping his back to the wall, staying as far from Dmitri as possible. A disappointed look passed over Dmitri's face.

"No harm will come to your friends. I promise. We just need to talk." Dmitri's stormy eyes bore into Oscar's with earnest.

No harm? He had seen what the dog did to Marcus. And Zara? Was Zara okay? Oscar shuffled further across the room; the door was so close.

"I really hoped that we would never have to have this conversation," Dmitri said, eyes shining as he shook his head ruefully, "but perhaps I always knew we would, and I've put it off too long."

"What are you talking about?" Oscar's words were thick and clumsy in his mouth.

"I want to help you, Oscar." Dmitri gave the slightest hopeful smile. "But you need to let me."

Oscar shook his head. Remembering the huge dog. The metal door in the basement. The desperation of Marcus' fading screams.

Nina's eyes.

He's the bad man.

"No." Oscar struggled to stand up straight. "You...you hurt people. You hurt Marcus." The words left his mouth with power and entered the space around them, sounding small and hopeless.

Dmitri's brow furrowed with concern. "Please, Oscar. You need to listen. You are in danger, and it's...complicated."

"No!" Oscar shouted, moving for the door with a staggering lurch.

A wave of dizziness hit him all at once, and his vision blurred. It was all he could do to let out a feeble cry as he grasped at the doorframe, leaning against it heavily.

Firm hands caught him by the shoulders, easing him down to the floor. Dmitri's face was close to his. It seemed to glow in Oscar's swimming vision.

Oscar felt his consciousness fading, like sinking into a bottomless black pool that he could not escape.

"I'm so sorry, Oscar," he said softly, the words settling over Oscar like a haunting lullaby.

And then, everything was gone.

9

INTERLUDE THE FIRST: THE CITY'S GOT TEETH

Harry Barlow had always wanted to visit London. His mother and father were a little bemused by this, given that Harry was only eight years old.

It started a few years before when his grandmother had come to visit. She had recently been on a coach trip to the city and brought him back a miniature London bus for his toy car collection. It was quite a lovely addition. Cool and metallic to the touch with the most beautiful Pantone red paint that shone when the light caught it just so.

Ever since, Harry was obsessed. His relatives, of course, made the most of it. They used the theme as an easy idea for Christmases and Birthdays alike, obligingly providing an abundance of London themed toys and presents. The picture books, toy cabs, and beefeater teddy bears only served to compound Harry's strange fascination.

It was Christmas Day when his dad announced that they would be visiting London on New Year's, and Harry was beyond excited. He spent most of Christmas deciding what he would take with him in his satchel, packing and unpacking several times before lunch. He then spent most of the afternoon asking the same questions about the trip over and over again. His planning was somewhat interrupted by the stream of noisy visitors. Still, he was so excited that he didn't even mind when his red-faced uncle mussed up his hair, or his pointy-nosed aunt painfully pinched his cheeks.

They stayed up late on New Year's Eve, watching fireworks out of the little window on the landing. Even after that, despite how tired he was, Harry could barely sleep at all. Despite his restless night, Harry woke up early on New Year's Day full of glowing energy and the joys of eight-year-old life.

Harry sat, enraptured, for the long monotonous coach journey from Leeds to Kings Cross. Sapphire eyes flickering, trying to catch every detail as it sped by the window, drinking in the surroundings. Memorising them, as if he might be able to retrace his steps in his dreams.

When they arrived at Kings Cross, Harry practically fell over his own feet in a rush to be amongst it all. It took several sharp bashes of strangers' baggage, briskly moving legs, and a thick aching ear from his mum to take the edge off of his excitement. Still, he drank in every detail, wide eyes starving for knowledge.

But the more he saw, the more Harry realised that this London was...*different*. Not just different from what he imagined or expected, but distinct from anything that he knew or anyone had said. All the people making the street swell were distracted and unaware. *Cold*. It was like they were in a different place than everyone else around them altogether, carefully avoiding each other's edges. Nobody was smiling or seemed happy. In fact, most people didn't even seem to see him at all. Nobody said *excuse me* or *hello*. Everybody was in a rush. As though they were all late for the same appointment but going different ways.

Worst of all, when Harry saw other children his age, they seemed different too. Walking blindly in a zombified stupor, gaze fixed ahead, harried by their busy parents. Eyes tight and mouths unsmiling. Harry got an uncomfortable feeling under his ribcage.

And then there was the city.

Billowing gusts of heavy smells beating him around the face like fetid breath, tall irregular buildings jutting up like teeth. As if he were standing in an enormous mouth, ready to swallow him up and make him become one with the millipede of people heaving through the crowded streets living inside its intestines.

It made Harry feel sick. His skin broke out in a cold sweat, and his insides felt like they might start melting inside him. His breath started to become raw and ragged in his chest.

This was London.

London didn't want *him* here.

Harry clung on to his mum's hand as they battled their way through a gauntlet of sights. Big Ben. Buckingham Palace. Nelsons Column. Each view seemed to shine a pale and dingy light on the reality of London. Drained of colour, life, and joy. Dark, smelly, and miserable like a broken memory of what it could have been. It all just seemed so...pointless.

By the time the sun had started to set, Harry felt thoroughly miserable. Everything he'd dreamed of ended here, in muted disappointment. The red London bus that his grandmother had given him seemed to weigh as much as the real thing might in his satchel. All he could think was how every one of his favourite toys and presents back home carried some part of this dirty prison. All of it was touched with the sickly overwhelming grey of London itself.

His parents had exchanged worried looks for much of the day. The journey had been expensive, and the night in the hotel meant that they probably wouldn't manage a trip to the seaside this year. Harry was usually a happy child, but something seemed wrong today. They quietly whispered between themselves about how it was probably because he was tired, or maybe he was coming down with something. They tried to brighten his day by buying him a bag of sweets and a small model of Big Ben. None of it seemed to lift his spirits at all.

The sun was hanging at its lowest point when they finally agreed to take him for a walk along the South Bank. The winter evening was crisp by the river, and their breath steamed the air from the spouts of their thick coats and scarves like chimneys.

"Isn't it lovely?" His mum's voice was hopeful as she gestured at the glowing lights of the city beyond the lapping river Thames. They stood by the railings, a small passenger boat lazily crawling ahead of them in the fresh darkness.

Harry gave his mum a tired half-smile that didn't meet his eyes at all.

"What's wrong, love?" Her arm curled around him. "You've always wanted to come here."

Harry shrugged, leaning into her embrace.

His dad had taken a few steps ahead and was leaning over the railings to look down at the river. "Hey, Harry, look! There are steps here." He turned his head to shoot a mischievous grin. Harry's friends said their dads were always at work, the pub, or watching telly all the time. Whenever Harry's dad wasn't at work, he loved to play trains with him or play tricks on Mum that set her to laughing or shouting in equal parts. There was always a twinkle in his eye and a smile halfway onto his face. "Shall we go down and get a closer look at the river. See if there's any Thames treasure down there?"

"No," Harry replied glumly, but his dad was already scooping him up, growling playfully. Harry wriggled, giggling in spite of himself as his dad squeezed him in his arms.

"Probably shouldn't, Greg," his mum's worried voice warned sharply. "There's all sorts down there. Needles and condoms. You can't even see properly!"

Ignoring her, his dad lumbered down the steps with Harry in his arms. "Bloody hell, give over, Sally. It'll be alright!"

Harry hung limp but wondered aloud, "What's condoms?"

"Here we are!" his dad boomed, ignoring his question and setting him down on the smooth grubby sand instead.

Harry looked around and immediately decided that this was probably the worst beach in the world. There were a few bits of litter around them, and what looked like a broken bottle lay in pieces nearby. Harry's eyes found their way to the inky water lapping gently at the edge of the ugly little beach.

His gaze travelled in wonder across its surface, discovering the reflection of the moon, whilst the river whispered before him, showing him its secrets. He felt his heart lift a little. The loud honking and talking seemed a little quieter down here, and the heavy dark wiped away the grey and let the city shine.

This was more like the London he had imagined. Majestic and magical, brimming with adventures and stories.

"Careful!" his mum warned, daintily descending the worn stone steps behind them. The wind blustered, laced with an icy chill. Mum's favourite powder blue scarf, which had been wrapped under her chin and up around her head to protect her hair, came loose. Caught by the thrill of the wind, it nearly flew away, but she deftly snatched out with a manicured hand to capture it.

Harry laughed.

"That's more like it, son. Save up some laughs, though. She still might tumble yet." His dad winked, voice low and conspiratorial. Mum righted herself and appeared to think better of coming all the way down to the ugly beach, remaining on the stone steps and trying to tie the scarf back under her chin again.

Harry felt his eyes pulled back to the inky water, like a second night sky beside him.

"What's that?" Harry asked, pointing at what looked like a dark green streamer bobbing close by.

"Probably just a bit of seaweed, son," his dad answered gruffly.

The wind blew again, harder this time and sharp with cold. Harry heard his mum curse loudly behind him with a word he definitely wouldn't be allowed to repeat. "Oh, bugger this," she moaned, "I'm not coming down there."

Harry looked back to his dad, who had made his way to

crouch beside the river. "Here look, Harry. I told you we'd find treasure." He picked something up.

Harry made his way over, carefully avoiding any litter. The dark sand was harder under his feet by the edge of the river, where it was wet from the liquid night's kiss. He stood by his dad, who proudly held out a grubby metallic disk.

"What is it?" Harry said, wonder creeping into the edges of his voice.

His dad rubbed his thumb roughly across it, and Harry saw that it was a coin. It wasn't like any coin he'd ever seen before, though. "I reckon it's an old crown, Harry. Can't see the date in this light, but it might be worth something."

He held his hand out, and Harry took it. It felt strangely warm in his chilled fingers.

"Mum, we found a crown!" Harry yelled, turning and moving for the steps to show her their treasure.

At that moment, the wind blew again.

If the gust that tried to claim his mum's headscarf had been a slap, then this was a powerful punch. On the steps, his mum's scarf, only just back in place, came free again. Too fast this time for her fingers to snatch back out of the air, it whipped away into the night like a strange bird taking victorious flight.

Behind him, Harry heard his dad cry out in alarm, and before he could turn to see why, his own feet tangled in something, and he fell. The grubby sand rushed up to meet him, and he let out a hollow yelp as it knocked the air out of his lungs, his precious crown still clutched tightly in his fist.

Harry tried to get up quickly, but his leg was snared on something. He tried to wriggle free, but whatever it was tightened. No, not just tightened. Something *pulled* Harry by his ankle. Harry twisted, half expecting to turn his head to see his dad, grinning and playful, grabbing at him. Instead, Harry's eyes bulged.

Something was wrong. Very wrong.

His dad had fallen into the river, and the look on his face was beyond terror. The dark, milling water seemed to churn and roil around him like it was alive. Something pale was wrapped around his throat.

Something that looked like a hand.

"Dad!" Harry squeaked. His dad's face began to sink underneath the inky river, his wide eyes never leaving Harry's.

"Da—" Harry tried to cry out again, but the violent wind struck again, battering his small voice back into his lungs.

His dad's face disappeared into darkness.

Whatever had hold of Harry's ankle tugged sharply, the dirty, rough sand grinding at his back where his coat dragged up. Twisting awkwardly, Harry saw the green streamer like seaweed he'd seen before had a hold of him, coiled around his leg tightly. It was dragging him.

Pulling him into the river.

Water colder than ice crawled forward onto the bank and gripped both of Harry's feet and ankles. Harry let out a terrified sob as the dark waters claimed him to the knees. He felt something else take a firm hold of him, snaking around his other leg, and then he heard a scream.

Hands grabbed him under his armpits, and he saw his mum's pale hair whipped around by another torrent of wind. Her face was a mirror of the wild terror he felt inside, and something else. Fury.

She pulled painfully under his armpits, but what had him by the ankle pulled *harder*, the river taking him up to his hips. His mum fell to her knees, clutching on to him and letting out a desperate sob.

The wind howled.

"Dad," Harry sobbed.

"No!" his mum cried out fiercely. He felt her hands pulling him so hard it hurt, her fingernails biting into him even through his coat. Slowly, she reclaimed him from the cold until it clung to only his ankles. Harry thought his mum had done it, saved him from whatever was trying to take him. Until he looked down.

From the darkness of the river, a pale hand, withered and sinuous with prominent dark veins, clutched at his leg. Harry knew at once that it was the hand that had been around his father's throat.

He tried to cry out but found that terror had taken his voice.

A face rose slowly from the river.

For a moment, he thought it was his dad. But the skin was too pale, eyes too cruel and dark. She smiled, her mouth a wide gash beneath her large crooked nose. Lank knotted hair inky black. Teeth stained with moss and rot. Water bubbled from her cracked, grinning lips.

Harry tried to scream but spluttered wetly instead. Water leaked from his mouth and nose.

His mum let out a gargled shriek behind him, her fingers digging painfully into him. Harry felt cold water splashing onto his face and knew that his mum was somehow drowning too. Drowning just like he was.

Just like Dad.

The river woman pulled. She pulled him to the river. Pulled him to *her*.

Her pale, withered hand closed around his wrist as she dragged him into the darkness, her face drawing close to his.

There was a thump on the earth beside them, and a flash of darkness moved in the night.

Harry saw the figure of a man with wild dark hair lunge at the river woman.

He saw eyes glow the colour of embers, lighting the man's face. A flash of teeth too sharp, and then the night lit up as the man, the *thing*, spat fire.

Harry closed his eyes, but he felt the flash of heat against his cheek as it burst into the night. He felt the searing pain in his hand as the flames touched them before he could jerk it away. He heard a guttural shriek, so unlike any sound that he had ever heard before, so otherworldly, that he knew it must have been the river woman. Harry felt her crushing grip release and heard a great splashing from the river.

Harry coughed and retched, the last of the cold dark water dribbling from his mouth. He gasped in the cold night air, clutching his burned hand to his chest in agony.

His frightened eyes searched the night desperately. He found only his mother, huddled close by, shivering and wracked with deep sobs.

No river woman.

No dark figure with glowing eyes.

And no sign of his dad.

II

OF LESSER KNOWN MONSTERS

10

THE PLAGUE OF DREAMS

Bright light flooded Oscar's eyes. He blinked groggily, his head thick and vision fuzzy, as he traced the light to the open curtains. The window was open too, and a sharp autumn breeze cut through the room.

His room.

A sharp, deep ache pierced in the back of his skull, like a hammered chisel driving deeper with each strike. *Worse.* He was going to vomit.

Oscar staggered out of his tangled blankets and across the room, almost tripping as they wrapped around his legs. He had barely made it through the bathroom door when he was falling to his knees painfully, nearly striking his face against the toilet bowl.

Several minutes later, he lay on the bathroom floor, cool tiles chilling his clammy back through the light fabric of his T-shirt. What happened? Why was he in bed, fully dressed? Had they been drinking last night? He clawed for memories, but they slipped through his fingers like fine sand.

He could remember being with Zara and Marcus. Had they been at a bar? His memory churned with fuzzy images of Zara laughing, Marcus falling over. They definitely didn't go out drinking like they used to, but had his alcohol tolerance really fallen this low? He couldn't even remember drinking, but the hangover was all too familiar.

He pushed harder into his memories, but the aching in his skull worsened.

Oscar closed his eyes and concentrated on his breathing instead, willing the ache in his head to go away.

He may have fallen asleep for a second or an hour, or he may even have just passed out a little bit. When he came around, he knew with absolute certainty that he needed to get up. His sweat had dried cold on his skin, chilling him through.

Weakly, he turned on the shower and fumbled his way out of his clothes. The water jarred him, a searing spray that seemed to tear through his skin. He washed as well as he could manage in his current state, then swaddled himself in a bundle of coarse aubergine towels. One around his waist, another around his shoulders, and a third hung over his head like a sinister purple hood. The pain still burrowed into the back of his head like a living thing, sharper now, but at least he felt more awake.

With brittle fragility, Oscar shuffled into the living room, his damp feet leaving prints across the laminate floor. His jacket was tossed haphazardly onto the couch. He lifted it, feeling relief at the familiar weight in his pocket. A quick search mercifully revealed he had made it home with both his phone and wallet. Oscar thumbed his phone screen to life.

Three missed calls from Paige.

He swept those aside with a touch; he really wasn't in the frame of mind to deal with *that* right now. A couple more swipes and Zara's face appeared on the screen, large and grinning. He needed answers, and she was probably the best person to give them. Rather than the melodic ring of the call connecting, he only received three dull beeps.

He tried Zara twice more, and Marcus once.

Both lines were dead.

Oscar put his phone down on the counter clumsily. The heavy *thunk* reverberated unpleasantly through his skull.

Come to think of it, weren't both of them supposed to be at work today? Oscar had the day off, but it was unlike Zara and Marcus to drink on a work night. There were parts of the hospital where there was no signal, but it was *extremely* unlike Marcus to have his phone switched off.

His phone buzzed on the counter, and he snatched it up.

Come to work.

— ZARA

Oscar tried redialling her number. Nothing.
He tapped in a message instead.

What happened last night?

— OSCAR

He waited for a few moments, hoping for a simple explanation for when the night went south. When coffee turned into beer. When beer turned into...whatever had made him feel this way. His phone buzzed again.

Come to work.

— ZARA

Oscar groaned.

It was going to take a lot more than a hot shower to wake him up enough for this.

~

THE HOSPITAL WAS *NOT* the place he wanted to be right now.

The lurid strip lights pierced his vision like screwdrivers. The ambient buzz of mechanical beeps, loud voices, and rattle of equipment being rolled down the halls set his bones on edge. The world seemed to move far too fast around him, an assault of overwhelming stimuli pounding at his ragged senses.

Mercifully, he soon found himself at the doors to the ward he and Zara worked at, 3b. His ears were ringing as he stumbled in, the bright lights casting rainbows like broken glass in his swimming vision.

"Oscar?"

He turned, finding the concerned face of one of the nurses that worked on the ward.

"Louise," he croaked, shielding his eyes weakly from the lights above.

The woman practically recoiled at his appearance, her eyes bulging in concern. "Oscar love, you look terrible! What are you doing here?" Louise was one of the older staff on the ward and had been there longer than almost anyone else. She was a warm woman with a motherly air, mouse-brown hair in a bob tucked neatly into her jaw, and eyes haunted with years of sleepless nights caring for other people's children.

"Zara," Oscar managed, his voice a broken rasp.

Louise shook her head, frowning. "She didn't come in today, love. Left us short. She's not answering her phone." She reached out a hand to his forearm, and Oscar stepped back, confused.

"She...she messaged me," he croaked weakly.

"Oscar, did something happen?" Louise's brow furrowed

deeply with concern. "Do you know where Zara is? It's not like her to not turn up."

Oscar tried to remember, but the aching in the back of his skull jabbed sharply, sending a prickling sensation all over his skin. He took a lurching step back and nearly tripped on his own feet.

"Come on, let's get you sitting down." Louise reached out again.

Before her hand caught his arm, another claimed his shoulder firmly. Thin fingers with a grip like iron.

"Not to worry," the voice behind him said smoothly. "I'll take it from here."

Fear bubbled distantly in the back of his mind as he dared to look over his shoulder.

Her angular face regarded him coolly, eyes like obsidian hammers. "Hello, Oscar," Doctor Ocampo said firmly. "I think you had better come with me and sit down. You shouldn't be here in this state."

Oscar tried to shrug away, but her delicate grip on his shoulder was relentless.

"Calm down." Her voice was velvet and steel. Without looking at Louise, she spoke to her, voice like a lashing whip. "Nurse, help me get him to my office."

"Doctor Ocampo!" a voice interrupted. One of the newer nurses that Oscar didn't recognise, her blonde hair was mussed and cheeks flushed pink. "The little girl in bed seven, she's missing! We looked everywhere!"

"What?" Ocampo snapped, casting an irritated glare that made the young nurse wilt.

"The security team is here. They want to talk to you," the frightened nurse squeaked, already edging away.

Doctor Ocampo tutted, her grip tightening painfully on Oscar's shoulder for a fraction of a second and then abruptly releasing him.

"Take him to my office," she commanded Louise brusquely, already striding away with a sharp click of heels.

Oscar watched her go, deep relief washing over him. But...someone had gone missing? That was terrible. *Bed seven?* Something prickled in his mind, and he tried to unpick it, but the ache in his head deepened again, causing him to cringe in discomfort.

"Go home, Oscar, love," Louise said softly beside him. "You shouldn't be here unwell. And no good can come of...*her.*"

Oscar watched Doctor Ocampo cast him a last sharp look over her shoulder before she disappeared into the room and thought that he might never have heard anything so wise.

IT WAS A DIM AFTERNOON, and a fine drizzle from the overcast sky kissed his clammy skin pleasantly. Oscar had managed to get off the ward before Ocampo got her hands on him, slipping out of one of the back exits of the hospital and into the grid of tired streets behind. A crowded maze of squat buildings, dingy from the foul fumes of the city.

Fragments of his memory edged together like poorly repaired glass as he picked his way down the pavement, his feet dragging tiredly. Piece by piece, he was trying to put parts that might have been beside something else together to make some sense of it. Nothing quite fit. Too much was missing. They had been out for coffee, and then they had gone for a walk for some reason. Blurry memories of loud noises and flashing lights seemed to swallow the rest. When he tried to think any harder about it, the sharp pain in his skull throbbed in alarm until he thought he might throw up again.

His phone buzzed against his chest in his breast pocket, and he fumbled it out and looked at the screen. Suppressing a groan, he answered.

"Where have you been, you little twat?" Paige demanded sharply on the other side.

"Sorry," Oscar answered numbly. "I've been sick."

"Urgh," Paige groaned.

Oscar cleared his throat, checking both ways before crossing the quiet street behind the hospital.

"I saw you still hadn't paid the electricity bill, so I did it this morning." Paige's voice rested ominously between acidic and smug.

Oscar groaned. "Sorry, Paige."

"It's fine," she replied quickly.

Oscar startled, almost biting his tongue, only in part because of Paige's unexpected response.

Up ahead, he saw Zara.

Her dark hair hung loose and wild, streaks damp and lustreless from the rain. No makeup, eyes staring flatly into nothing.

Oscar froze. Something was wrong. He couldn't remember the last time he had seen Zara not looking fresh and preened.

"Oscar?" Paige said against his ear.

Up ahead, Zara turned jerkily and began to walk away with a rapid, lurching gait.

"Yeah?" Oscar answered, starting to follow Zara.

"Oscar...listen. I need to sell the flat," Paige said.

The words slid into Oscar's chest smoothly, like a too sharp blade. So quick, he barely felt them. *That isn't good.*

Up ahead, Zara darted around the corner, not looking back.

"Paige, I need to go." Oscar's voice was small and brittle.

"Oscar, did you hear me?" Paige demanded sharply.

"Speak later," Oscar mumbled, hearing the start of an angry reply before he quickly hung up and stuffed the phone in his pocket.

When he rounded the corner, he had to squint before he saw Zara. *There.* Up ahead on the other side of the road. "Zara!" he yelled; it came out a hoarse cry that painfully increased the pressure in his skull.

Oscar moved to cross the road, but a sharp, sudden screech and a blaring horn made his heart leap practically out of his mouth, and he cringed defensively. Angry shouting rose from the car that had nearly hit him. Panicked, Oscar dashed the rest of the way across the street.

Ahead, Zara disappeared around another corner, to the right. Oscar followed as fast as could, but when he turned the corner she was gone.

Gone.

Then he caught a flash of movement. Not on the street but beside it. At the edge of one of the buildings, he spotted her. She turned, damp hair flicking out as she fled.

The small shop looked like it had been closed for a long time, its windows covered with steel shutters. The little alley beside it was half blocked with a pile of soggy, moulding boxes and had the distinct stench of cigarettes and urine. Oscar made his way through it quickly, holding his breath, and found a small opening at the back. A small courtyard of sorts...if a grotty little backspace with cracked mossy slabs and a few bins in it could be called that.

Zara stood at its centre, hair lank and messy, shielding her downturned face.

"Zara?" Oscar stepped forward.

She looked up, and he froze. A shiver ran up his back. Something was wrong.

Zara was wrong.

Her eyes were darker than their natural cocoa brown, darker than any brown he had ever seen. Darker than black.

She looked at him with those dead, black eyes and smiled. Her mouth was too wide, her teeth too large and flat.

Panic bubbled in Oscar's chest, and he staggered back. "Zara?"

He hit something. At first, he thought it was the wall, but

walls don't have hands. Hands that firmly grip you and move you aside.

Oscar let out a yelp of surprise, clutching at the figure, his fingers finding the thick damp wool of a charcoal overcoat.

Pale eyes fixed on Oscar's. A dark shock of hair, and the faintest whisper of a smile.

Dmitri?

11

THE WRONG ONE

O scar had no time to speak.

No time to ask any of the hundred questions that bloomed in his aching mind.

Zara let out a noise unlike any he'd ever heard her make before. Unlike any noise *anyone* made. A shrill, gurgling, wail. Her black eyes flashed, and her mouth split her face in a twisted mockery of a grin.

She lunged for him. Fast. *Too fast.*

Then Dmitri was there, his broad shape moving between them in a blur. He moved low, picking up momentum despite the short distance, and his shoulder connected solidly below her ribcage. Zara tumbled back with a winded snarl, falling into the row of dustbins with a clatter.

"Zara!" Oscar cried, taking a step forward. Whatever was happening, this wasn't right. He couldn't let Zara get hurt.

"Get back." Dmitri cast him a fierce glance, eyes flashing. "This is *not* your friend."

"What's...what's *wrong* with her?" Oscar stuttered. *And why are you here?*

A memory bloomed, overwhelmingly clear. A memory of something that had never happened.

Dmitri looming over him in an unfamiliar room with murky green walls. Those same stormy eyes and concerned frown fixed on Oscar.

I'm so sorry, Oscar.

Oscar stared at him in a stupor. Before them, Zara rose from the pile of scattered rubbish, and Oscar turned to look at her, aghast. "Zara. I..."

The closer he looked, the more wrong she was.

Her clothes were faded, like the colour had been almost all rinsed out. Her hair too dark and coarse, skin a few shades short of her rich tawny brown and closer to a muddy grey. Her dark eyes were bereft of warmth and life.

Zara let out a snarl, her mouth opening far too widely. Large enough to cover his face. His throat. She clawed out at the air between them threateningly.

Her hands.

Had her hands been like that before?

Her fingers were grotesquely long, a funhouse mirror's reflection of what her hands should have been, tipped with long ragged nails. Oscar imagined what they might feel like tearing into his flesh.

Whatever words might have found their way into Oscar's mouth turned to ash on his tongue instead.

She moved. There was no grace, only feral power. Unbridled purpose.

Dmitri was there again, as fast as she was, seeming to anticipate her movement. He caught her arm and twisted, putting his body behind her and shifting his weight. Dmitri's body pivoted, and he drove her up against the wall with jarring force. Unfazed, Zara snarled, this time not at Oscar but Dmitri.

This is all so wrong. Everything is so wrong. Oscar's heart was trying to pound its way out of his throat. "Zara, stop. It's me!" Oscar cried hoarsely.

Zara screeched again, her teeth gnashing terrifyingly close to Dmitri's unflinching face.

Then her body *deflated*, like a withering balloon. Her shoulders collapsed in on themselves sickeningly. Oscar let out a gasp of horror. Just as quickly, she expanded. With a guttural roar, she unfurled in Dmitri's grip, pushing him aside viciously and sending him stumbling back.

"Zara, stop!" Oscar begged, voice shaking. He fell back against the wall behind him, hands raised, cowering.

Zara's eyes shone with bloodlust, and she lunged.

She was so close he felt the hot stink of her breath, sweet as rotten fruit.

Oscar closed his eyes, waiting to feel those flat teeth closing around his skull. Feel the ragged nails ripping into him. Instead, he heard a low grunt. He stayed in the darkness a moment longer, wondering why he was not dead, then slowly opened his eyes.

Dmitri. Again, he had gotten there in time. He was latched onto her, body hunched, arms wrapped roughly around her head.

Oscar's stomach dropped.

Dmitri looked wrong too now.

His eyes.

They were no longer the stormy grey of before. Instead, they seemed to burn a flickering orange in the grim lighting. Like failing embers. His woolen overcoat was wide open, and his shirt torn at the chest, dark blood blossoming there. He pulled viciously at Zara's head. She let out a strange gurgling yelp, arms thrashing in wild rage.

"Stop," Oscar croaked. The burning in Dmitri's eyes intensified, and he let out a low growl, and just for a moment, Oscar thought he saw the flash of pointed teeth.

Dmitri pulled again. More savagely this time. Zara twisted desperately in his grip.

"STOP!" Oscar cried.

Dmitri pulled once more, putting his whole body behind the force of it, and there was a sickening wet pop.

Zara's body slackened, her head twisted at an unnatural angle.

Panting, Dmitri loosened his grip, and Zara's body dropped with a grotesque, heavy finality. Her head connected with the concrete, bouncing with a disturbing dull thud.

Oscar's body buzzed with numbing agony. With coring loss.

And then, Dmitri's burning eyes turned to him.

Oscar squeezed his eyes shut. Curling his body up on itself, he willed it all to stop. Prayed that he would wake up. That none of this was real.

Zara.

"Are you hurt?" Dmitri's voice was gentle. Oscar opened his eyes and found him close, crouching beside him, eyes no longer burning. Now they were their normal grey once more. Oscar realised for the first time they looked like they were moving, swirling slightly. Cold and ominous as storm clouds skimming the sky. His dark hair hung in damp threads around his face.

"Stop," Oscar repeated weakly, raising a feeble shaking hand.

Dmitri's brow furrowed in concern. "It was not your friend. Look." He gestured toward where her body had fallen.

Oscar did.

And his jaw dropped.

She was...*sinking.*

Oscar watched as Zara slowly seeped into the earth, the colour of her clothes and her dulled brown skin shifting to closer match the concrete as she did. It only took a few seconds, and then she was gone. A shadowy stain remained in her place, only slightly darker than the slabs had been before.

"What's happening?" Oscar choked out.

"Everything is okay. You are safe," Dmitri said softly.

Oscar shook his head. What did he mean? What was happening? Something had been wrong with Zara, *but it had to be her*. He'd seen Zara almost every day for the last three years. Seen her laugh, cry...

And now she's gone.

"Please come with me. I will explain everything," Dmitri said gently, reaching out.

Oscar stared at his large hand, streaked with blood.

Quickly, Dmitri shifted, offering his other hand, which was only slightly cleaner.

Oscar's heart lurched painfully in his chest, ready to give up. He could not bring himself to reach out. To take Dmitri's hand. The hands that had killed Zara just moments ago.

"Just come with me. Everything will be okay," Dmitri whispered earnestly.

Oscar shook his head.

Dmitri sighed and gave a small rueful, smile. "Of course." He reached inside his breast pocket. "I should have known that you would need space to consider. But I fear now is not the time for space." He withdrew a flat brassy tin about the size of his palm. Popping open the lid, he pinched something out of it with his fingers before moving his hands toward Oscar's.

Oscar flinched, but nothing happened. Then his eyes caught sight of some fine, downy hairs, gently settling on the back of his hand.

Pale as the moonlight.

TAXONOMY OF MONSTERS:
THE BRAG
(EQUUS SYCOPHANTAM)

Who knows what form this imp will take?
What mischief it now means to make?
He twists and turns his wretched shape,
To find what is his favourite jape.
He takes you high up on his back,
And then begins his fierce attack.
He bucks and bolts and will not trek,
With hopes to toss, and break your neck.

— JIM PHILLIPS, DATE UNKNOWN

12

THE POISONED CUP

The rhythmic march of a ticking clock.
Oscar thought distantly that it sounded far too slow.

Tick.

Tock.

His thoughts came to him as sluggish as the ticking clock.
Lazy light filtered in from somewhere beside him.

All he knew was the steady ticking of the clock and a strange
serenity that was rapidly ebbing away. The suspension of everything. Total absence. Distant curiosity crawled into his waking
mind, and the clock seemed to tick ever more quickly.

The deep ache in his head was slowly thrumming back to life
as the room seemed to waken around him in flashes of lucidity.

Tick
Tock

The clock was old fashioned but well kept. Its broad face a dingy cream, scattered with Roman numerals.

The scent of stale air. And something else. Deep and rich, a little spicy.

Soft cushions against his back.

Wallpaper. Ornate ivory and peacock blue patterns dancing together, faded dull with time.

Thin sheets against his skin, coarse and cool.

Tick... Tock.

Memories started to return. Separate and distant, closer to echoes than truth. The feeling of the cold rain drizzling on his face. Eyes like glowing embers. A girl he knew, loved, sinking lifelessly into the ground.

Zara.

Tick. Tock. Tick. Tock.

And then, all at once, he was *there.*

Where *there* was, Oscar did not know.

He took a gasping breath, sitting bolt upright, searching for an anchor of recognition. The room was dim with only the pale daylight spilling in through the grimy window to his right. He sat on a four-poster bed, ornately carved from rich dark wood. The sheets were crisp and white beneath him, newer than anything else in the room.

His eyes skimmed around like a smooth stone skipping on a still pond until they landed on the figure sitting in the corner. Leaning forward, watching him intently over steepled fingers, black hair hanging in strands over his eyes, was Dmitri.

A flash of panic blossomed in Oscar, but he forced it down quickly. *If he was going to hurt me, it would have happened by now.*

"Are you okay?" Dmitri asked, his voice barely more than a whisper.

Oscar shifted on the sheets. "I'm...not sure."

Dmitri gave him a sympathetic look. He spoke in that calming voice again, his accent lengthening the vowels very slightly. "What do you remember?'

Oscar took a slow breath, his voice shaking as he spoke. "You killed Zara." The words burned his mouth like acid.

Dmitri shook his head gently. "That was not your friend."

Oscar chewed his lip as his mind wrestled with itself, trying to make sense of the situation.

"Your friend is here. Both of them are. They are safe," Dmitri said.

Oscar's mouth opened, flapping in confusion. *Both of them? Marcus?* "Where are we?"

"My home," Dmitri replied, tilting his head slightly, curious. "You...don't remember anything else?"

Oscar shook his head slowly. He tried to sort through his thoughts once more. The throbbing in his head intensified.

Dmitri pointed beside Oscar to the bedside table, the same dark wood as the bed. On it sat a short tumbler and a cup, delicate and fragile looking. Like most things in this house, it didn't seem to fit with the rest. It reminded Oscar of the cups his Great Aunt Joan had served tea in when he was little. Thin china with a scalloped edge, though in this case, the gold piping seemed to have completely worn off even if the faded flowers remained on its face.

"You should drink," Dmitri murmured. "It will...help you feel better. Then we will speak with Zara." His eyebrow twitched slightly at that last part for some reason.

Oscar picked up the cup, his eyes leaving Dmitri for the briefest of moments. He regarded the contents suspiciously. "What is it?" he asked, as the warmth of its contents spread through his fingers. "And what was...*that,* if it wasn't Zara?"

He met Dmitri's eyes as he took a sniff. It smelled...bitter? Earthy.

"Hawthorn mostly. Some agrimony and mugwort. A little marjoram," Dmitri said, eyes fixed on the cup in Oscar's hands. "Oh, and I put a little honey in it," he added, looking down, as though suddenly bashful. "To make it taste better."

Very slowly, Oscar took a tentative sip and...*Oh, dear sweet, gentle baby Jesus*. It was all he could do not to let it all spill back out of his mouth and into the cup. It was so bitter and *thick*. The honey came after, adding a sickly sweetness to what tasted like...*stagnant puddle water?*

Dmitri leaned forward, watching with earnest.

Wincing, Oscar swallowed. Perhaps the slowest gulp of all gulps taken since the dawn of time. He tried to give Dmitri a smile but suspected it was somewhat marred by his twitching left eye.

"I know it tastes bad, but if you drink it all, you really will feel much better."

"Guuuuuurrrghhh." Oscar's stomach rolled in protest at the thought.

"If you do it quickly, perhaps that way will be better," Dmitri offered helpfully.

"You could have just shoved it in my mouth while I was asleep," Oscar groaned miserably. "I wouldn't have minded."

Dmitri's eyes widened, and he spluttered like he'd been the one to drink the muddy concoction instead.

Puzzled by his reaction, Oscar snatched at an errant thread of courage and swigged the contents of the cup in one. He was good for it, too, until the gritty final gulp hit his mouth. He forced it down and gasped, close to retching.

Dmitri watched him, confused. "You didn't need to take the dregs," he said softly.

"Oh, God." Oscar moaned, burying his face in his hands as the flavour roiled on his tongue, and something scratched inside his throat. "Water?"

Dmitri gestured beside him again to the same place, and

Oscar remembered the short tumbler of water there, too. Oscar picked it up and drained it in one go. It didn't clear the taste from his mouth, but as he set the glass back down, he realised his headache was gone.

Just gone. Like the deep throbbing ache hadn't been there since he woke up today. But then...

Everything
Came.
Back.

Oscar stared at Dmitri, eyes wide.

"Breathe," Dmitri said softly.

He did it. Blood seeping through bandages. That's the bad man. Frightened eyes, full of certainty. Mixed light and dark leaves churning beneath his feet. The lonely humming of the tall fridge. Too many locks on a thick steel door.

Oscar's chest heaved; his clawed fingers bunched the sheets between them.

"Breathe," Dmitri commanded more firmly, standing and striding over to where Oscar sat on the bed.

Oscar's chest burned, his vision swam, dark seeping into its edges.

The giant dog's mouth closing around Marcus' head as his muffled screams faded down the corridor, arms and legs thrashing desperately.

"BREATHE," Dmitri roared, hands gripping Oscar's shoulders, his face inches away.

Oscar collapsed back into the pillows and took one long ragged gasp.

Then another.

He closed his eyes, his body sagging into the soft cushions, and started to shiver. He felt the sheets being lifted over him, and he kept his eyes closed tight, trying to sort through the overwhelming jumble of memories.

After a few moments, he heard a click and knew that Dmitri was gone.

He had been so close that Oscar could feel the heat of him.

And now he was gone, and Oscar was all alone.

THE BEAST'S BARGAIN

O scar lay huddled in the covers, a cocoon separating him from the strange reality outside, until the shivering in his bones had subsided completely. He remembered everything, but none of it made any sense. Fear for Zara and Marcus wrestled with disbelief at all the things he'd seen. Mistrust of Dmitri collided violently with the fact he had saved him in the alley.

How can any of this be true? How can all of it be true at the same time?

Finally, the door creaked open, and Oscar peeked out of his fragile nest to see Dmitri slowly enter. He glanced from beneath his lashes coyly, at odds with the truths Oscar now knew. *Strange to see a wolf looking so sheepish.*

Dmitri said nothing, closing the door gently behind him, and standing patiently until Oscar spoke.

"Where are my friends?" Oscar asked, his voice little more than a whisper.

"Here," Dmitri replied. "Both safe and well. Just a little shaken."

"The dog...Marcus." Oscar shook his head, remembering its jaws swallowing his friend's head and shoulders.

"Ed was as gentle as he could be. It was too much, I understand, but I could not risk any of you getting away. It could have put them, or you, in far greater danger."

Oscar chewed his lip, trying to process that. Finally, he asked the question. The one that had surfaced in his mind over and over.

"What are you?"

Oscar expected Dmitri to laugh. To look at him incredulously. Instead, he met his eyes, watching for the slightest reaction. "It's complicated."

Oscar pulled the sheets tighter around himself. He had dismissed one idea several times, but it was hard to ignore. It all made too much sense, even before what had happened. His perfect skin, his pale eyes, his thick dark hair...

"Are you a..." Oscar ventured, his voice brittle, "vampire?"

Dmitri did something then that Oscar had never seen before. He burst into a sudden laugh, rich and amused. It made him look younger. He shook his head. "A vampire." He chuckled softly. "I suppose...the accent?"

Oscar blinked, his cheeks burning. "Your teeth."

Dmitri grunted and ran his tongue over his teeth, which were only as pointy as they ought to be right now. "When I fought the fetch?" he mused.

Oscar frowned, confused by the word.

"A fetch. You might think of it as a doppelgänger."

Doppelgänger. Is that what that thing that looked like Zara had been?

"I am not a vampire," Dmitri said softly, the ghost of a smile still on his face. "What you think of as vampires do not exist."

Oscar shook his head, feeling lost. "As far as I was concerned until today, a lot of things didn't exist."

"True enough." Dmitri nodded, moving smoothly across the room and toward the foot of the bed.

Oscar was forced to release himself from his cocoon or else

lose sight of Dmitri, and he had no intention of doing that right now. He sat quickly upright, watching as Dmitri moved to take the chair by the window.

Oscar realised that Dmitri's shirt was still stained with dark blood at the chest from what happened in the alley. "You're hurt."

Dmitri shrugged, unconcerned. "It's nothing." His gaze fixed on Oscar. "I need to apologise to you, Oscar. For many things, but first, for this. I have not had this discussion with anyone for a long time and with very few people at all who do not share my... unique situation. So, I may not explain this in a way that you can appreciate." He tucked an errant strand of dark hair behind his ear. It had dried now and was clumped together slightly in thicker strands than its usual perfection. Dmitri looked pensive for a moment before speaking again. "Do you believe in life from other planets?"

Oscar's jaw dropped. "You're...an *alien*?!"

"Perhaps that is one way of thinking of it, though not exactly true in the typical sense. Many people believe the concept that we are alone in the infinite universe is absurd. Even that is human arrogance. The truth is that there is much of *this world* that is not understood, let alone infinity. The current understanding of time, space, and reality itself are little more than idle postulation compared to the reality."

"I...don't understand," Oscar admitted quietly.

"There are...beings. Beings that share this world your people call your own. Some may have seen the truth of over the years, spawning the myths and bedtime stories."

"Monsters?" Oscar breathed.

A muscle in Dmitri's jaw jumped. "That is a word that has been used. But that implies a certain...expectation. The truth is, these beings might be found anywhere. Undetected and living peaceful lives. Driving buses, running businesses, making music..."

"Working in labs in hospitals?" Oscar murmured.

Dmitri's eyes fixed on his, the grey of them swirled like smoke blowing in the wind.

Oscar swallowed. "Is that what that thing was? It looked like Zara. I thought..."

Dmitri's lips twisted in a sneer. "Fetches are disgusting creatures. Barely fully-formed things cobbled together from half-shadows. They rob the appearance of..." His eyes touched on Oscar's, and he stopped short. "*Others*. It gives them a strength they do not deserve."

"Was it...evil?" Oscar's voice was little more than a squeak.

Dmitri leaned back in the chair, rubbing the shadow of stubble on his jaw with one hand. When he spoke, he sounded tired. "Few things in this world are evil. Some that are, are human, others not. In the case of the fetch, I suppose it is relative. Does the antelope think the lion evil?"

"Probably."

"Does that make the lion evil?"

Oscar bit his bottom lip thoughtfully.

"Fetches are rare. Much rarer than lions. But they have no motive that would make them a friend of humans, though they are rarely so aggressive as the one you met today. So, I suppose that you might think them evil."

"Are all...*monsters*...evil?" Oscar ventured slowly; eyes fixed on Dmitri.

Dmitri's eyes flashed up to meet his. "No, we are not."

A chill ran up Oscar's back, and he felt goosebumps form on his arms that had nothing to do with the cold.

We.

Oscar's heart raced in his chest.

I have to do it. I have to ask.

"Did you...hurt the little girl at the hospital?" He blurted out the words before he could convince himself not to.

A dark shadow lingered over Dmitri's face.

Oscar pushed on, his voice shaking. "The little girl on the ward. She said...that you were a bad man. That you hurt her."

"She is not human either," Dmitri said darkly.

Oscar's mind reeled from the words. *He did it.* Oscar had seen her, held her hand in his. *Dmitri cut the little girl.* She was all alone, her parents gone. *But she...wasn't a little girl?*

This was too much. "I want to see Zara and Marcus." His voice was shaking. *We need to get out of here.*

Dmitri's expression became stiff. "Soon. Your friends are...difficult." Dmitri's brows knitted in consternation. "It is important you understand something first."

Oscar pulled the covers tightly around himself, as tiredness suddenly threatened to overwhelm him. The pounding in his chest was easing even if the goosebumps had not gone away. If Dmitri had hurt the girl, then Oscar had to get out of here. Get them all out of here. Dmitri was a *monster*...so, why did Oscar feel so calm?

"I want to help you," Dmitri insisted gently.

Oscar blinked, waiting for him to go on, but Dmitri struggled to find the words.

"You were in danger. Before you came here. I know that someone...*something,* was hunting you. But it is like no creature I have encountered before."

Oscar's voice was thick and dazed. "Me? But why? I'm not important."

Dmitri's gaze locked back on to him, pained. "You should not say that."

Oscar's heart skittered in his chest. *Really? Now?* The man had literally just confessed trying to kill a little girl before he kidnapped Oscar and his friends. *Not to mention coming out of the monster closet.* Yet his steady gaze still gave Oscar butterflies that threatened to shred his guts.

"I...I did something to you. To make you forget," Dmitri confessed.

"What? How?" Oscar blinked. The sleepiness that had overcome him before seemed to be subsiding again now.

"It's...complicated." Dmitri frowned, dissatisfied with his own response.

"Magic?" Oscar dared to guess.

The hint of a smile crept back onto Dmitri's face. "Magic and science may be better bedfellows than either one would ever care to admit." His gaze drifted from Oscar's uncomfortably. "I tried to do the same to your friends, but it didn't work on them."

"Why?"

"It doesn't work on everyone. Some people are resistant. It depends on certain things. Usually, it's because of a particularly strong will."

"Oh. It didn't work on them, but it worked on me?" Oscar wondered softly.

"Too well." Dmitri grunted. "I have never met anyone who succumbed as you have before. It was like you wanted it."

Oscar felt his cheeks burning. When he looked up at Dmitri, he thought that his face looked flushed, too.

"So, you made me forget...but then I was at home?"

Dmitri's eyes fled his gaze guiltily. "I took you there. I wanted to try and lure out whatever was hunting you, and putting you in your own home seemed best."

Oscar's mouth hung open. "You went into my flat?"

"I apologise. I understand that this is a violation, but I was taking you there from my home, which you had not been invited into either." Dmitri's grey eyes remained elusive.

Well...that's true.

"Wait, how did you know where I lived?" Oscar wondered out loud.

"As I say, something has been hunting you. I may have ensured you reached your home safely on more than one occasion."

Oscar's heart skipped a beat. Dmitri had been...following him?

"I used your friend's phone to get you to expose yourself. To see if it flushed out what had been following you. I...I understand this means I was using you as bait." Dmitri's voice was stiff. "But I need you to know that it was only so I could track what was after you. To keep you safe."

"From the doppelgänger? Or...what did you call it, a fetch?"

"Perhaps. But I still think there is something more. Something...stranger."

Oscar shook his head, numbly. "Why...why didn't you tell me?"

"Do you think you would have believed me if I had?"

Oscar shook his head again. He wasn't even sure if he believed him now.

Dmitri's eyes fixed on his with that intense, earnest stare. "If your friends had not been resistant to my ability, I would have set you all back as you had been before. Continued to watch you from afar, just like before. But since you all took it upon yourselves to break into my home, I was left with little choice. The fetch made it somewhat easier, at least. I had hoped if you were vulnerable, what hunted you may show itself, and the scent of my ability on you likely aggravated the fetch even further. I hoped it would go some way to convincing you of the truth."

Dmitri's...scent? On me? Oscar felt his cheeks growing warm again.

"I need you to understand, Oscar, I just want to make sure you are safe."

"Why?" Oscar breathed.

Dmitri's mouth hung open, and his eyes searched Oscar silently, completely dumbfounded for the first time Oscar had ever seen. "I...because I can. Because I need..." He shook his head, looking down at a loss for words.

Oscar swallowed. "And...my friends?"

"I need to...try talking to them again." Dmitri shifted uncomfortably. "When I tried to explain before they were not particularly...receptive. I was hoping you would help?"

Oscar's imagination ran through a variety of scenarios in fast forward in his head, none of them ending with kind words or happy plans. "You want to tell them...*everything?*"

Dmitri's paused for a long moment, looking troubled. "Everything...sounds like a good start."

TAXONOMY OF MONSTERS: THE ALKROW

(AVEM MULIER)

P'raps thought a bird upon first glance,
Flee now, while you still have the chance.
She swoops from high,
You soon shall die,
The sky will host your final dance.

— THOMAS CLEARY, 1898-1929

❧ 14 ❧

THE AROMA OF LIES

The dog waited in the hallway.

It wasn't the dog that Oscar had seen before. The one that had swollen and grown impossibly and dragged Marcus away. This time he recognised the breed. A doberman.

"Ed," Dmitri said softly.

The large dog let out a low whine and cocked its head, one pointed ear twitching.

Ed? Isn't that what he called the other dog?

"Your dog..." Oscar began, turning to Dmitri.

"As much a dog as I am human."

Oscar nodded; that made sense. A wet nose pushed its way between his fingers, and he nearly jumped out of his skin, snatching his hand up to his chest.

Ed sat beside him, giving him a patient look, tentatively pawing the floorboards.

"Well, he might not be a *normal* dog. But in many ways, Ed very much does remain...*dog*. Your human tales might call him a mimick-dog." Dmitri smiled.

Swallowing, Oscar slowly reached out his hand and touched the silky point behind the dog's left ear. Ed leaned his head forward, ambling excitedly toward the touch before his long wet nose was snuffling Oscar's palm again.

"He likes you," Dmitri said encouragingly.

Suddenly, Ed collapsed in on himself, like a balloon with its knot undone. Oscar barely had time to blink in surprise before a doberman puppy was bounding excitedly around his legs.

Oscar looked at Dmitri, amazed. "He can change?"

"There are limits, but yes." Dmitri watched Ed thoughtfully. "He does not usually warm to others so quickly."

"He was a puppy when I first met him downstairs when..." Oscar trailed off as Ed rubbed clumsily against his shins.

He remembered the vast jaws closing around Marcus' head, and a cold, lead weight dropped in his stomach. *That was...this dog?* He cleared his throat. "I want to see them, please."

Ed stilled before him, tilting his head and letting out a low whine.

"Of course." Dmitri led the way down the hall, to the furthest door. Oscar followed, carefully stepping around Ed, who watched him with interest.

As he passed the bannisters, Oscar peered down the familiar stairs. The upper floor was as tired and run down as the rest of the house—with the exception of the bedroom he had woken in. *Dmitri's room?*

"You...you actually live here?" Oscar followed the threadbare rug that led him to stand beside Dmitri. "It's so...cold," Oscar finished awkwardly, not wanting to seem rude.

"It is...a space that I use to base myself. I do not get cold easily," Dmitri said, cheeks slightly pink again. He drew a long key out of his pocket and leaned forward to twist it in the lock of the door. "Your friends are in here. I will let you deal with them. I do not wish for them to become...hostile." He looked troubled as he replaced the key in his pocket.

Hostile? Oscar almost smiled at that. He didn't have to wonder as to which one of them had caused Dmitri trouble.

Oscar reached forward and opened the door.

"What the..." Zara's voice burned with fury as the door opened. Her tone quickly shifted to elation. "OSCAR!"

He barely had time to lay eyes on her before she collided with him, knocking the air out of him with a *whoomph*. "Hey," he managed weakly into a face full of teal-streaked hair.

Zara quickly let him go, gripping him at arm's length, eyes scanning his body and searching for signs of harm. Eyes, the warm brown of autumn leaves just fallen. Oscar's heart sang. *It's really her. She's really okay.* "I'm glad you're here," he choked out.

"I'm not!" Zara said, voice taking on a keen edge again. "This creep has had us locked up in this room for the last day." She stared daggers over Oscar's shoulder to where Dmitri stood in the doorway. "Are you okay? Did he hurt you?"

"I'm fine," Oscar said, peering beyond Zara. Sitting on the floor beside the rusty looking daybed with a skimpy yellowed mattress was Marcus. He did not have his glasses on, and he was huddled in on himself, holding his knees to his chest to make himself as small as possible. He gave Oscar an anxious look.

"He's fine," Zara said, squeezing Oscar's arms. "A bit shook up. Some dog spooked him."

As if summoned by her words, Ed—still a puppy—marched merrily into the room, oversized ears twitching.

"Shit!" Marcus yelped. In a flash, he was up from the ground and half sprawled on the bed. His eyes bulged. "Stay away from that thing!"

Ed's ears drooped, and he took a tentative step back.

Oscar cringed. Slowly, he reached down to give Ed a tentative scratch. He still wasn't quite sure what make of the dog...or whatever he really was, but he seemed to be harmless enough. *For now, at least.* This was the best way to show Marcus that he wasn't in danger.

"NO!" Marcus cried. "It gets big! It tried to kill me! It's not a dog, it's a monster!"

Oscar gave him a sympathetic look. "Yeah...there's a lot of that going around. But he's okay, see?"

Ed panted, his tongue lolling out as Oscar rubbed his head, but Marcus only shuffled further back on the bed, aghast.

"You." Zara's voice was hard as steel, her chin raised and eyes flashing at Dmitri in a way that told Oscar nothing good was coming. "You drugged us. Drugged us and trapped us in your creepy house. Let us go now, and we won't go to the police." Her nose twitched at that last part. Zara could be fierce, but she was not a good liar.

Oscar looked at Dmitri, who returned Zara's gaze levelly.

"What...what happened to you, Zara?" Oscar asked.

"Ask him," she spat angrily, jabbing a finger at Dmitri. "One minute, I was at the front of the house, and his car rolled up. There wasn't exactly anywhere to hide, so I tried to tell him that there had been an accident nearby, and Marcus was hurt."

"You tried to lie and buy your friends time," Dmitri corrected.

Zara's eyes flashed, her mouth twisting irritably. "Not a complete lie. And hardly the worst thing that's happened around here lately," she snapped acidly. "Either way, the next thing I know, he takes something out of his pocket, my head's all fuzzy, and I can't think straight. He must have jabbed me with something. Next thing I know, I was here with Marcus blabbering like a hot mess about some hallucinations he had. Door locked, bars on the window."

Oscar saw she was right. Fine, twisted metal bars the same pale colour as the walls blocked off the window.

"Not a hallucination. It ate my glasses." Marcus' voice trembled, his eyes still fixed on Ed.

Zara continued, "Then this creep comes in, tells us we're in danger, and says he's *protecting* us. Tells us he didn't drug us but used some kind of...stink-magic."

Oscar looked at Dmitri, puzzled.

"Pheromones," Dmitri said, as though that explained everything.

"Exactly." Zara folded her arms and arched an eyebrow. "Stink-magic. Also known as bullshit. We were here just being curious. His dangerous house tried to eat Marcus, then he came back and drugged and kidnapped us."

"That is...correct. For the most part," Dmitri said thoughtfully.

Zara's nostrils flared dangerously, and Oscar jumped in. "Zara. I think he's telling the truth."

"What the fuck, Oscar?" Zara's eyes widened.

"About the stink-magic?" Marcus' voice was low.

"No, not the...stink-magic. Well, maybe. I mean, he did something to me too, but..."

Zara and Marcus exchanged a significant glance.

Dmitri cut in. "I tried to explain this before. Pheromones are capable of much more than you think. What I did...can do...it is an advanced form of modulation. Signalling neurotransmitters into a specific response. Relaxation, alertness. Small amounts typically make people more suggestible, heighten specific emotions. A heavy dose can cause a loss of consciousness with a temporary effect on memory."

"Are you saying you can change people's memories?" Zara said, looking at him sharply.

"No. That is far beyond me. But generally speaking, if the brain is tampered with and memory affected, it will remap to provide itself with logical explanations. Typically using parts of other memories to path things together. Just like people change their own memories to avoid a painful or frightening truth. Lie to themselves until they believe it as truth. And if they can't explain it, they block it out."

"Like the forest people," Marcus whispered.

Three sets of eyes joined Ed's in staring at Marcus.

Marcus cleared his throat. "There are several reports of people being lost in the forest for days. Weeks even. When they come back, they don't remember anything. It's all just...gone."

"Perhaps," Dmitri agreed.

"If that's true, then why didn't you just stink us out? Have our brains make up a story?" Zara raised her chin at Dmitri stubbornly, folding her arms across her chest.

"Some people are immune," Dmitri replied, shifting uncomfortably. "A strong-willed or highly perceptive person. Genetic predisposition can affect it, too. Certain medications, herbal remedies...paranoia."

"Bullshit," Zara said flatly.

"I...I don't think so, Zara," Oscar said.

"What exactly happened, Oscar? Where have you been?" Zara asked.

"I forgot what had happened. Woke up at home. But then I got...a text from your phone telling me to come to work."

"He took my phone." Zara glowered at Dmitri.

"Well, I went, and when I left...I saw you. But it *wasn't* you."

Zara shook her head, and Marcus whispered something from the corner that sounded suspiciously like *stink-magic*.

"Anyway, I followed you, but not...because it really wasn't you. It was a monster, all grey-looking and with a big mouth and pointy nails. Dmitri said it was like a doppelgänger, but it was called a fetch."

Zara pressed the back of her hand on Oscar's forehead, then her fingers found their way to his wrist to check his pulse.

"And then Dmitri showed up. Made me stop panicking somehow and brought me back here." Oscar's mind stumbled over the last part. *How did that happen? What was in that little box?*

"What happened to the...*thing*?" Zara scowled.

"The fetch?" Oscar said.

"Stop trying to make the fetch happen," Marcus said weakly, his heart not in it.

"Oh," Oscar said, awkwardly. "Dmitri..."

"Killed it," Dmitri finished.

Zara's eyes flashed to Dmitri, narrowing.

"It hurt him. It was trying to kill me. He had to," Oscar explained.

Zara's eyes took in the bloodstain on Dmitri's chest, and her eyebrow quirked slightly. "In any case, this doesn't sound right, Oscar. I think he's given you something, made you think things. Think they're real."

"He didn't," Oscar insisted. "I saw it."

Dmitri cleared his throat from the door "Technically, I did give you something," he admitted. "I did not want to use my ability on you again, given your previous...extreme reaction. So, I used some fur from a Ditherfox I procured. That's what I used on your friends, too. It obfuscates the passage of time. At least for humans."

"What?" Oscar asked, turning to Dmitri. He wasn't sure he knew what half of those words meant.

"He's not well, Oscar," Zara murmured.

"It is harmless in small amounts. It just...helped me..." Dmitri struggled to explain.

"Drug us?" Zara finished.

Dmitri's eyes dropped to his feet. "I'm sorry. I thought I should be honest."

"No, it's okay," Oscar said. "We need to understand..."

Zara scoffed.

"Whatever is real and what isn't...how do we know he's not just making you say all this?" Marcus said from the bed. His eyes had finally left Ed, but he sat stiff with tension, as if ready to bolt at any moment.

"Exactly." Zara eyed Dmitri sharply. "Leave us alone. Let us talk with Oscar without you here."

Dmitri frowned, his eyes meeting Oscar's for a long moment.

Oscar felt his cheeks flush and nodded.

"Very well. I will go and..." He looked down at his torn bloody shirt. "Get cleaned up. I will leave Ed to keep watch, so please...just talk, yes?"

Zara scoffed again, her eyes flashing to the puppy, mouth twisting like she couldn't believe her luck at being left on those conditions.

Before retreating through the door, Dmitri spoke once more. "Ed. Veghea."

Ed responded with a yip, and then his small puppy body bubbled, bloating rapidly before their eyes.

"What the...oh shit!" Zara gasped, stumbling away. The back of her legs hit the edge of the bed, and she tumbled onto the mattress beside Marcus.

Just when Ed looked fit to burst, the swelling stopped, and he settled. He was still in his doberman shape but fully grown once more, with lean, corded muscle under sleek black fur. He gave a low ruff, so deep it seemed to reverberate in Oscar's chest, and padded to the door to keep watch. His intelligent eyes took in Marcus and Zara on the bed, then moved to Oscar before his tongue drooped out happily. Oscar couldn't help but smile.

"I told you so!" Marcus whined, trying to retreat even further onto the bed.

Zara's eyes were fixed on Ed, her mouth working soundlessly.

"So anyway," Oscar said, biting his lip, "I think Dmitri is telling the truth."

THE TAINTED URN

Zara tried to reason it every which way possible, reeling off a list of potential drugs, conditions, and medications that frankly gave Oscar a new appreciation for her knowledge.

Finally, after she had ruled out shared hallucinations for the third time, she sat back on the bed beside Marcus and scowled at the half-closed door.

There was a gentle tap on the door, but by the time Oscar got there, all that sat outside was a carrier bag filled with various packaged sandwiches and bottled water. Oscar's stomach growled, and he brought it into the room and set it on the bed. "Dmitri must have fetched them whilst we were talking."

Marcus was already rummaging through the contents and selected a packet, tearing it open and taking a ravenous bite. His eyes never strayed far from Ed, but there was a new light in them now. A luminous glow of exhilarated vindication. "If monsters are real, imagine what *other* things are," he said, through a mouth full of half-chewed bread.

Zara was prodding through the contents of the bag, eyeing it suspiciously.

"Not *normal* monsters," Oscar said. He was sitting cross-legged on the wooden floorboards, only a few feet away from the bed. "Dmitri told me that things we think of as monsters, like vampires and stuff, aren't real at all. But there are different things."

Zara narrowed her eyes at him. She had taken one of the bottles out and was checking its seal scrupulously.

"Like what?" Marcus leaned forward, eyes wide.

"I...don't know," Oscar admitted. "He just said that you can't always tell, and they're everywhere, and not all of them want to hurt us."

"And Dmitri is one? What kind?" Marcus' eyes burned with curiosity.

"I don't know," Oscar said again. "I mean...when he fought the fetch, his eyes glowed, and his teeth looked...sharp."

"You need to stay away from him, Oscar," Zara said bluntly. "I saw how he looks at you, and nothing good comes of any guy with glowy eyes and pointy teeth. Particularly one who locks people in his house, drugs them, and claims to control people using BO."

Oscar felt colour rush to his face. *Dmitri...looks at me?*

"Os, I'm serious. This guy needs to not be the latest in your line of bad boyfriends. He's dangerous. You'll have more to worry about than him ghosting you. You might end up an actual ghost. As in *dead*."

Oscar frowned and took the first sandwich he found out of the bag. No matter what was in it, he was so hungry he'd eat it.

"We need to know more." Marcus' voice brimmed with excitement.

"We need to know *less*," Zara snapped, giving him a disapproving glare. "Have you forgotten why we came here? That he cut up a little girl?"

"Dmitri told me that she isn't a little girl," Oscar said, taking a bite and resisting the urge to gobble the whole thing up.

Zara rolled her eyes. "And normally monsters admit to cutting up little girls right away! I don't suppose he cleared his name of all the local disappearances, too, did he?"

Oscar swallowed with difficulty. "No, he didn't."

Zara sighed, folding her arms. "We need to be realistic, even if the situation isn't. We need to get out of here, and all be safe. That's number one."

"Agreed," Marcus said.

"Of course," Oscar added.

"So why don't you go talk to...Count Stankula." She pulled a face. "Get us the golden ticket out of here. Tell him whatever it is he needs to hear short of, 'Yes, Dmitri, we will join your secret child cutting cult.' Christ, tell him we will if it gets us out the door."

"Okay," Oscar agreed, cautiously.

"After that, we do what we need to do. Reassess, keep our mouths shut, stay low." A shadow of concern passed over her face as she met Oscar's eyes. "We need to know if someone...*something* really is following you like he claims. All I know is that we can't trust him."

Marcus looked sullen and disappointed but did not object.

"He helped me, Zara. That thing that looked like you, I'm pretty sure it would have killed me if he hadn't been there," Oscar said.

"Don't trust him, Oscar. Do you hear me?" Zara spoke slowly, using the words like a hammer to drive the message into his head. "Even if that *was* real, you'd never have been in danger if he didn't put you there."

Oscar nodded silently.

"We will wait here with Scooby *oh-god-please-don't*." Zara eyed the hound, whose large body was curled on the floor in the centre of the room. He let out a curious *arf* in his half snooze.

"Maybe you could come with me?" Oscar suggested uncertainly.

Zara glanced at Ed doubtfully. "Let's see," she said. Slowly, she moved to the edge of the bed. Her feet touched the ground, and Ed's eyes opened, his head lifting with interest. It wasn't until she stood and took a half step forward that a low growl reverberated deep from within him.

Zara quickly stepped back and sat back on the bed, looking a little pale. "Looks like you're flying solo."

Ed looked up at Oscar, his tongue lolling out again as he panted.

"Okay." Oscar straightened his back. "I'll...see what I can do."

"And fast, Oscar," Zara added stiffly through her teeth. "I had to pee in that vase over there, and I really don't want to have to do that again."

❧ 16 ❧

THE CONSUMING HEAT

Oscar retraced his steps across the landing, floorboards creaking tiredly under his feet. Dmitri could be anywhere, but he figured that he would try the room he had woken up in first.

"Oh," he squeaked as he entered.

Dmitri stood by the wardrobe, wearing only dark jeans, still glistening from his shower. His dark hair was slick back with wet, but Oscar found it hard to notice anything other than his chest, lean and powerful, a subtle scattering of dark hair in the middle.

Three livid scratches ran across his pectorals, disappearing into the groove of his sternum. His broad chest tapered down to his lean, toned waist. Oscar knew everybody technically had abdominal muscles, but...he didn't know they could really look like that. Wasn't that all just lighting and CGI?

"I'm sorry," Oscar garbled, his tongue suddenly several times too large for his mouth.

"It's fine," Dmitri said blandly. One hand swept up to brush a strand of wet hair behind his ear, offering a flash of round bicep and thick, dark underarm hair before it fell back to his side. "I heard you coming."

"Oh. Okay then. Well, I'll just go." Oscar sidled back through the door.

Dmitri looked confused. "It's fine. Tell me what happened."

Oscar's eyes wandered back to the wounds on his chest. "Those scratches...do you need to see someone?"

Dmitri shrugged. "The bleeding has already stopped."

"But...maybe you should cover it up with a bandage or something. Stop germs from getting in?"

Dmitri's eyes sparkled in amusement. "If you think so. In the drawers beside you."

Oscar cleared his throat, twisting around quickly and pulling out the top drawer, the old wood catching as he did. Sure enough, there were several dressing packs he recognised from the hospital.

"You stole these?" Oscar asked, scandalised.

"Employee benefits, no?" Dmitri smirked.

"They're expired. By like...three years."

Dmitri shrugged. "It's fine. Bandages don't really go out of date, they just have to put that on there."

Oscar gave him a doubtful look. "I can...help if you want," he offered, though he worried that his tongue might drop out of his head at any minute. Fortunately, it seemed to want to stick to the roof of his mouth instead.

Dmitri looked at him for a moment, then simply sat at the edge of the bed.

Oscar sat beside him, and Dmitri leaned back slightly, resting on his elbows to allow him access to the wounds, and displaying his...*perfection*.

Oscar fumbled the packaging, dropping it on the floor, and mumbled an apology. He scrambled to pick it up, forcing his eyes to focus on the angry cuts on Dmitri's chest. *His perfectly sculpted chest*. This close, he could feel the heat coming off of Dmitri. Smell that smoky citrus smell.

"Are you okay?" Dmitri asked.

"I'm fine." Oscar jumped, heat rushing to his face.

"Feeling better after the tea?"

"Well, I'm not sure. I suppose the tea helped, but I imagine that everything feels better once you've tasted that tea, if only because it's not in your mouth anymore."

Dmitri's face split into that grin again, guileless and wide, the years fading from his face; even if those shifting grey eyes still looked far too old for him. "I'm sorry. The ingredients are very specific."

Oscar's face grew hotter. "No, I'm sorry, that was rude. My headache is completely gone. I feel much...clearer." He managed to get the dressing pack open without spilling its contents onto the floor and started to pull on the sterile gloves.

"I meant are you okay in general," Dmitri replied. "Today has been...difficult."

Oscar shrugged, taking care not to meet Dmitri's eyes. His thoughts were a mess, he didn't remember the last time his hands weren't shaking, and all he wanted was to lie down in a dark room. Only now he didn't trust the dark quite so much anymore.

"I'm fine. What else can I be? I'm happy that Zara and Marcus are okay. Scared that you said something is after me. Grateful that you helped...*are* helping us. It's just been...confusing. It still is. All the forgetting made things harder."

Dmitri cleared his throat. "I'm sorry that I made you forget. It was the only way. It could have been much more dangerous if I had let you leave instead."

Oscar chewed his lip, pulling on the second glove. Something had been troubling him, something that came to mind back when he was talking to Zara and Marcus. "You did it to me again, didn't you? When I woke up, and you were telling me everything. You stopped me from being scared."

Dmitri gave him a guilty look. "I did. You were frightened, and I was worried. I didn't even realise I was doing it at first; it was just the smallest amount. I stopped as soon as I realised."

Oscar swallowed. "Please don't do that to me again. I think I can trust you, so you can't do things like that. Even if they seem right at the time."

Dmitri's shoulders sagged, and his eyes dropped. "I apologise. I will not do it again, Oscar."

Oscar felt his cheeks flush. "You were...worried about me?"

Dmitri met his eyes, just for a flash, and nodded. Oscar's stomach flipped.

Oscar gently pulled at the edges of the deepest wound. Dmitri did not flinch, but the scratch looked deep even if it wasn't bleeding anymore. "It looks like you cleaned it already. Do you think you need antibiotics?"

"I don't think I will need them," Dmitri said softly, that imperceptible smile returning.

Oscar began to apply a layer of gauze across his chest. The skin felt so hot. "It feels like you're burning up, you might have a fever."

"I'm always this warm," Dmitri said softly. "It won't get infected because I don't get sick. I usually heal quickly."

Oscar grunted. He hadn't thought of that. That maybe Dmitri being...*different*, things didn't really work the same. He remembered his amused look when he had suggested that his wound be dressed and felt a rush of embarrassment.

Oscar worked quietly anyway, fingers tracing across the sculpted, burning lines of him, until the last part of the adhesive dressing was pushed down, and he started to peel off his gloves. "I'm sorry, it might pull the hairs when you take it off."

Dmitri, who had closed his eyes peacefully as Oscar worked, opened his eyes and gave him a small smile. "Thank you."

Oscar bundled the unused dressings together and leaned over to set the used pack on top of the dresser. He found he could barely bring himself to turn back around. "You must think I'm an idiot," he mumbled.

"What?" Dmitri sounded surprised.

"For the dressing. For everything."

Silence lingered, and Oscar fixed his eyes on the floor. "You're different. Not like us. I'm sorry I don't understand what I'm supposed to do. I never do, really."

Oscar's voice faded as he felt warm fingers wrap around his own, taking his hand from his lap. His heart lurched in his chest as Dmitri took his hand in both of his larger hotter hands, fingers closing and squeezing gently. Oscar found those pale eyes fixed on his own, brow knitted in concern. "Please stop that."

Oscar did, closing his mouth so quickly his teeth clicked. The look on Dmitri's face was pained.

"Oscar. How do you not hate me? I poisoned you. Kidnapped your friends. Murdered a doppelgänger of one you love right in front of you." He shook his head. "All of this, all of the horror and lies from a...a monster." Dmitri's mouth twisted around the final word like it was bitter in his mouth. "Yet, you wake up here, stroke my strange dog, listen to my impossible words, and...try to take care of me."

Oscar shifted on the bed, conscious that Dmitri still held his hand.

"You asked me what I am. But I ask you. What are you that you can forgive this? That you could ever begin to trust me, let alone want to help me? How many people, after the day you have had, do you think would be sitting here right now?"

Oscar spoke, his words thick. "You didn't call."

Dmitri tilted his head, confused.

"When we went for coffee. You left, and you never called. And you ignored all my messages."

Dmitri closed his eyes and took a slow breath, releasing Oscar's hand. After a long moment, he opened them again, meeting Oscar's with earnest. "Now you understand why. I could not bring you into *this* if I could avoid it. I suspected you were in danger, but I didn't want to bring you closer to the flame."

"But why?" Oscar shook his head. "Why do you care? Why were you worried?"

Dmitri's head dropped, at a loss for a reply.

Oscar was suddenly aware of how close they were sitting and the heat radiating from Dmitri. His vision felt hazy, his head thick with a familiar feeling. *Desire*. The urge to pull Dmitri closer was overwhelming.

Distant alarm bells rang in his head.

Pheromones.

"What are you doing?" Oscar croaked.

Dmitri's head tilted, confused.

"Are you...doing that thing?" Oscar swallowed. "Pheromones?"

"No." Dmitri moved closer, eyes searching and concerned. "I'm doing nothing, I swear."

The urge intensified; Oscar practically felt dizzy with it.

"I know what pheromones do..." Oscar swallowed thickly. "I feel..." His cheeks burned, eyes travelling over Dmitri's bare muscled torso.

Dmitri looked mortified and moved back. "Oscar, I would never do that. Not like *that*. I swear to you. Whatever you are feeling...it is not me doing it. Anything you are feeling is...it's just you."

Oscar's heart pounded like it wanted to burst from his chest. He reached out.

"Oscar..." Dmitri began, eyes shining with intensity.

Dmitri's wet hair felt thick and silky between Oscar's fingers. The heat of his chest, pressed against his own, burned through his clothes. He saw Dmitri's eyes widen as their faces came together, and their lips collided. Oscar's nose squashed against Dmitri's cheekbone clumsily.

Nope.

That wasn't right.

Dmitri stiffened and pulled away, hands on Oscar's shoulders.

Deep shame tore into Oscar, and his face felt like it had completely drained of blood all at once.

"Oscar." Dmitri's voice was low, his body shaking slightly. His eyes were shut tight as though in pain as he spoke each word carefully. "You cannot do that. You have no idea...it is not a wise path to take."

Oscar stood up. His legs felt too light as he staggered toward the door, voice quivering. "I'm sorry. I thought...I thought you wanted to."

"Want?" Dmitri snarled, low and bitter. "Want is a childish game. I do not *want*. Want is a candle beside the bonfire of *this*." He opened his eyes, no longer pale but that flickering burning orange.

Panic jabbed at Oscar's insides.

"Since I first saw you...I have *needed*." Dmitri shook his head as if trying to shake the thought away. "I stayed away to keep you safe. Safe from whatever was hunting you. But also from this. Safe from me."

"Dmitri—"

"Everything about you from the moment I first saw you calls to me. Your presence sings in a world full of silence. I have lived for so many years and never before felt like *this*. You should stay away from me. We need to make sure that you are safe. I have a...source that we can check with. After, I will watch over you. Do not ask any more of me. Do not tell anyone of this. If others get involved, it might keep me from being able to keep you safe."

His broad shoulders slumped, and he hung his head, dark hair falling like a curtain to cover his face.

Oscar stood frozen by the door, eyes still on Dmitri, motionless. His feet wouldn't move.

Need.

Has anyone...ever?

Slowly, to Oscar's own amazement, he took a step forward. He dropped to his knees before Dmitri, face level with his drooping crown. Very gently, Oscar reached forward with both hands, his fingers lacing through damp locks, and tilted Dmitri's face upward. His eyes no longer burned; their pale grey was distant, sorrowful.

"Can I kiss you?" Oscar's voice was softer than a whisper.

Deafening silence hung for eternity, Oscar's heart pitched down a bottomless pit, their eyes fixed upon one another.

"Please," Dmitri breathed, closing his eyes.

Lighter than a butterfly, Oscar touched his lips to Dmitri's, feeling his full and bountiful bottom lip between his own. It lasted barely a second before he moved back.

Dmitri looked into his eyes, searching. Oscar had no idea what for, but in that moment, more than anything, he hoped he found it. Found him.

Dmitri's fingertips ghosted Oscar's face, touching delicately down his jaw and cheekbones like he was a long-lost priceless treasure, rediscovered and coveted anew.

"I don't want to go," Oscar whispered, his voice vibrating in time with his racing heart.

Dmitri's kiss was nothing like Oscar's.

Oscar's kiss whispered chaste anticipation and tentative restraint.

Dmitri's was deep, hungering desire. A ravenous man picking gently at the feast's offering as not to overindulge too quickly.

Oscar ran the tip of his tongue over Dmitri's, and the larger man shivered. He gripped under Oscar's arms, and like Oscar weighed nothing at all, he pulled him up from his knees and onto the bed. *Onto him.* He twisted, pulling Oscar beneath him, pinning him with his weight and heat deliciously. Calloused hands found Oscar's wrists, pushing them together and holding them above his head with one of his own. Damp hair fell onto Oscar's face as starving lips feasted on his jaw, his throat, his collarbone, leaving a burning trail.

Dmitri's free hand roamed, sliding over his body as teeth

scraped his neck. Oscar bit his lip, arching his back and gasping, as Dmitri's fingers ran down his side, thumb latching under the hem of his T-shirt and pulling it up. In moments, Oscar was free of its confines, slim, pale torso exposed to the cold room until Dmitri enveloped him in his embrace once more, flesh on burning flesh. *What am I doing? This is all so quick, but...*

All cogent reasoning left his mind as Dmitri's hot mouth covered his nipple. The catch of teeth caused a whine to escape him. Dmitri's eyes opened, glowing once more with flickering heat.

Panic and excitement warred in Oscar. This felt so right, so good, but *those eyes*. His heart gave a thrill when he caught the flash of too sharp teeth grazing down his hip. "I should shower," he blurted awkwardly, remembering his barely arbitrary attempt when he awoke this morning.

Dmitri pushed his face into the sparse hair at Oscar's chest, breathing him in and shivering again. "You smell perfect," he growled, pushing himself up on *those arms* to look down at Oscar.

Oscar's heart galloped, eyes drinking Dmitri in. The way his bottom lip pouted, begging to be kissed, his angled jaw, tousled dark hair, faintly glowing eyes...

"We should probably stop," Dmitri said, his voice a rasp, eyes taking in as much of Oscar as he could beneath him.

Oscar's breath was heavy.

We should stop.

We should stop.

But...

"I don't want to."

Oscar reached up, sliding his hands around the nape of Dmitri's neck, at the same time his legs moved around Dmitri's waist, pulling him into him. Their bare torsos collided, and Dmitri covered his mouth in a crushing kiss, their lips rediscovering and reclaiming. Oscar's hands travelled down Dmitri's back, feeling the muscles there move.

"Is this okay?" Dmitri growled, fingertips pushing down under the rear of Oscar's jeans, parting both denim and underwear from flesh.

"Oh God, yes," Oscar moaned.

Dmitri growled into his throat with absolute agreement.

TAXONOMY OF MONSTERS: THE LUBBER-FIEND
(HOMINUM PRODIGIUM)

*"The blood of our kind has grown thin in this world, in no small part due
to some entering trysts with the wretched humans. This may result in
offspring, often causing the demise of the carrier. One common product is
what we have come to call the Lub. Lubs are large in size and carry
features of their stronger sire: extreme hirsutism, horns, or a tail. Lubs are
known to have a particular predilection toward chores and bargains."*

— EXCERPT: THE REVENANT'S ARCANUM

❧ 17 ☙

THE TRAITOROUS TONGUE

"What happened?" Dmitri's voice was thick like drawling honey. Oscar watched his face as he spoke. *Serene.* His eyes were closed, thick lashes paired as one, as bonded as their naked bodies beneath the sheets. "To your parents?"

"They left," Oscar replied. Neither the question nor answer nettled him now. Some things just *were.*

He remembered the dark empty chasm of loneliness, confusion, and rejection that had almost swallowed him up. He'd moved around that void so often now, it was reflex. Like not stubbing your toe on the coffee table when walking through your house in the dark.

"Mum was a pretty well-known art historian. Dad was a Botanist. They travelled a lot. One day they just...didn't come back. They got listed missing, but they'd planned to leave. Booked the tickets and everything. We were on our own after that." His voice was monotone and flat like he was making a shopping list. *What other way is there to say it now?* These wounds had long since closed, scabbed, and scarred.

"We?" Dmitri pressed.

Oscar sighed. "Me and Paige. My sister. They were going to

put me in care. My aunt helped out for a while, but Paige was just about old enough to get parental responsibility, so I was really lucky. She dropped out of college to work and support us."

"That sounds hard."

"It was. I...owe her a lot."

"You must be close?"

Oscar chewed his lip. "Not really. I don't know if we ever really were. When I finished school, I got a job so she could go back to college. Paige is smart. I think she got all the good at everything genes."

Dmitri took a deep, steady breath, his chest expanding and lifting Oscar's head where it rested. "You are good at many things, Oscar."

Oscar thought for a moment that he might be teasing or making a lewd comment, but there was no edge of sarcasm or playfulness to his voice. "I don't know. Good at making a mess, maybe. Good at forgetting things..."

"Good at being kind. At being *good*. Helping people," Dmitri interrupted gently.

Oscar closed his eyes and buried his face in the crook of Dmitri's throat, breathing him in. He smelled slightly different now, deeper, and richer. The smokiness of his scent seemed stronger, mixed with the salt of sweat. Oscar liked it.

Dmitri's fingers feathered their way up his spine. "Are you okay?" he asked, his words a low rumble. Oscar felt Dmitri's head turn, the soft pressure of his lips and scratch of stubble at his forehead.

Oscar forced a smile to his face and looked up at Dmitri. "Of course. I'm fine."

Dmitri's pale grey eyes fixed on his, searching.

Oscar wasn't sure how much time had passed from the fervent touches and shared breath, until now, almost full darkness outside. Their voices were low as if louder words might shatter the illusion of what they had shared. Crack the fragile shell of whispered promises and whimpered pleading. *Complete with all new sticking together skin.*

Oscar *did* know that if he hadn't needed a shower before, he definitely did now.

Unfortunately, Dmitri had already mentioned, his shower only ran cold. Oscar never had the stomach for cold showers, even if lying with his head on the carved muscles of Dmitri's chest made him feel like he might just need one. For *other* reasons.

Oscar was becoming increasingly conscious that Zara and Marcus still waited down the hall, with Ed keeping them ill at ease. "So, what now?"

Dmitri sighed. "What I want, or what needs to be done?"

"I thought want was a childish thing?" Oscar smiled.

"Oh, I suppose it is." Dmitri smirked. "But we should probably get you dressed before it matures back into need again."

Oscar chuckled. "Yeah...I don't think that can happen again for a little while."

Dmitri stiffened beside him, voice becoming serious. "I hurt you?"

Oscar's cheeks flushed. "No. Well...it...you were perfect." *Maddeningly patient, and...thorough?* "It's just...it had been a while. I think I'll need to...recover a little."

Dmitri relaxed slightly against him.

"Is being good at *that* one of your powers?" Oscar asked playfully.

Dmitri pulled him closer with the arm hooked under him, warm flesh pressing together and his soft lips catching Oscar's tenderly. "It might be," he purred.

Oscar laughed, only giving him the weakest push of protest.

"In truth, it's been some time for me also. Far longer than for you, I guarantee."

Oscar's eyes widened. "Really? But you...you're so..." He trailed off, blushing.

Dmitri grinned, pulling Oscar close again.

"We should go. Zara will be angry," Oscar said.

"True. She is quite...intimidating."

"She can be, I suppose. She's tough but usually right. I think...I think today is the first time we have ever disagreed with each other. About you, I mean."

Dmitri grunted. "She is wise. I think if the situations were reversed, I would agree with her. But the circumstances are quite...unique." He brushed his lips against Oscar's once more, sending a shiver across Oscar's skin.

Sighing, Oscar peeled himself away from Dmitri's warmth, wriggling out of the tangled covers. Away from Dmitri's heat, the chill of the room gripped him, adding urgency to his hunt for his scattered clothing. As he got dressed, he sensed Dmitri's eyes upon him and cast a furtive glance to confirm. Pale grey eyes scrutinised Oscar in a way no one had before. A stare frank and intent, studying to memorise every detail. Oscar awkwardly found himself rushing even more to get into his clothes, covering his nakedness by twisting his body away.

"Why are you hiding?" Dmitri drawled lazily. "There isn't a part of you I wouldn't know by taste or scent alone now. Though I am keen to test that theory."

Oscar felt his face heat and got a prickling sensation across his skin.

That is...probably true.

"It's weird, stop watching," he whined, hopping to pull on his jeans quickly.

Dmitri flashed that rare wolfish grin that lit up his eyes like sparks instead of embers. "I *am* quite weird. So that explains it."

Oscar laughed, quickly pulling on his T-shirt. "Do you think...they heard?"

Dmitri's grin turned to a thoughtful frown. He closed his eyes for a moment and put his hands behind his head. The display of flesh and lean muscle made Oscar feel like he should look away because something so appealing must be forbidden. "I'm not sure," he admitted, jolting Oscar out of his lustful stare. "They're very quiet. If they're talking, it is a whisper. The walls are thick in this house, and we were...as quiet as we could be."

Oscar grunted, then after processing the words, looked at Dmitri in surprise. "You can hear them from here?"

Dmitri opened his eyes and nodded slightly.

Oscar frowned. "We're going to have to talk about the things you can do. I feel like I need to make a list."

Dmitri nodded again. "We will talk as much as you want..." He trailed off, brows knitting.

"But?" Oscar added.

"It will be later. We should speak with your friends first, and you need to meet with my contact. What to do next is...far beyond my expertise. My contact will be able to help us understand if you are still at risk. We should go to her tonight."

"Sounds...ominous?"

"It is," Dmitri replied flatly. "She is a fate-reader. She can glimpse probable futures and might help choose the right path. She can tell us if you are in danger still. Well...if she feels like it."

Oscar's eyes widened again. "Really?"

Dmitri smiled. "She is not the strangest of things we will speak of, trust me."

Thoughtful, Oscar turned, looking for a mirror, and failed to find one anywhere in the room. He knew his hair was probably a mess, kicked up at the side from dried sweat. He settled for trying to blindly tame it.

Beside him, Dmitri rose from the bed. Oscar's eyes could not help but gravitate to him, and his stomach filled with something much bigger than butterflies. *Monster butterflies, perhaps?* Unhurried and without shame, Dmitri rose from the sheets, like a living sculpture and stood thoughtfully.

The quickening of Oscar's pulse made him wonder if perhaps he *wasn't* completely worn out.

As if he could hear his thoughts, Dmitri smiled.

Oscar's mouth became very dry. "Can you...read my mind?" His voice was panicked.

Dmitri placed his hands on his hips, eyes sparkling. "Not at all. But I can hear your pulse quicken. Feel your body temperature rise. Smell your—"

"Okay, enough." Oscar waved his hands, blushing and averting his gaze. "Just put some bloody clothes on."

WHEN OSCAR RETURNED to the room at the end of the hall, it was indeed very quiet.

Zara pointedly ignored his entry; she had found a piece of string and was absently casting it across the floor. Ed was still a doberman, but much smaller now. Not quite a puppy, he rolled around, trying to bat at the string and catch it with disproportionately large paws. Marcus still huddled on the bed, watching the game with interest. Empty packets and bottles scattered the bed beside him, giving Oscar hope that Zara had decided to eat and drink.

When Oscar closed the door behind him, Zara finally looked up, her eyebrow arched. Ed caught the string and started tugging at it with mouth and paws.

Oscar cleared his throat. "We...talked."

"Oh." Zara pursed her lips. "We know. We heard you *talking*. In fact, I'm surprised you can walk after all that talking."

Marcus snorted.

Oscar felt his face grow hot and rubbed at the back of his neck, staring at his feet.

"When I said convince him to let us go, I didn't mean like...*that*." Her scowl was marred by the look of concern in her eyes. "Are you...okay?"

"I'm fine," Oscar said awkwardly.

"Good." Marcus grinned. "We thought he was killing you at one point."

Oscar felt his face burning even more. At this rate, he would have a higher body temperature than Dmitri.

"Stockholm syndrome," Zara grunted.

"Not even!" Oscar answered defensively.

Zara shrugged, careful not to meet his eyes again. "I guess it doesn't hurt our odds of getting out. Will he let us go now?"

"Not yet." Oscar chewed his lip.

"What?!" Marcus sat bolt upright on the bed, outraged.

Zara pulled at the end of the string again, taking it from the Ed's clutches, and quickly cast it out. It landed on Ed's nose, and he batted at it with both paws. She gave Oscar a level look. "What's the condition?"

"He wants us to meet...one of his friends," Oscar said.

"Frankenstein?" Zara replied, pursing her lips.

Oscar ignored her comment. "A fate-reader."

Marcus leaned forward excitedly, eyes leaving Ed. "Fate-reader? Is that like a fortune teller but...real?"

"That's what it sounds like. Dmitri says we can check with her to see if there's any more danger."

"And after that, he will let us go and leave us alone forever?" Zara asked.

"I think so," Oscar replied. *Is that what I want?* "I mean...I guess it might depend on what the fate-reader says."

The idea of not seeing Dmitri again pressed against him, an uncomfortable weight on his chest. He still had no idea who Dmitri was. *What he was.* And he could still smell Dmitri on himself. Almost feel his lips against his own. The sensitive flesh at his throat, his thighs, still felt like it was still glowing from the coarse scratch of Dmitri's stubble. But it wasn't just that. It was more than touch.

Oscar couldn't stop thinking about that honest smile, like a layer of wrapping-paper half torn from a gift, barely revealing the hidden contents. Dmitri was...so much more than he had ever thought if that were possible. And to just stop now? Nothing more? Oscar didn't know if he could, or even if he even wanted to, but maybe it would be for the best.

Zara cast the string out again. This time Ed caught it, snapping his teeth around it excitedly. He rolled, pulling it completely from Zara's fingers as he doubled in size.

Marcus' eyes snapped back anxiously to the swelling form of the strange dog thrashing the piece of string around.

Zara watched too, her face a stubborn mask. "I guess we have no choice."

DMITRI WAITED at the other side of the hall, fully dressed in a clean white T-shirt and the dark jeans from before tucked tidily into brown leather boots. He raised his eyebrows hopefully as Oscar closed the door behind him. Oscar felt a stab of bashfulness, sharp uncertainty at the apparent difference between the man that stood before him and the one he had been in bed with not long ago. The space between them felt like a gulf as Oscar shuffled forward awkwardly. "They agreed."

Relief flooded across Dmitri's pale features. "Good."

"Are you sure your shower doesn't run hot?" Oscar asked, looking down at his crinkled T-shirt.

"I'm sure." Dmitri winced apologetically.

"I feel gross." Oscar sniffed himself.

"Trust me, you are anything but gross." Dmitri stepped forward, taking him by the hips and closing the impossible gap between them. Oscar's heart leapt as Dmitri's lips pressed against his with thrilling familiarity. "I could have showered, but I could not bring myself to wash you off of me."

Oscar found himself grinning into the larger man's lips.

"We should speak with your friends. Downstairs. I do not want them to feel like prisoners any longer," Dmitri said.

Oscar nodded, realising he should probably mention something else. "They...uh...heard us."

Dmitri shrugged. "No matter."

"It doesn't bother you?"

"Why should it? It doesn't bother people for others to hear them scream in pain or anger. Pleasure is the product of choice, so why should there be any shame in the outcome?"

"I suppose..." Oscar was conscious that Dmitri likely wasn't the one they heard anyway. From Oscar's heated memory, he was mostly low growls and whispers.

Dmitri finally let Oscar go, and he felt cold and loose again like he was flapping around in empty space. As Dmitri passed, his fingers caught Oscar's, taking his hand. Oscar's heart soared.

"Ed, aici," Dmitri said as he popped open the door. There was a scrabble of claws from the other room, and Ed rushed onto the landing. As he ran, he shook his body, his coat lightening and softening, ears drooping. When he reached his master, he was closer to a chocolate labrador.

Footsteps followed, and Zara appeared at the door, jaw set, and mouth in a stern line.

"So," Dmitri forced a stiff smile closer to a grimace, "let's talk."

"Fine," Zara said, narrowing her eyes. "But I'm using your bathroom first."

THE DEVIL WITH THE DETAILS

Z ara sat at one side of the dusty old dinner table, arms folded tight, face severe. Her mustard-coloured coat was pulled over her shoulders loosely, like a surly but colourful mafia boss. Marcus was beside her, thumbing a deep gouge at the table's edge thoughtfully, finally managing to keep his eyes away from Ed for more than a few seconds. Ed, for his part, was by the door, wagging his tail and staring back at Marcus like this was a brilliant game he had devised. Dmitri had taken the seat on the opposite side of the table to Zara. After a brief moment of panic at the prospect of choosing one side to sit over the other, Oscar awkwardly shuffled to the seat at the head of the table. *Probably best to stay in chair Switzerland for now at least.*

Zara's eyes briefly glanced over as Oscar settled, cool and guarded, before they quickly found their way back to their previous task of staring daggers at Dmitri.

"What is it exactly that you want from us?" she asked bluntly.

Taking turns to use the bathroom to refresh themselves hadn't softened her edge any. After having been locked up in a room for the last day, Oscar didn't really blame her. He had been surprised to find Dmitri's bathroom was the best kept room in the house, clean and the contents organised—almost spartan. Zara had washed her face; she looked even more tired without her makeup on.

Dmitri met her gaze thoughtfully, choosing his words with great care before finally answering, "Nothing."

Zara's face flashed indignation.

"That is...I want nothing from you for *me*," Dmitri said. "I only want to make sure your paths are safe. Something was hunting Oscar, and we need to know more to ensure his safety and yours."

"And then?" Zara prompted.

"And then...if the threat has passed, you can go. I will leave you alone," Dmitri answered, eyes drifting to Oscar, shining with an emotion he couldn't place.

Zara sniffed loudly. "That sounds good to me."

Oscar's skin prickled cold, and that weight pressed on his chest again. The weight of losing something he had barely even found.

"We need rules." Zara's voice cut through his thoughts. "No drugs. No lies. No locking in rooms. No stink-wizardry. No magic fucking rabbit fur."

"Ditherfox fur," Dmitri corrected, tersely. "It is extremely rare, and I have none left."

Zara's eyebrow quirked.

"And even if I did, I would not use it again," Dmitri added hastily.

"Why do you even care what happens to us? If you're a...whatever you are," Marcus asked, his eyes bright with interest.

"I'm different from some of the others."

"How? What exactly are you?" Marcus leaned forward, his voice growing bolder.

"It is difficult to explain." Dmitri shifted uncomfortably. "I am not human. I do not wish to confuse matters by telling you too much too quickly."

"Try me," Marcus begged. "You're a different species altogether? Like an undiscovered mushroom in the Amazon?"

"That is a nice way of thinking of it," Dmitri answered, a small smile on those perfect lips. "But there are many of us, some as different from each other as you and a dog."

"Oh, Marcus isn't so different from a dog sometimes," Zara muttered drily.

Marcus waved an irritable hand to silence her. "You're saying there's not only a species but an entire taxonomy? An ecosystem not known to anyone?"

"For the most part. Obviously, humans have encountered and documented some of our kind, mistakenly assuming that they are...organic to this world. The Anglerfish is an obvious example. But not all of us can be seen and sensed at all times, and most reside on a different plane altogether."

Marcus sat back, face slack and eyes like saucers. "This...is amazing. What about ghosts?"

"Perhaps human paranoia. Occasionally parts of the veil may weaken; someone might see a flicker of something that they should not. A strange shape or a flash of darkness that mirrors an action on the other side."

Oscar's skin tingled. *Like flecks?*

"What part of the spectrum do you fall on?" Zara asked darkly. "Ghost? Wolfman? Vampire? Magical flying hell witch with snake hair?"

Dmitri eyed her levelly. "I am...on the more human side of things, obviously. For the most part, at least. Do not mistake this for what you see in movies or read in trashy novels. In reality, there are few things so...pedestrian as those depict."

"I like trashy novels," Oscar mumbled.

Dmitri's face showed the flicker of a smile.

"And other than the knockout gas, what else can you do?" Marcus leaned forward intently. Oscar recognised the look. Marcus' brain was recording every detail.

Dmitri looked uncomfortable. "That is not the purpose. It is...not gas."

Zara snickered.

"Nothing that would harm you. I am stronger, faster, and heal quicker than you. I do not depend upon sleep nor food in the same way."

"And you don't do anything terrible? Like, eat babies or anything?" Marcus asked, sounding more interested than afraid.

Dmitri took a moment in thought before he replied, voice sombre. "I have not always been like this." His eyes found Oscar, watching for a reaction. "For many years, I was...a victim to my base urges. A slave to my power and nature. I know I cannot blame myself; I was simply being my beast. One of a pack of lions amongst gazelle."

"You did eat people?" Zara's voice was hoarse.

"No." Dmitri paused, frowning. "Well...maybe a little bit once. But that was a long time ago, and it was really more of a sexual thing."

"Woah," Marcus breathed. "I have questions."

"No. It is irrelevant. Human flesh is not my sustenance. I neither crave nor enjoy it. That is not to say this is true for all of my kind. In any case, I knew that I needed to live right if I were to be satisfied with who I am. I cannot undo what I have done, and I will not pretend not to have done it, but I will do better each day. Better by myself, and better for others. So, I kept watch. On the news, on patients at hospitals, on the internet. For unusual circumstances, disappearances, strange events. And I...I try to keep balance."

Zara's eyebrows shot up. "Are you saying that you're a good monster that hunts bad monsters?"

Dmitri nodded, eyes shining with intensity.

"Wow." Zara leaned back, suppressing a smile.

"It's so...nineties prime time TV. Now we need a love triangle." Marcus beamed.

Dmitri looked uncomfortable, his eyes finding Oscar's, searching for a foothold in the conversation again.

"Why do you live...*here?*" Oscar asked, trying to change the subject. "It's like it's been abandoned."

Dmitri's pale cheeks coloured. "As I said, I do not have the same requirements as you. I do not need heat or light. I do not need food or sleep as often. The location was for convenience, but there is a chance that I may have...neglected my residence. I have had...*other* things to attend to, and you are my first...guests. Human ones, anyway."

"Explains the welcoming party," Zara grunted.

"Why do you have a spider-hole that locks up like Fort Knox?" Marcus asked keenly.

Dmitri looked confused for a moment, and then realisation blossomed on his face. "Ah, yes. Well...that functions as detainment of sorts. Though one of my more colourful non-human guests recently rendered it somewhat ineffective, by creating a new roof."

"We noticed," Zara said drily. Dmitri cast her a puzzled look.

"The baking powder!" Marcus burst out. "We saw it in your sad little garden. What's all that for?!"

Dmitri paused for a moment, looking uncomfortable, his eyes flickering to Oscar and back to Marcus. "I use it when I wash. It helps neutralise my...distinct scent." His cheeks coloured. "Without it, I would be more easily detected by others of my kind."

So that was the smell? Smokey and acidic. Well, maybe that makes a lot of sense. "Don't they *hate* you? For turning against them?" Oscar asked softly.

Dmitri shook his head. "It is not just about keeping the balance for human's sake. For my kind too, balance is important. Too many humans harmed, people missing, strange events...people become suspicious. They begin to pry. Our kind do best in the shadows, and if I can trace events, so can others.

Many of my kind are grateful for the peace I keep; some others even do the same. Some...despise me. I am not a welcome guest in what you would call the community."

"What, like you can't go down to the local monster bake-sale without getting bullied?" Zara sniped.

Dmitri's eyes showed a flicker of hurt. "It is not a pleasant thing, to feel alone in this world. I'm sure that is something all here can perhaps appreciate."

Zara fell quiet, her eyes dropping to study the table.

An uncomfortable silence fell over the room, but Oscar noted that some of the tension seemed to have dissipated at least.

That was shattered when Zara spoke again, brandishing three simple words like a blunt weapon. "The little girl."

Dmitri looked at her, face an impassive mask.

"Nina," Zara growled.

Dmitri shifted in his chair, leaning forward and speaking. "That," his voice was low, "is not a little girl."

Zara's face darkened, and she leaned back in her chair, eyes becoming distrustful again. "I saw her. Talked with her. Took her pulse and dressed her wounds. What do you expect me to believe?"

"The truth," Dmitri replied.

Zara's eyes narrowed, waiting for him to continue.

"Are you saying she's evil?" Marcus said excitedly. "Like, possessed? Do we need an old priest and a young priest, because I saw that movie and it didn't work out so good."

Dmitri shook his head darkly. "The thing that seemed to be a girl is not. There are creatures that have been noted in human myth. Various names are used in different places. Ghoul, spirit, ghost, acheri. That is what it is in part, this thing you call *Nina*. A pale reflection of what it is."

Zara was shaking her head in disbelief.

"Acheri," Marcus repeated, testing the feel of the word.

"It can change its shape to present as she does, seeking to

spread illness and death. Particularly to the young. It is a vile creature."

"A shape-shifting ghost who kills children?" Marcus whispered. Oscar hated the edge of excitement in his voice.

"And you can prove this?" Zara demanded, voice as cool as her stare.

"Yes, by destroying it." Dmitri's voice was low and dangerous.

Zara shook her head slowly, her eyes flashing angrily. "Those wounds..." Her eyes wandered over to Ed, who was now breathing heavily in the doorway, apparently asleep.

"Ed was not involved," Dmitri said.

"A knife?" Zara asked.

Dmitri shook his head. "Human weapons only do so much. The way our bodies are composed, particularly this creature...it usually needs to be something from the same world as us. Otherwise, it's not right. Even if you shot her, should the bullet manage to cause damage, her cells might knit together again as quickly as you unmade them."

Zara narrowed her eyes "Then what?"

Dmitri shifted uncomfortably. "I was not fast enough to finish the job is what is important. It eluded me. Fooled the staff at the hospital to protect itself, the very place I work. That must have been a taunt. I wanted to get it out. While it's there, it can sicken the children."

A foggy memory surfaced in Oscar's mind, one that had been muddled into the overwhelming resurgence of all the others. He blurted it out immediately. "She's gone!"

Zara's eyes met his warily. "Gone?"

Oscar nodded, clawing back what he had overheard at the hospital. "She disappeared from the unit. They were all looking for her earlier today."

Zara quieted at that, eyes tight and jaw clenched as if considering how those pieces fit into this horrible puzzle.

"Can you track it? How do you find them?" Marcus asked,

practically bouncing on his seat. "Do you have like...a special sense?"

"Yes and no," Dmitri answered with a frown. "Sometimes I can smell our world on them, or sense that they are...different from humans. Sometimes they leave no sensory trace, and I need to track them through more...human means."

"Like a detective?" Marcus said, hopeful.

"Like a detective," Dmitri admitted warily.

"Monster Detective," Marcus whispered in awe.

Dmitri gave him a crooked smile.

"Okay." Zara's voice was firm and decisive.

Dmitri gave her a curious glance.

"Okay," Zara repeated. Oscar recognised the stubborn set to her jaw. She had made up her mind. "Let's go and see this friend of yours."

TAXONOMY OF MONSTERS: THE MIMICK DOG
(CANIS GETULUS)

"First noted by humans in their sixteenth century, this four-footed beast is of unknown origin. Little is written of how old the species is, or how many there are, due to their elusive nature. It is known that this creature is able to take other forms, usually of a similar physiology. It remains unclear whether it is able to do this by simple contact, or if it has fed upon those it mimics."

— EXCERPT: THE REVENANT'S ARCANUM

❧ III ❧
BY THE MOON UNBLESSED

❧ 19 ❧

THE BOTHERED BUGGE

"A graveyard? GRAVEYARD?" Zara practically spat as she pulled her coat tight around her in the cold night air.

"Maybe he's going to kill us and leave our bodies here." Marcus sounded oddly detached, as he peered through the railings at the tombstones within.

"It is not a graveyard," Dmitri corrected helpfully, "it is a cemetery."

"Same thing," Zara grunted.

"Not at all," Dmitri said. "Cemeteries have no association with the church."

Oscar's palm made it almost all the way to his face before Zara bit back.

"So, you expect us to feel safer because a monster is taking us to a place full of dead people, and there's NO holy protection?"

Dmitri flinched as she named him *monster*. His face was stiff and voice brittle when he replied, "I have told you. I do not want to hurt you; I am trying to help you. When you have seen the Bean-Nighe, we will be able to rule out any further danger. Besides, 'holy ground' has no bearing at all on protecting anyone from our kind. In fact, a good number of powerful religious lead-

147

ers, both past and present, are not human; including one of your recent popes."

"That's reassuring," Zara grumbled. "But also, strangely makes a lot of sense."

"The bean what?" Marcus asked, turning around. The moon reflected on his wide dark eyes, shining with curiosity.

"The fate-reader. She is the Bean-Nighe," Dmitri replied.

"Weird name." Marcus grunted. "Why does she live here?"

"She doesn't," Dmitri said, earning him a hard look from Zara before he continued. "This is just a crossroads. An access point into her domain. This cemetery is the place where the veil is thinnest between our worlds in London. Second only to another location in the Scottish Highlands on this island. There are a few other such locations in the world."

"Lucky for us that you live so close," Oscar mused.

Dmitri's eyes caught his, grim and dutiful. *Oh. Not luck. He...keeps watch?*

"How do we get in?" Marcus chimed impatiently.

Dmitri cleared his throat and gestured to the wall beside them. "Just here."

Zara looked at the wall, and then fixed Dmitri with a level gaze. The wall was pale solid stone, at least six feet across and eight tall, separating the black painted iron fencing topped with spikes like arrows aimed at the skies either side.

Dmitri strode to the wall and immediately began tapping the bricks, with peculiar specificity. Oscar watched, curious. *Four times on the top palest brick, twice on one with a strange crack running across it on the lower left.* Dmitri's shoulder blocked what he did somewhere on the right, and as Oscar moved to get a better view, he saw Dmitri press his palm flat against one of the bricks in the middle. As Dmitri moved his hand away, the wall *changed*. Nothing moved per se; there was no grinding of stone or physical disappearance. Instead, it was as though the perspective *shifted*. Like a magic eye puzzle suddenly realised or optical illusion revealed. Instead of a solid wall, there was now a narrow opening, revealing the cemetery's bare trees clawing at thin clouds bathing the cold, fat moon above.

"What did you do?" Oscar gasped.

"I revealed the parallax," Dmitri explained. "It was built into the wall when the cemetery was developed. A back door of sorts, for those who know how to use it. Go through quickly, it will close again in less than a minute and will not open again for an hour or so."

"What the fuck?" Zara said, eyes narrowing. "I'm not into this at all. Is there a train to a problematic wizard school through there, too? If so, I'm out. I'm not sure how welcome any of us would be, and Marcus *definitely* won't want to go there."

"Quickly," Dmitri urged again, stepping through backwards, the narrow gap catching his shoulders.

Marcus was the first to follow, as quick as a flash before Zara had further chance to object.

"Marcus," she hissed, rushing after him, bubbling with low curses that Oscar didn't quite catch.

Oscar watched her, chewing his lip nervously. They hadn't had a chance to talk yet, and he felt the wound between them, hot and tender. Still fresh. He knew she must feel like he had betrayed her, but was she really mad because he and Dmitri...

"Oscar," Dmitri said firmly.

Oscar jolted to his senses, and with visions of the wall closing in on him as he did, quickly followed through the gap.

A breeze rustled through the trees, like icy breath, and Oscar shivered. Realising that Dmitri was watching the gap in the wall behind him, Oscar turned and marvelled as the puzzle unsolved itself, tilting back into place soundlessly, leaving a solid wall again.

"What would happen if you were standing in there when that happened?" Oscar wondered aloud, shivering again, this time nothing to do with the cold.

"You would end up on one side or the other, depending how far through you were," Dmitri said. "Probably nothing gruesome."

The tension in Oscar eased a little.

"Probably?" Marcus echoed.

Dmitri shrugged. "As many volunteers care to test the theory as you would imagine."

"That was a good question," Zara grumbled. "Should have asked it earlier." Her eyes caught on Oscar's, and he gave her a small smile. He thought she mirrored it, but it may have been a trick of the moonlight.

"So now we find the Bean Eye?" Marcus asked excitedly.

"Bean-Nighe," Dmitri corrected softly. "And not yet. The entrance to the Bean-Nighe's location is constantly shifting. I need to seek help from another. A guide."

"Just how many friends do you have living in this cemetery?" Zara asked darkly.

"Living, only two. If either could be called a friend. Dead, many more." Dmitri sounded wistful.

Zara side-eyed Oscar.

"And where do we find the Guide?" Marcus asked.

"He's already here." Dmitri smiled. "Good evening, Gax."

Oscar looked around, seeing no one. Fallen leaves rustled in the breeze.

"Evenin' Dmitri," a voice, deep and guttural like the croak of a frog, responded.

Oscar's eyes searched for the source. Marcus gasped, and Zara stiffened before he saw it for himself. Standing not even two and a half feet tall, 'Gax' as Dmitri had called him, was a monster. Much more the type of monster that Oscar would have expected, in fact. His skin was a mottled green, glistening in the night like wet leaves. His squat body with thick rolls of flesh was covered in patches of moss. What was left was covered in what looked like old burlap, dark and stained. He regarded the group with wary eyes, shiny and black as beetles, over his long nose and beard like damp hanging weeds.

"We're looking for the Bean-Nighe," Dmitri said.

"Course you are." Gax shrugged, sounding disheartened. "Why else would you bother comin' to see me."

"Well, we could have looked ourselves." Dmitri smiled slyly. "But, I was hoping you'd give these humans a tour on the way."

Gax hummed, a sound somewhere between a ribbit and a groan, and his mouth parted, splitting his face in two and showing square yellow teeth. "Why not 'ey? Not that often we get 'uman's in 'ere that I can talk to, and there ain't no sort quite as stupid as 'em."

Dmitri chuckled, and Zara shot him a look like knives. Marcus meanwhile was studying Gax with utter fascination, getting gradually closer, his mouth hanging agape.

"Keep a good distance, Marcus," Dmitri warned. "Gax is a Bugge. Their skin is highly poisonous to humans."

Marcus jumped back a couple of feet but continued to eye the creature curiously. "A Bugge?"

"Typically considered as a type of Goblin, I imagine. Bugges have been around for a long time," Dmitri explained.

"Forever," Gax croaked.

"They're also where the myth of the 'Bogey Man' originates." Dmitri shot the Bugge a playful half-smile.

Gax bristled. "'ere that was jus' Bernard and ain't none of us liked 'im. We got better things to be doin' than wanderin 'round 'umans 'ouses looking for cupboards to 'ide in."

"Don't we all," Dmitri replied.

"Not all," Gax quipped, and Dmitri hummed in agreement.

"Bernard the Bogey Man," Marcus whispered in amazement, wide eyes shining in the moonlight. Gax cast him a sharp, irritated look.

"Any news, Gax?" Dmitri asked in a low voice.

The Bugge's discerning eyes scanned the three humans. "Nothin' yet. No change."

Marcus sidled over to where Oscar stood as the pair continued to talk in hushed voices with Zara glaring at them suspiciously.

"Don't worry about Zara," Marcus whispered, nudging Oscar. "I like your new boyfriend."

Oscar blushed. "He's not..."

Is he?

"I don't think he's evil. I've got his trousers on."

Oscar turned to look at him in confusion.

Marcus shifted uncomfortably on his feet. "I made Zara swear to never tell, but there's a reason I didn't have to pee in the vase. It might have happened when the dog got me..."

"Oh."

"But when I woke up, there were some clean trousers left for me. They're a bit baggy, but the way I see it, no one evil would have left me clean trousers. I don't think he's Satan's bitch boy, is all I'm saying." Marcus smiled awkwardly.

Oscar felt the sudden urge to hug him and wondered if it was the strangest relationship blessing anyone had ever received.

"Righ'!" Gax's beetle black eyes moved around the group again. "Let's be goin' then, 'umans. See if I can teach you a bit before Beanie 'as 'er fun." With that, he waddled unceremoniously into the bushes, apparently taking for granted that they would follow.

Marcus grinned at Oscar and dashed after the Bugge. Zara watched him with a troubled gaze before following, arms folded and jaw set. "Marcus, don't get too close," she chided.

Ahead, Gax's croaking voice took on a lecturing tone. "Over 'ere we have some dead people. They all died. As borin' as it sounds; they di'nt do much, then they died. 'Umans."

Dmitri's fingers found their way smoothly into Oscar's as they followed behind, and Oscar's heart skipped in his chest in the way it seemed to have learned to in these last few hours. The way he had forgotten it could. "Interesting tour guide today," he murmured.

Oscar grunted, picking his way carefully on the uneven ground. "Aren't there...cameras or guards or anything?"

"A couple." Dmitri shrugged. "But only in certain areas. The biggest worry is other visitors, of the less monstrous kind. Sneaking in to vandalise or take drugs and the like. But Gax has a bond with this place; that's the Bugge's trait. They connect with a place on a deeper level than any other thing. He knows the second that anyone or anything sets foot on these grounds. Senses every whisker on every cat, every worm in every corpse."

Oscar looked at him with disbelief, the moonlight catching on Dmitri's pale skin like marble. "That's amazing. He knows where everything is?"

Dmitri smiled mysteriously. "Everything that is living. There is irony in his chosen dwelling."

Oscar chewed his lip, stepping around a tombstone. "What was that before? When you asked him if there was any news?"

Dmitri's brow furrowed for a moment before he replied. "There are...things you might not believe if I told you. Probably even when you see them for yourself." His eyes met Oscar's. "I will do my best to be completely honest with you as often as I can, but I don't want to...overload you."

Oscar tried to smile. "That's reassuring."

"If I told you everything, with no limitations, you would never sleep again. Some humans have seen things they shouldn't, learned things they wished they hadn't. The descent into madness isn't linear. I told you I would protect you, and I would keep that promise. I will protect your mind, body, and soul." Dmitri's hand squeezed Oscar's fingers, and Oscar's heart skipped another beat.

"Is this place why you live here?" Oscar asked.

Dmitri cocked his head, eyes sparkling.

"Before...you said you lived in that house for convenience.

And then you said this place was where...it was thinnest. The veil?"

Dmitri's mouth quirked in the ghost of a smile. "You are more perceptive than you give yourself credit for. Yes. This place is an area where certain supernatural activity may be more common. It does mean unfortunately that there have been a number of grizzly deaths in the area over the years."

Well, that explains the unsolved murders.

"Well, she was a poet you see," Gax croaked up ahead. "Should've give'er away really, writing summat called 'goblin market,' but 'umans refuse to see even the simplest things sometimes. Truth was, she were one of us. A typ'a banshee is probably close to what you'd call 'er."

"There are Monsters buried here?" Oscar whispered to Dmitri.

"A fair few," Dmitri replied. "I told you I had some friends here." His eyes shone sadly.

"Friends?" Oscar asked quietly. Small creatures of jealousy gnawed at his guts. "And...ex-boyfriends?"

"Ex all-sorts," Dmitri mused.

"How many?" Oscar asked. He hated the words even as they left his mouth, and definitely did not want to know the answer.

Dmitri gave him a flat, appraising look. "A conversation for another time, perhaps."

Oscar grunted, eyeing the gravestones. They all looked...*ancient*. "Dmitri. How...how old are you, exactly?"

Dmitri took a slow breath, looking up at the moon. "I'm as old as my tongue and a little older than my teeth."

Oscar frowned. "That's what my grandma used to say."

"Jonathan Swift." Dmitri smiled. "Wrote a very famous book, centuries ago."

"Oh...an ex?" Oscar probed.

Dmitri chuckled, his fingers squeezing Oscar's. "No, iubite, I never met him."

Oscar shot him a quizzical look. *What did he just call me?*

The distance between them and the others was increasing, and Oscar realised that very subtly, Dmitri's hand weighed on his, drawing him back, slowing their pace to increase the distance between them and the others. "You should have taken the cold shower." Dmitri's voice was low.

Oscar felt a jab of self-consciousness and looked at Dmitri, whose gaze was fixed ahead where the Bugge was now laughing about something, a sound like a drain clearing. Oscar thought he heard him saying something about...*lizard people?* Oh no, Marcus was probably quizzing him on one of his conspiracies.

"I can smell you. And myself on you. It is maddening." Dmitri's face remained impassive, but his voice was a husky growl. "It is a good thing we are not alone, or I do not know if I could resist having you again right here."

Oscar's heart lurched in his chest, and he felt heat blossom across his skin despite the cold around him. Up ahead, the others rounded a corner around a worn old tomb, briefly out of sight. Boldly, Oscar pulled Dmitri aside, his back colliding with the side of the crypt. Dmitri was already on him, his full lips enveloping Oscar's hungrily, his hands a crushing embrace around his ribs. One of Oscar's hands pressed into the space between them, sliding up Dmitri's shirt to touch his burning, hard body. Dmitri gave a low growl, pressing against him so Oscar could feel his urgent desire.

"'old on," a voice croaked loudly. "We got stragglers. 'Ent up to no good either."

Dmitri broke this kiss, his eyes burning into Oscar's as he stepped away quickly. The night closed its jaws around Oscar again in the absence of Dmitri's heat.

Oscar turned to see Gax rounding the corner of the crypt, jet-black eyes fixed on them. "Jus' cos you 'ent dead don't mean you 'ave to carry on like that round 'ere to show off." He flashed yellow teeth in a strange smirk before he turned on his heel and waddled off. Oscar moved first, and as he rounded the corner, he saw Zara watching him with a scowl. Marcus seemed far more interested in their surroundings.

As Oscar followed the Bugge back to his friends, with Dmitri close behind him, Gax stopped abruptly. A strange shiver ran through his small body, which set some of the tangled moss hanging from one of his pointed ears shaking.

"Something's...wrong," Marcus said faintly up ahead.

"Gax?" Dmitri prompted from beside Oscar. "What is it?"

The Bugge turned its head very slowly, shining eyes large in alarm. "Somethin's ere." His voice was shrill. "Somethin' none of us wants to run into."

THE GUARDIAN OF THE VEIL

The pace the Bugge set was hurried now. His stumpy waddle moved ever faster through the overgrown grass, weaving between tombstones with more agility than his frame suggested possible. Dmitri shadowed him closely and was speaking in a low, urgent voice that Oscar could barely hear as he struggled to keep up in the darkness.

"Is it what I think it is?" Dmitri asked.

"I reckon." Gax's voice was sharp and high with panic. "'int never seen 'im meself, but not felt anythin' like it before. Fits with the whispers I've 'eard."

"So, then it's true. The gateway *must* be here. After all these years..."

"Aye," Gax replied, his voice hoarse.

There was a rustling in the bushes beside him, and Oscar near jumped out of his skin, eyes wildly searching for the source.

"Cat!" Gax stated loudly, barrelling forward. Oscar caught a glimpse of a ragged tortoiseshell cat, fat from mice, dashing between the bushes.

"Where is the Bean-Nighe?" Dmitri growled urgently.

"Not far now. 'Round the old Egyptian avenue a few rows back," Gax ribbited.

There was another rustle in the bushes up ahead, and the Bugge and Dmitri froze.

"Cat?" Marcus asked, voice high with hopefulness.

There was a low growl. Something about it seemed to resonate with Oscar's core, his insides vibrating inside of him in a way that made him feel like his knees might just give out.

"Not a cat," Gax croaked.

"The Bean-Nighe will protect you. Follow Gax." Dmitri's voice was stone.

Gax darted to the right, dashing between two tombs, and Marcus bolted after him, with Zara close behind. Oscar moved to follow but saw that Dmitri still faced the direction that the growl had come from, back straight, expression dark and determined.

"Dmitri," Oscar breathed.

"Go!" Dmitri barked, taking off his overcoat and tossing it over a tombstone beside him. He bristled with anticipation and his eyes alight, flickering brightly with the promise of flames to come.

The low growl rumbled again, like rolling thunder far too close.

Whatever is making that sound is big...

Oscar couldn't stop himself from turning to look.

Immediately, he wished he hadn't.

It was almost dog-like in appearance if the dog were the size of a bull and made of slabs of raw meat. Something between ears and horns adorned its massive head, like a fleshy crown. Its eyes *burned*, a blaze beside Dmitri's embers. Its mouth opened, splitting its head in two and drooling thick dark slobber, showing teeth longer than fingers and sharper than glass that filled its massive maw.

Every muscle in Oscar's body froze, and horror took hold.

The beast lunged.

A dark shape barrelled into it with a roar. But the beast was too big. Quicker and stronger than its attacker. It twisted, rolling to the ground, and latching onto it with its massive jaws. Latching onto *him*.

Dmitri roared in agony as large, jagged teeth sunk into his shoulder, blood gushing freely and soaking his white shirt half crimson all at once. With his free arm, he pounded at the beast's face furiously, earning little more than a blink. The beast dug in, shaking his head and rattling Dmitri like a doll. Then a massive hand clamped onto the beast's muzzle, long thick fingers dark with hair, nails black and clawed like talons. Not Dmitri's hand, only...it *was* Dmitri's hand.

Oscar realised something was happening...Dmitri was *changing*. Not growing the same way that Ed had grown, like a bubbling well, but with the agonising shifting of bones, the sickening twist of muscles and flesh. His body twisted and bulged, shirt tearing at the back and arms. The smell of burning grew stronger. Like Dmitri's charred cedar but overpowering now. Like a forest alight.

Steam rose from his body, clouding the night around him as if he was going to burst into flames at any moment. His face turned to Oscar, and Oscar's stomach dropped. Dmitri's jaw was stretched painfully forward, nose flattened into his flesh, his eyes ablaze. "RUN," he roared.

An ocean of panic flooded into Oscar. Filling every space that the horror had carved out. He turned and fled into the night.

OSCAR'S HEART hammered in his chest, his breath coming in ragged heaving gasps, the edges of his vision blurring white. His legs pumped as he ran through the gravestones and past the tombs, feet slipping on the damp grass. What he had seen was burned into his mind like a fresh searing brand.

Dmitri's flesh and bones shifting as he changed. No. Changed back. Back into what he really was. It wasn't just glowing eyes and pointed teeth...

Dmitri really is a monster.

Other memories followed. Those bright eyes looking up at him, pointed teeth catching at his inner thigh, fingertips digging into his shoulders. His legs wrapped around Dmitri's waist, fingers tangled in thick hair damp with sweat, ragged breath shared mouth to mouth like they were one animal.

But *this* is what Dmitri was?

Oscar's mind struggled with what he had just seen. Trying to reconcile the gentle man with the disfigured beast. Suddenly, all he could imagine was Dmitri on top of him, but the way he had just seen him. Long, wet tongue trailing thick spit on his skin, hot breath at his neck. That grotesquely stretched muzzle opening over his face as clawed fingers tore at his flesh.

A figure shifted in the darkness not far ahead, and Oscar's heart faltered. For a second, he was so sure he would see flaming eyes and teeth like broken glass. Instead, it was Zara, her round face paler than usual and eyes wide. "Come on," she panted, dashing forward and grabbing Oscar's hand. She didn't wait for a response, and Oscar's breath burned in his chest as she tugged him down a cracked cobblestone path, past some graves that were little more than rubble. Sharply, she yanked him to one side, between two of the bigger mausoleums.

Zara was out of breath. Oscar could see her skin shining with perspiration in the dull light. "Are you okay?" she gasped, looking back the way they had come.

"I'm fine," Oscar managed, his voice hoarse. "But...Dmitri..."

"I'm sure he knows what he's doing, Oscar." Zara peered out from the gap where they huddled over Oscar's shoulder. Her eyes bulged. With both hands, she grabbed him bodily and pulled him further down the gap, wedging them chest to chest as tight to the corner as they could both fit.

"Wha—" Oscar began, but her hand clamped roughly over his mouth. Zara's eyes were not on him but staring out of the mouth of the gap between the mausoleums, into the night. Oscar followed her gaze and whimpered into her smothering palm.

The massive shape of the beast padded heavily into the opening they had passed through moments before. Steaming breath from its dripping jaw filled the night around it as it stalked on powerful limbs corded with raw muscle.

Every instinct in Oscar warred. He did not know if he should collapse to the ground and play dead or run as fast as his legs would carry him. Luckily, Zara's grip stopped him from doing either. Her breath was low and steady against him as the beast tilted its head and sniffed the air. Its burning eyes scanned the darkness, drifting unerringly toward them. There was a snap somewhere in the distance, and the beast's head twisted around in the direction of the sound.

Slowly, the creature took a step in the direction of the noise, sniffing the air once more.

I could not bring myself to wash you off of me. Oscar remembered Dmitri's words. That thing could smell them. Smell them both all over each other. And it was...confused?

Making its decision, the bulky creature let out a low rumbling growl and bounded off into the darkness. Zara sagged against Oscar. "If I die here, tell that asshole Dmitri I pissed in his vase. This is all *his* fucking fault."

THEY STAYED like that for as long as they dared until they were sure that the thing was gone. But not so long as to give it time to come back. As Oscar's breathing returned to normal, his thoughts clung to Dmitri. He was clearly no match for that thing, and dread of the inevitable clawed at Oscar, his concern shredding away his disgust at what he had seen before. Dmitri was sacrificing himself to save them.

Oscar remembered that wide, boyish grin that he had never seen before. It had been so new and honest. He suspected that Dmitri hadn't smiled like that in a long time, and his heart ached to make him smile like that again. Not to lose him so soon. Not like this.

Worse, Oscar knew there was nothing he could do. He was helpless. And he was going to lose Dmitri, just like everyone else. Everyone but Zara and Marcus.

Finally, Zara led the way, silently shuffling from their narrow hideaway. They took a right of the branching path and down a smooth, cobbled slope. Sturdy stone pillars proudly supported a grand ornate arch as they passed into an alley of sorts, lined either side with tombs in varying states of decay. Each rusted door was hauntingly beautiful, dark metalwork in various, intricate patterns suggesting the grand status of the eternally resting residents. The walls and gates rose high, framing the wisped clouds and pale stars above, the edge of the moon peeking gamely as if to watch what they might do next. A rattling noise startled Oscar from his brief reverie; at one of the gates on the right, he saw Marcus.

Marcus' lean figure was yanking at one of the doors doggedly, whilst the dumpy little Bugge beside him croaked irritably. "I tol' you, if she don't want you in, she won't 'ave you in. She can sense the Guardian's 'ere an' not 'appy. Prolly won't open 'er door for all the cats in 'ell."

As Oscar and Zara drew near, Gax's black eyes shone at them as he shifted on his feet guiltily.

"Are you *sure* this is it?" Zara asked, her breath still ragged.

"'ow bloody dare you," Gax harrumphed. "Don't get me comin' out there tellin' you where things are in your own 'ouse." He put on a simpering high-pitched voice. "Ohhhh are you sure your door's at the front of the 'ouse?! Maybe you forgot where you 'as it?!"

Marcus pulled again at the door, impatiently. The loud rattling gave Oscar the urge to look around him for fear of the beast. Zara moved closer to get a better look at the gate.

"What was that thing?" Oscar asked, voice trembling.

The Bugge gave him a sullen look. "The Guardian," he croaked. "'e patrols places the veil is at risk o' breachin'. 'e's not bin seen in centuries though. Din't know 'e'd be so..."

"Big?" Oscar tried, then for good measure added, "Scary?"

"Oh, I knew 'e'd be them things. Don't get to be Guardian' of the bloody veil being a fluffy little sweetling 'int it. I was goin' to say angry. Must be that we were right. We 'ad an 'unch that the gateway was 'ere..." Gax trailed off, his mouth hanging open and growing very still. His black beetle-like eyes grew large, and a low squeak escaped his gaping mouth.

Oscar heard a low rumbling growl behind him and turned to see the massive shape of the beast stalking under the archway, powerful haunches holding its body low to the ground. Twin furnaces for eyes fixed upon him.

"'ello there," Gax croaked, voice high with panic. "'ow are you this evening, Master Guardian? I imagine you 'ent 'ere looking for trouble or—"

The beast gave a snarl that cut off the Bugge, causing him to yelp in alarm.

"Bugger this!" Gax cursed beside him and dove to the ground. There was little more than a damp pile of leaves, but the Bugge's squat body collapsed, slipping between the gaps in the cobblestones with an odd squeaking *pop*, leaving nothing behind at all.

The beast's growl grew louder as it stalked forward on its massive paws, each tipped with a claw the size of a butter knife, caked with grime and blood. *Dmitri's blood.*

"Marcus," Oscar whined, backing away from the beast. The orange flames of its eyes blazed. His back connected with something soft, and Zara whimpered against him.

The door rattled louder behind him. "I'm trying," Marcus cried.

For a moment, Oscar wondered if he should run. When it had first emerged, it had shown no interest in Dmitri, not until he had charged right into it. *Is this the thing that was hunting me?* The beast's glowing eyes were fixed on Oscar once more.

He imagined running. Dying. Buying his friends a chance to escape. But his feet felt stuck in the earth like they were embedded in the stone. He was a coward. A useless coward that was going to die just the same either way.

The beast crouched, moving to pounce, massive teeth bared. Oscar knew it would at least be quick. He wondered numbly if he would even have time to scream.

Suddenly there was a grating noise, and Zara collapsed behind him. Oscar lost his balance, staggering back and then falling painfully, cold stone rushing up to meet his back. There was a clattering of iron as the gate swung shut behind them. No sooner had it shut than the beast collided with it with a wretched crunch, the collision so thunderous that dust, debris, and loose mortar fell from the stone around them.

The beast's snarling muzzle filled Oscar's vision, bright burning eyes wild with bloodlust. Marcus let out a cry behind him, and he heard Zara scream, felt her body shaking against his. The beast struck the gate once, twice, three times but it somehow held fast. A thick dark glob of spit came through the bars and landed on Oscar's leg, just below the knee. The liquid immediately felt scalding hot, and he yowled in surprise as he felt it burning against his flesh.

"Ohgodohgod," Zara sobbed behind him.

Something heavy connected with the side of the beast, and it let out what was surprisingly close to a yelp as it was forced to its side, a twisting, writhing mass of muscle and too many snapping teeth.

Oscar caught a glimpse of what had hit it.

Who had hit it.

Oscar only caught the briefest of glimpses in the pale moonlight, but he knew it was him.

Dmitri's body was larger, his bulky shoulders hunched with muscle, and face unrecognisable. His shirt was torn to tatters, flesh dusky grey and streaked with blood.

In a flash, he moved again, leaping at the Guardian. In a flurry of jaws and claws, the mass of muscle and death rolled out of view.

"What...the fuck...was that?" Zara gasped.

Oscar's reply was so quiet he didn't know if she heard it. "Dmitri."

The sounds of snarling and struggling were growing more distant, leaving only their rasping breath breaking the silence, and Oscar's heart lurching painfully in his chest. "Is everyone okay?" he choked.

"Nope. Nope nope nope. Definitely not okay," Marcus mumbled from the darkness at the back of the tomb.

"I've been better," Zara groaned beside him.

Oscar's eyes scanned around the small tomb that they had tumbled into. Most of it was hidden by darkness. Just damp, mossy stone and an empty Coke can and crisp packet that had probably been cast through the bars of the door.

Cold fingers closed around his wrist.

"So, what do we do now?" Oscar asked.

"Are we locked in?" Marcus asked, moving past him to the gate and giving it a tentative push.

"I wouldn't be surprised," Zara said darkly, moving to stand beside him.

Oscar was just about to reply when he realised.

If they're both there...then whose hand is this? His eyes travelled down to his wrist, dragging through thick layers of dread.

The fingers that reached out of the shadows beside him were

pale as the moonlight. He opened his mouth to cry out in alarm, but only a cracked squeak escaped.

Ever so slowly, a face advanced from the pitch beside him. Hair the dirty orange of a half-rotten fruit, face narrow and soft, pale as the bony hand that gripped his wrist. She would have been beautiful, perhaps she was still, but...*her eyes*. Lidless and lashless, they sat on her pretty face like two great orbs, round and a brilliant white, with neither iris nor pupil.

Her delicate cupid's bow lips curled in a secretive smile.

"Hello, Cricket."

❧ 21 ❧

INTERLUDE THE SECOND: THE HERO THAT NEVER WAS

Parked not far from the cemetery wall that Oscar and his friends had been led through was a battered old Ford, its black paintwork mostly covered by rust and filth. Sitting inside, watching keenly through its grimy windows, was a man. He was nearer to forty than thirty, though his dark, untidy hair only had a few strands of grey close to the temples.

He was handsome, in a typical sort of way. Prominent chin, sapphire blue eyes, and a thick shadow of beard growth on a strong jawline. He was, however, more than a little unkempt. The stains on his stonewash jeans had been there for more than a few weeks, and their top button was permanently undone to stop it digging into his belly. His faded black T-shirt was covered in crumbs, sporting the remnants of a band logo he hadn't listened to for years. A heavy camera sat in his lap.

He rolled an old coin across the back of his knuckles, a trick he had picked up years ago before it turned into a comforting habit. The car stunk with the stale, heady fug of fast food and flatulence. He didn't care about any of that. He was doing important work.

He was doing *surveillance*.

This was the man that Marcus called his *online contact*. The man who called himself Barloh.

Barloh had first come across Marcus in an online group a couple of years ago. After several hours discussing whether the government was dosing water to hold killer viruses at bay, Barloh realised the kid was smart. After that, they shared intel when they could. Barloh had been impressed at how well the kid covered his tracks. He hadn't been able to ID him until a couple of days ago when he came to him with something new. Something very interesting.

Dmitri Roburt Tza.

The kid had compromised himself in sharing the information —that told Barloh how serious he was. He gave Barloh access to the guy's files at the hospital, begged him to pull everything he could on him. And Barloh had.

What the kid didn't know was that Barloh worked for the Police. Nothing so simple as plodding around the streets with a daft bobby hat on; he didn't even need a badge. Of course, he didn't *have* a badge. He hadn't earned one. But Barloh told himself that was just a triviality. Beneath him. *His* work was important.

Barloh's *official* duty was to track down data to be used as evidence. He had back doors into more systems than you'd like to imagine. But his *real* work, the work that he wasn't paid for, was off the books. *Way off the books.* It took him all of an hour to find more than he needed to know about the kid or *Marcus* as his name turned out to be.

Twenty-four. Patchy educational record but impressive test scores. ADHD. No previous criminal charges. Transgender.

That last one had been a shock. It might even have been enough for him to decide to ditch the whole thing and cut ties with the kid if not for what he found on Tza.

Or to be more accurate, what he hadn't.

Nothing.

No images on file, no passport, no national insurance, no

financial ties. Absoloutely nothing. The guy was a ghost. Barloh had only read about this kind of thing, never seen it himself. He had to cross-reference old public records before the name popped up on property records. He knew that it was unequivocally a sign that something terrible was happening, especially when the suspect had a *foreign* name.

He shared the address with the kid, but he kept the only other piece of information he had to himself.

The name on the records was from over ninety years ago.

Either there had been a Dmitri Tza Senior, or this guy was a con.

It made Barloh's teeth itch.

When the kid had found the data about unsolved murders close to the location, Barloh had been impressed. He'd clearly taught the kid well. He pulled the images of the killings. A few messed up stabbings, the vics sliced up pretty nasty. Half looked like whoever had done the deed set their dog on them afterwards. Necks swollen and torn, hands bloody and ruined where they'd tried to protect themselves.

So, he sent the kid on his way, eager to hear back how it went. Eager to find out the truth about Tza. Worst case scenario, this might give Barloh a bust by proxy—sending a canary into the mine, so to speak.

And then the canary went quiet.

When the kid hadn't checked in like they'd planned, Barloh started to worry. That hadn't lasted long before he was excited instead.

This was it. He was going to make all those assholes in the office sorry. They wouldn't be laughing at him when they thought he couldn't hear anymore. He would be the one laughing. He was going to catch a killer.

He already had the address from the info the kid sent over. He walked up and down Kinmount street for the better part of an hour before he gave up. The skies had turned dark, and he had just closed the car door when he saw them, walking out of some overgrown path at the side of the road.

The guy in a dark coat must have been Tza, a pretty-boy with slicked back hair and an angular jaw like some kind of European fashion model. A tall, wiry black kid with a narrow face came next; Barloh recognised this as *Marcus* immediately. A girl who looked like she might be pretty if she smiled more and washed the crap out of her hair and a skinny pale guy with big eyes followed. He had no idea who *they* were, so he snapped a couple of pictures with his camera to check later. They never even looked in his direction. He smirked. The advantage of never washing your car was it look unused, sedentary. Clean vehicles drew attention, but most people overlooked his battered old Fiesta.

When they set off down the street in the opposite direction, Barloh itched to go and check out the house. That must have been where they came from. But instinct told him to follow them instead.

He waited until they were out of sight and slipped out of his car, following on foot, not trusting the old banger to keep quiet. He had managed to keep sight of them all the way to the cemetery, but then they just disappeared.

He walked back and forth three times before he caught the sound of voices inside.

They'd gotten in somehow.

He scanned around, looking for an opening, finally contenting himself with pushing his face between the bars to try and get a better look.

He could see the kid, *Marcus*, standing just through the bushes. The girl was beside him, looking sour. He shifted slightly and saw something that made his stomach turn to ice. He was so shaken he completely forgot about the camera around his neck.

A minute later, they walked away, deeper into the cemetery, their voices fading into the night. Barloh tried and failed to clamber over the wall. After scuffing his leg on the second attempt, he went back, fetched his car, and parked it up beside the spot they had somehow gotten through. He'd been there close to two hours now. But he was still grinning like a fool because of what he'd seen. *Proof*.

Proof he'd been right all these years. Proof that the psychologists, the doctors, everyone had been wrong. He just needed to keep following these people. Obviously, they'd been sucked into a cult or something. He knew if he stuck close, he could finally get his evidence that *they* were real.

Monsters were real.

22

THE EYES OF THE MOON

"Oh my God." Zara's voice was barely more than a whisper. "The Bean-Nighe," Marcus murmured.

The Bean-Nighe's mouth turned up in a pleased smile. "Humans searching low and high, to answer who what when and why, take care of what you ask the Nighe, for she won't tell a single lie." Her voice was shrill with an irregular singsong quality like a stumbling nursery rhyme.

A pregnant pause hung in the darkness.

"What the fuck?" Zara whispered.

"Hey," Marcus offered in his most charming voice.

"Really, Marcus?" Zara snapped. "*Her?*"

Marcus shrugged, and the Bean-Nighe continued to give them the same fixed smile. The moon shone through the gate, catching her pale face, making her large eyes seem luminescent.

Then, just as slowly as she'd appeared from the shadows, she began to seep back into the darkness that flooded the edge of the small tomb. Her bony fingers released Oscar's wrist grudgingly. Her hand turned, finger curling, beckoning them to follow into the blackness before it too disappeared.

"What do we do?" Zara whispered hoarsely.

"Follow her." Marcus' voice was practically dreamy.

Outside, there was no sound. No sign of the beast. *No sign of Dmitri*. Zara met Oscar's eyes as she pushed the gate. It opened easily now. A path to freedom...or to hungry jaws waiting in the night.

"Dmitri said we had to do this. To make sure we are safe from whatever was happening. Whatever was after me." Oscar swallowed.

"Dmitri said a lot of things," Zara said tersely, looking out into the darkness. "But last I saw him, he didn't exactly look like he was...playing for our team anymore."

Oscar deflated, remembering Dmitri's twisted body. Those inhumanly long arms and massive clawed hands. *He can't have been lying. This must be the right thing to do.* Oscar cleared his throat. "Let's just do this one last thing. And then we will go home."

Zara eyed him doubtfully. "I don't know, Os. If the going's good, maybe we should just get out. Nothing good has come of this so far, and—"

Marcus stepped forward into the shadow.

One quick, decisive stride, and it swallowed his body whole.

"Marcus!" Zara cursed, pulling the gate closed again with a clatter. She started toward the darkness, ready to snatch him back, but pulled herself short, eyes flashing angrily.

Oscar chewed his lip, staring into the shadows. "We should stick together."

Zara gave a single angry nod, and he saw that it wasn't just anger in her eyes. *Zara was scared*. It was the first time he had ever seen it, and judging by the look on her face, it was something she certainly wasn't comfortable feeling. Oscar reached over and took her hand. She squeezed it tight.

"Let's get it over with then," she said darkly.

Together they stepped forward into the darkness.

And it *was* total darkness.

A darkness that filled all of Oscar's senses, just for a moment.

For one single stride, he felt nothing. Not his feet on the ground, nor the chilled night air on his skin. Zara's hand was gone, and the smell of stale moss and stone vanished. Even the sound of his own breath. His heartbeat. He was nowhere, and there was nothing.

And then as quick as he was gone, he was somewhere again. But a *different* somewhere. A profound sense of otherness from any place he had ever been before.

The warm dancing light of candles bloomed around the room, casting a glow on the hard earth beneath his feet, giving shape to the busy shelves that crowded the flat stone walls. Knick-knacks, books, and trinkets crowded every flat surface, all useless things presented as prized ornaments. A golf ball next to a rusty trumpet, propped against broken remnants of a vase beside a twisted hubcap. Betwixt the shelves, lines hung. Fine metallic wires adorned with a selection of tattered clothing and scraps of fabric.

"Who thinks that they go anywhere is neither here and neither there," the Bean-Nighe cooed.

Oscar's eyes found her, crouching on the ground beside a sturdy table that looked to be made of solid stone. She stood, triumphantly waving what looked like a doll, mostly perished through the middle. It was closer to a rag with one arm and a head attached.

Now that Oscar could see her in full, the Bean-Nighe truly did dance a jagged knife-edge between beautiful and terrifying. Her pale limbs were sinuous and long, moving with irregular grace, like a puppet dancing on the strings of a drunken puppeteer. The fabric that covered her body, only slightly paler than her flesh, billowed in an unseen breeze, like frothing cream.

"We've come to have our fates read." A ragged note of fear clung to the edge of Zara's voice. Oscar realised with a start that not only was she no longer beside him, she was on the other side of the room. Zara's arms were folded tightly across her chest, eyes wide, but jaw squared and proud. Marcus stood not too far from her; his eyes were wide too, but his grin said this was more awe than fear.

The Bean-Nighe's pale orbs turned on Zara, mouth twisted in a cruel smile that sent a chill up Oscar's spine. "Oh. She *is* an impatient one. Not all are so keen to hear how they end."

"Dmitri said you'd help us," Oscar said hopefully.

The Bean-Nighe laid the rotting doll down with great care on the stone table in the centre of the room. "You don't want to hear about death, but everything is about death. From joy to bones to hate to breath, it's all a game right up to death."

"I think we should leave." Zara turned, searching the shadows to pass back through, but only finding solid wall.

"The Gwyllgi still waits." The Bean-Nighe grinned, showing small teeth as pearly white as her eyes. "Sneaky puppy."

Zara took a shaky breath and turned back to the Bean-Nighe, sharing a wary look with Oscar and Marcus. "Gwyllgi?"

The Bean-Nighe shrugged. "Gwyllgi, Barghest, Beast of Many Places. Cerberus even." She gave a simpering giggle. "All are right and wrong at once. The only thing certain is his teeth. He's not a bad boy, really; you just need to get to know him." She sighed, and with her next breath, the darkness in the room seemed to pull toward her, all of the candles sputtering and flickering at once.

Oscar stepped back as she stretched, standing straight for the first time. She seemed...*bigger*. Bigger than any of them. *She must be close to seven feet tall.*

"You," she demanded, raising an imperious finger and pointing directly at Marcus. "Come here." His eyes bulged nearly as big as hers, and he shrunk away.

As quickly as she had loomed, she giggled, moving in a swaying gait with those willowy limbs. The room seemed to brighten again, the candles growing bolder. "Come on!" she trilled, waving at him coyly.

Marcus took a tentative step forward, pushing aside a gauzy shirt that hung from one of the wire lines. "Marcus," Zara warned, but the Bean-Nighe's long fingers had already reached out and snatched his, as dark as hers were pale. Marcus stood stiffly as the Bean-Nighe clutched his hands, her moonlike eyes fixed upon him. Then, she began to hum.

Zara cast a wide-eyed look at Oscar and mouthed an obscenity.

The hum was not quite a tune. It was too irregular and out of pitch to really be any kind of song. The Bean-Nighe let out one final high-pitched note—closer to a shriek—and then burst into a rapturous giggle. "Oh, that was easy! Thank you!"

Marcus frowned. "You're welcome?"

"Next!" The Bean-Nighe declared, dropping Marcus' hands abruptly.

"Wait...aren't you supposed to tell us something?" Marcus shook his head, confused.

The Bean-Nighe tutted. "Sometimes. Not all fates are the same, so not all that is supposed is the same as it is supposed to be." She grinned. "But I did almost forget that I was meant to give you something."

Her long pale hands cupped his face and brought it close to hers.

"Marcus," Zara hissed.

The Bean-Nighe placed a tender kiss upon his forehead.

Smoothly, she released him, his body sagging away dreamily. She took a deep breath, and the candles flickered once more. "Next!" she declared again.

"Dmitri said you were supposed to tell us if we were in danger. If we could go back to our normal lives," Zara said sharply.

The Bean-Nighe's expression turned sour. "The girl is last. She asks the same questions over and over. It bores." She sighed heavily. "Very well. This one's fate is his fate; it chose him before he ever came here. His path will be easier for this meeting, but he will live the same."

"And...my end?" Marcus ventured with a gulp.

The Bean-Nighe's mouth flickered a dangerous smile. "Not telling. Too much fun. Shouldn't spoil it." She winked teasingly.

Marcus let out a strangled gasp, and his lip wobbled as he moved back to stand beside Zara.

"Next!" the Bean-Nighe repeated, impatience heavy in her voice now. She pointed at Oscar emphatically. Swallowing, Oscar stepped forward more boldly than he felt, and raised his hands obligingly.

The Bean-Nighe shook her head. "Not you, not for you. You're too tricky. I noticed when I let you in. I need to use a different door for your secrets, gentle Cricket." She hummed, fumbling at her waist. With a flourish, she produced a knife, its long silvery blade only as thick as a thumb that came to a wicked point.

Zara gasped but held her tongue.

The Bean-Nighe leaned forward, and with a pale finger and thumb, deftly lifted a lock of coarse hair away from his forehead. With terrifying speed and accuracy, the blade flashed, and she held a chestnut tuft in her fingers.

She began to hum again, leaning over the stone table to hold the hair above the flame of the nearest candle. The fire caught it, and the hair sparked and singed in her fingertips, letting out an acrid smell. Oscar wrinkled his nose, but the Bean-Nighe leaned forward and breathed deeply, tipping her head back. She held the breath for what seemed like an age, until Oscar wondered if she would keel over blue. Finally, those eerie orbs turned back on Oscar, mouth a straight line.

"Inconclusive," she said flatly.

Oscar frowned, confused. "What?"

"Tell friend Dmitri that you are a funny bunch he chose to send. One with a fate clearer than stars, another whose path breaks more times than it folds. Your path, Cricket, is shattered. Scattered, like lost pebbles amongst the endless woods." She used the wicked knife to scratch her head thoughtfully. "Only time will tell. But I have something that won't help."

"Won't help?" Oscar asked, confused.

"Oh, not at all. Unless you can make it. Keep it close just in case it doesn't make things worse, though," the Bean-Nighe whispered secretively, before skipping away to rummage in a pile of things in a battered old suitcase by the wall.

Oscar looked over at his friends.

"What's that?" Marcus asked, gesturing to a bone propped against the wall beside him. It looked like a femur but almost as tall as he was and as thick as his neck. Part of it was shaved away like it was being whittled.

"You'll see." The Bean-Nighe waved a distracted hand as she continued to rummage.

"We need to get out of here," Zara mouthed.

When Oscar looked back, he startled. The Bean-Nighe was standing inches away from him, though he hadn't seen her move, and was holding something. A rusty hunk of metal shaped like a 'T' with a nobbled ball on each end. She thrust it out at him excitedly.

"Oh," he took it in both hands, "thank you?"

"The blade is missing and cannot be reforged," she said merrily. "But that doesn't mean you can't stab people with it. You just need to *really* want to do it." She coiled a lock of hair thoughtfully around one bony finger. "You're not much the type for that, though, are you, Cricket?"

Oscar frowned. "Why do you keep calling me Cricket?"

The Bean-Nighe grinned. "*Chirping.*"

"What..." Oscar began.

"Next!" the Bean-Nighe proclaimed, waving her hand at Zara.

"I—"

"NEXT."

Oscar bit his lip and stepped back, gripping the rusted hilt in both hands. He stood beside Marcus, who rubbed his forehead where the Bean-Nighe had kissed pensively.

Zara strode forward, shoulders stiff and face serious.

"The damsel in distress," the Bean-Nighe sang.

"I don't know about that," Zara replied grumpily.

The Bean-Nighe tilted her head. "Let's see..."

A pale hand flicked forward and touched Zara's. The finger-tips had barely made contact when something like pain flickered across the Bean-Nighe's face, and she let out a low hiss, yanking her hand away as though scalded.

"What?" Zara asked, face aghast.

"Ohhhhhhh." The Bean-Nighe's voice was low and distant as she stared into space. She made a clucking with her tongue. Abruptly, she stalked across the room and snatched an old bottle filled with a cloudy looking liquid from one of the shelves. She swayed across the room toward Oscar and Marcus, past Zara who was still standing waiting.

"What did you see?" Zara asked.

The Bean-Nighe shrugged, popping the cork free of the bottle. "Nothing."

Abruptly, she tipped the contents of the bottle onto Oscar. He tried to jump back, but one of her pale hands shot out to his shoulder and held him firm. The cloudy liquid glugged out of the bottle and onto his leg, where it fizzed strangely against his skin. *The spot where the Gwyllgi's saliva landed.*

"Just a bit of this so that you don't die before anything interesting happens." The Bean-Nighe offered a haunting smile.

"W...what?" Oscar stuttered as she popped the cork back in the empty bottle.

"Poisonous saliva," she cooed. "Most people it would have killed already, but for you, it might have taken a little longer. You would still have been dead dead dead as a dead thing, though. A shame, too. Normally such a nice fellow, the Gatekeeper. Something must have driven him wild tonight. Perhaps he doesn't like Crickets."

Oscar watched her numbly as she swayed back and set the bottle back down on the shelf. *A nice fellow?* Was she really talking about the creature that had chased them?

"Nothing?" Zara repeated icily from the centre of the room.

"Nothing I wish to share. Except this." The Bean-Nighe smiled wistfully. She began humming quietly and began to sway on the spot, staring into nothingness. After a moment, she jumped a little, realising they were all still there. "Ah, yes." She moved back to the shelves, rifling through an old crate.

"Why do you have all these things?" Marcus asked, eyeing the junk lined up on the shelves.

"Fates," the Bean-Nighe replied tiredly.

"Fates?" Marcus echoed.

"Of course, you ask, my sweet one." She looked up from her task for just a moment. "Yes, items instrumental for the fates of others. A ball of a child who would have cured deadly diseases rolled into the road for them to be struck by a car before it might happen. A phial of blood that carries a plague that would end humanity. A box tripped over to fall down a stair and break thy neck. Treasures. Treasures that are the gilded key to someone's making. Or unmaking."

"Doesn't everything play a part in that?" Zara asked.

The Bean-Nighe grew still for a moment. "Perhaps I misjudged you," she said slowly. "Aha!" she cried triumphantly, holding something up.

The paper was creased and grubby. Oscar had to step forward to see it. Drawn roughly in what looked like a child's crayon, was... "A duck?"

"A duck...with three feet?" Zara added.

"No! Completely wrong!" The Bean-Nighe grinned. "A three-footed duck."

"Of course," Zara replied drily. "And what should we do with this?"

The Bean-Nighe swayed across to the stone table and blew out the closest candle. "You might find it. Or it might find you. Or someone that found it might find you before you can find them." She sighed. "So many questions. I grow weary." She blew out another candle, and the room dropped deeper into shadow.

"You must have seen something about my fate." Zara sounded torn as if she didn't want to ask the question at all but couldn't help herself.

"Nothing is a must. Only maybe." The Bean-Nighe smiled sadly. She leaned heavily on the stone beside her, her pale orbs taking them all in again one by one. "Your fates are...exhausting."

"Could you just—" Zara began, but the Bean-Nighe blew again, on no particular candle, but Oscar felt the whisper of breath all around him. Every candle in the room flickered and died, snuffed out at once.

He cried out in surprise but could not hear himself as the void swallowed him. His hands reached out only to find he no longer had hands in that moment at all, and then when he did, they found only stone.

23

THE SHADOWS OF DOUBT

The crowded darkness forced Oscar's breath to come in short, panicked gasps. His fingertips traced coarse stone, dry wood, damp moss...until they found a narrow gap. Pressing his face against it, he found the sky. Less than a sliver of moonlight and a wisp of clean air, but it was there. A door.

Tucking the rusty, bladeless hilt under one arm, he pushed against the door. Hard. It finally gave way, splintering open with the crunch of wet rot, though not by much. Just enough for him to squeeze through, the rough edge scraping his chest uncomfortably. Oscar gulped the fresh night air, drinking it in gratefully.

Marcus was sitting on the ground outside, his head in his hands. As Oscar panted, his friend looked at him dazed. "Were you stuck in a crypt?" he asked.

Oscar nodded numbly.

Marcus pointed, and Oscar saw one of the other nearby tomb's doors had been pushed ajar.

"Are you alright?" Oscar managed, offering a hand to help him up.

"I'm...okay," Marcus replied tiredly. "Getting a headache.

Tired. Weirded out. But I'm okay." He took Oscar's hand and let him pull him up. "Any sign of Zara?"

Oscar shook his head.

As though summoned by her name, a voice rang out angrily in the night. "You nobheads better get over here, or I'm leaving right now."

Marcus grinned.

Together they rushed toward her voice, following the curved sloping path until they found her, looking tired and bedraggled.

Oscar grabbed her in a fierce hug.

"Where were you, bitches?" she grumbled.

"In crypts, up there." Marcus wrapped his long arms around them both.

"Lucky," Zara mumbled. "I thought I wasn't going to be able to get out where that weird pasty bitch stuck me." Oscar spotted a heavy stone coffin close by, the worn lid half out of place. The thought made him shiver.

Marcus released his grip on them and scanned their surroundings. "Do you think that big naked bear dog thing is still here?"

"Let's not stick around to find out," Zara said.

Marcus nodded. "Agreed. I think it's this way?" He began to lead the way into the maze of headstones.

As they picked their way through the darkness, Oscar realised that Zara was watching him with concerned eyes. "Are you okay?" he asked.

Zara blinked. "I don't know. This is all...a lot. I mean, part of me is not convinced this isn't just a really fucked up dream, the rest of me is mostly terrified. What about you?"

"Dmitri...he was fighting the Gwyllgi," Oscar said softly.

Zara gave him a guarded look.

"I'm sure...well...maybe he's okay," Marcus offered over his shoulder. "If he is, he will be looking for us. The best place to meet is back at his place."

"I'm going home," Zara said flatly.

Oscar looked at her in despair.

"I'll go with you to Dmitri's," Marcus offered. "I want to make sure he's okay."

"You just want to look through Dmitri's secret things for weird clues," Zara sniped.

Marcus gave her a narrowed side-eye. "Two things can be true. Besides, we need to get out of here first. Did you see what he did with those bricks?"

"No," Oscar admitted.

"I did," Zara replied thoughtfully, "but on the other side. Even if I remember it right, the way out might be different."

"Shame there int' no one 'ere to 'elp you," Gax croaked.

Oscar startled so hard that both of his feet left the ground. Zara let out a yelp of surprise and snatched at his hand.

"Jesus, Gax!" Marcus yowled.

The squat, leafy Bugge stood not two strides away, beside the crumbled remnants of a tombstone.

"Gax," Oscar breathed, heart still hammering in his chest. "Where is Dmitri?"

Gax's face grew grave. "The Gwyllgi 'as messed things right up. I can barely feel a bloody thing at all anymore. Some kinda forbiddin'." He growled, eyes scanning the night.

"Well, we very nearly never felt a bloody thing at all ever again when you left us for it to eat," Zara grumbled.

Gax's little head tilted back, a stubborn expression appearing on his face. "I ain't a coward. Just know 'ow to pick me battles. Ain't no sense in me stickin' round when I'm no 'elp just to get gobbled up. I'm a right good size for gobblin' see." He gestured to himself with both stubby hands.

"A Goblin for gobbling." Marcus snickered.

"Exactly!" Gax agreed, looking pleased that at least someone understood. "But I'll consider it a favour owed that I left you. Bugges take that sort of thing awful serious."

"So, you don't know where Dmitri is?" Oscar moaned.

Gax looked thoughtful. "Well the Gwyllgi must've gone. I am startin' to get a feel on things again. And there's a couple o' things 'ere. One feels familiar, so that might be 'im."

"He's alive?" Oscar breathed.

"Might be. Can't tell 'ow alive or for 'ow long."

Oscar turned to Marcus and Zara. "We have to help him," he begged.

"Oscar...we need to get out of here. Get somewhere safe," Zara said stiffly. "He's not even sure if it *is* Dmitri. Gax, can you get us out of here?"

"It's him," Oscar pressed. "It must be. Gax, please."

The Bugge looked between them, black eyes glittering in the moonlight. They came to rest for a moment on the rusty hilt in Oscar's hands curiously. Finally, he gave a slight nod. "You three jus' follow the path' round there to the left. Go right at Marx an' straight on at Michael. That'll take yeh back to the wall. I'll go see what's 'appenin and meet you there."

Oscar moved to touch the little Bugge's shoulder in gratitude, and Gax jumped away. *Oh right. Bugges are highly toxic to humans.* Embarrassed, he contented himself with a nod instead. "Thank you, Gax."

"Thank me later when everythin's alright," he croaked, then looked around the darkness with narrowed eyes. "Jus' be careful. Go straight to the wall. Somethin's...not right 'ere."

Oscar was about to thank him again, but the Bugge slipped into a pile of leaves, disappearing just like before with a wet smacking noise like slapping loose flesh.

"Right," Zara said, eyes fixed on the spot where Gax disappeared, expression a mixture of disgust and amazement. "Let's get the fuck out of here then."

∼

THE CEMETERY WAS MORE CHALLENGING to navigate without their unusual guide.

Oscar was grateful when Zara's fingers linked with his again in the darkness whilst Marcus tentatively explored ahead.

"Listen, Os." Zara's voice was uncharacteristically soft. "I'm... this is all so much. None of this makes any sense. But more than anything, I'm *scared*."

Oscar looked at his friend in surprise. He didn't know if he'd ever heard her say *that* before.

Zara's eyes were shining with tears in the moonlight, tawny cheeks flushed.

"Zara..."

Zara shook her head fiercely. "Let me finish. I'm not just scared of all the shit that's been happening. I'm scared for *you*."

Oscar's eyes widened, and he opened his mouth to speak, but she kept going.

"I feel terrible. I should never have made you go and sit with Nina, I just thought...with her parents not being around, you would know what to say. I know that was wrong. That wasn't okay to put you in that situation without talking about it first. I'm scared that I made you vulnerable and then..."

She trailed off, searching for the right words. "I've been acting like a bitch, but it's because I don't want to see you get hurt. After the problems coming out to my family caused...you were always there. I know Marcus feels the same. Any time I've needed you, you've been there. Even when I didn't know I needed you. *You* are my family, Oscar. And I had to watch when you got fucked around by Rami and all the other guys...but Dmitri? It could be so much worse if..." She trailed off, looking hopeless.

"Zara," Oscar said. "It's okay..."

"I saw him, Oscar. What he *really* is."

Oscar froze, his jaw clenched.

"I know you trust him, but I don't."

Oscar searched for a reply. Images of Dmitri, earnest and

tender, blurred with what he had seen Dmitri become, branded into his memory.

I stayed away to keep you safe.

Safe from whatever was hunting you. But also, this.

Safe from me.

"I...think he's good, Zara." Oscar swallowed. "Everything he's done seems to be to protect me. I don't think...I don't think anyone has ever looked at me like he does before." Oscar pictured those shifting grey eyes, intent and penetrating. Like they were seeking to unravel every secret Oscar held just so he could know. Just so he could see. "I feel like...like he sees something in me that no one else has. I don't know what's going to happen. If he's alive, and he can...go back to how he was before, then I guess I need to talk to him. But I don't think I want him to go away, Zara. I...I like him."

Zara smiled sadly and yanked him into her arms, squeezing the air out of him.

"I'm sorry, Oscar." She sniffed against his shoulder. "I can't stand the thought of losing you, but that doesn't mean I should push you away. I love you, Booboo."

Oscar smiled into her hair, his heart squeezed by her words as tightly as his body by her grip. "I love you too, Zara."

As quickly as she took him in her arms, she pushed him away, eying him fiercely, tears still shining in the moonlight. "But I still don't trust Dmitri. If you do, that's fine." She rubbed her tears away. "But I'll be here watching to make sure nothing bad happens. Those perfect cheekbones will not save him from my fury."

Oscar smiled. "Deal. I mean, if he's not..."

Zara winced. "Giant Hellhound chow?"

"Right at Marx, straight on at Michael!" Marcus exclaimed ahead, pointing excitedly.

He was right. Oscar saw it. The wall. It was difficult to tell from any other segment of wall in the cemetery in the darkness, but it did have a strange familiarity.

Marcus was already there, making a show of pretending to kiss the bricks.

"Careful, you'll get cemetery in your mouth," Zara warned.

"Bitch, my body is more cemetery than water right now, and there's nothing your science can do to fix it." Marcus laughed.

"Soap is science," Zara countered.

"Alas. I have been defeated," Marcus conceded with a bow.

Despite himself, Oscar felt a grin find its way onto his face. Now all they needed to do was wait for the Bugge to get back with Dmitri, and they could leave.

Marcus' face grew serious, and he stiffened. "Did you hear that?"

Oscar and Zara exchanged nonplussed glances. "What?" Zara asked.

"Shh, listen," Marcus urged.

Oscar listened, straining to hear more than the sound of the breeze in the branches above.

Then he heard it.

Small, faint, and weak, but definitely there.

A mewling cry, like a kitten? Or perhaps...

"Help," the tiny voice begged.

Zara's eyes widened.

"Where's it coming from?" Oscar asked, voice strangled as he searched the darkness.

"Please. Help," the voice begged, slightly louder this time,

"It sounds like a child," Zara gasped.

Marcus shook his head rapidly. "Gax said—"

"It's a child!" Zara repeated, shooting Marcus a horrified look.

"Maybe we should just take a quick look?" Oscar chewed his bottom lip.

"Of course we should!" Zara said, eyes wide.

"Please help," the voice sobbed again.

"Marcus...you stay by the wall for Gax. Oscar, let's go." Zara squared her shoulders and strode forward through the overgrown grass with Oscar close behind. They had to take a couple of turns and clamber through some spiky bushes with gnarled brittle branches that snagged at Oscar's clothes, but soon the crying got louder.

Zara reached over and gripped his wrist painfully, giving him an urgent look. Oscar clutched the cold metal hilt tightly in both hands. Hopefully, it was at least heavy enough to hurt something if he threw it hard.

As they parted through the narrow trees, they saw her.

Oscar didn't recognise her at first. Not until Zara said her name. "Nina?"

She was right. That thick dark hair and those anguished eyes. She still wore her hospital gown, though now it was splashed with mud and torn. Nina sat shivering on the ground, arms wrapped around her knees, sniffling. "Please...help," she whimpered miserably.

"Nina!" Zara cried, and the little girl looked up.

Her dark eyes were red-ringed and face tear-streaked. "Zara?" she mewled.

Zara let go of Oscar's wrist and rushed over to her as quickly as she could.

"Zara, Dmitri said..." Oscar was torn. This felt so *wrong*.

He watched as Zara gathered the small shivering girl into her arms. "Are you okay? What happened? Oh, Nina, you're freezing!" Zara was already taking off her coat and wrapping it around the girl.

"I don't know." Nina sniffled. "It was the bad man. He's trying to trick you; you have to believe me." She shivered.

Zara looked at Oscar, her mouth agape with horror.

"Oscar!" Nina whined, reaching out weakly toward him. Oscar froze in place, his feet rooted to the ground. Her dark eyes shone with misery, and her bottom lip quivered. Dmitri had said she wasn't human. Said that she was something more, something terrible. But the way she huddled in Zara's arms. The fear in her eyes. The hopelessness and need for somebody, anybody to be there. To protect her. Tell her everything was going to be okay. She was all alone. Just like Oscar had been.

He took a slow step forward.

Had it all been a lie?

"Oscar, stay back!" a voice roared from behind him. Oscar twisted to find the source, and a tall, dark shadow moved amongst the trees.

Closer, Gax waddled forward quickly, black eyes wide, mouth open showing his square yellow teeth. "'ere! Look out! That 'int a little girl!" he shrieked.

Oscar spun back, his mouth opening to shout out, but his words turned to ash in his mouth.

The girl in Zara's arms looked up at him, her face split in a broad smile.

Zara stared at Oscar, her golden-brown eyes wide and mouth half-open in surprise. The little girl's arm was buried in Zara's chest up to the elbow, except it was no longer an arm, but an oily slick of darkness.

The girl pulled the writhing tentacle of shadows loose, and Zara twitched and fell lifeless to the earth with a heavy thud. Not a drop of blood, and no visible wound, but Oscar knew with terrible certainty that something awful had just happened.

"Zara!" The cry finally left his mouth, strangled and harsh.

Nina, or whatever Nina was, twitched jerkily. Her skin took a dank greyish tinge, and she started to darken, deeper and deeper into a coiling mass of faceless shadow.

"Get back, boy!" Gax cried.

The tumbling mass of inky dark hissed at Oscar. It moved in a flicker, disappearing and reappearing at once much closer than it had been less than a moment ago. It was close, so close Oscar could feel the sapping cold emanating from it. Leeching at his warmth. The monster's shadowy tendrils reached toward him, then a flash of bright light split the night.

Billowing flames lit up the night, and the shadows that had been inside the little girl let out a shriek, flickering away into the darkness.

Oscar looked beside him for the source of the fire. The sight was like icy blades in his guts.

Dmitri.

His body was twisted. Inhuman, towering close to a foot taller than before, his flesh pale with a ruddy tinge, hair loose and wild. His nose was flat, face stretched at the jaw, muzzle like. He was barely recognisable.

Eyes like lanterns fixed on Oscar, burning into his soul. Dmitri opened his mouth, showing a mouth full of pointed teeth, flames still licking his lips.

"I told you to run."

TAXONOMY OF MONSTERS: THE JOROGUMO
(MULIER ARANEA)

More secrets than eyes.
A fine web her beauty weaves.
Shun her final kiss.

— THE TRAVELS OF KOHARU

❧ 24 ❧

THE BROKEN THREAD

It was a little after midnight when they arrived at the hospital. The blinding flashing of the blue lights piercing the dark was still all Oscar could see when he closed his eyes.

He remembered how she looked. Skin ashen, face slack. Almost like the fetch. But this wasn't some twisted version of Zara. This was her. His friend. His best friend. His family.

He had watched them put the tube in her mouth. He wished he hadn't. Maybe then he could still picture her how she usually was. Bright, bold, warm, and spiky.

The coiling mass of darkness that they had called Nina had fled when Dmitri appeared. Flickering away with a hiss into the darkness. Dmitri chased her. *Chased it*.

Oscar called the ambulance on his mobile. He didn't know what else to do.

The police had come too, of course. He should have guessed by the way the call operators made him repeat his location three times. Thankfully, the officers had been kind whilst the paramedics swarmed around Zara. The police said that prosecution for trespassing would be up to the cemetery. From the distracted way the officers watched the paramedics work on Zara, Oscar guessed they only expected to come here for loiterers or vandals. He took the opportunity to tuck the rusty hilt into the waistband of his jeans under his T-shirt.

Oscar didn't care about what trouble they got into. He just watched them squeeze the bag to make Zara breathe. He didn't care what happened to him as they hoisted the gurney and loaded her into the back of the ambulance.

When the officers led them out of the cemetery, Oscar looked back into the dark. He thought for a moment that he might have seen something. Seen *him*, a twisted figure with long arms and broad hunched shoulders—taller than any man should be—watching from the darkness.

If you get other people involved, I may not be able to protect you.

Well, Oscar hadn't told anyone anything, and Dmitri hadn't protected Zara.

Now he needed to do everything he could to help her.

An older police officer, a woman with short greying hair and flinty eyes, drove them to the hospital. Oscar thought she was probably a woman many people feared. Still, he could feel nothing but gratitude as he and Marcus sat in the back of the warm police car to the hospital. *Their hospital.*

When they got there, everything felt wrong. Like a horrible nightmare he had woken up from but then slipped straight back into the second he closed his eyes again. Oscar always avoided the emergency room whenever he could. It felt different there. Ragged. Too many people danced on the edge of life and death. The worst day of everyone's life come to be. *And now it's our turn.*

A weary-eyed middle-aged woman in a dark blue nurse's uniform greeted them in reception. She fussed with her untidy auburn hair whilst she spoke with the officers.

"Seems like you three were up to no good," she said baldly when the officers left, casting keen eyes between Marcus and Oscar. "My name is Mandy. We'll make sure your friend is looked after; they're in resus with her now. Her family is on their way."

Oscar felt the urge to crumple in on himself, imagining Zara's family rushing around their house, pulling on warm clothes to come to the hospital.

To come to the hospital because Zara was...

What would he say to them? What *could* he say?

"You need to tell me what you were taking," the nurse, Mandy, eyed him sternly. "That gives us the best chance of helping your friend."

"What?" Oscar shook his head, confused. *Oh. Drugs?* "N...nothing. We weren't doing anything like that."

Mandy regarded him doubtfully, tucking in her chin. "You need to be honest. It could save your friend's life."

"No!" Oscar snapped. "Nothing. We don't do that, it just...happened."

The nurse's pale blue eyes fixed on his. "Does your friend have any heart conditions? Epilepsy? Any allergies you know about?"

Oscar shook his head, blinking. "No...I don't think so."

"Usually these collapses are to do with drugs. It could be her heart, if not that. Might be something no one ever knew she had until the right trigger." Mandy's expression seemed slightly more sympathetic now. Softer.

"Okay," Oscar said numbly, remembering the dark coil driving deep into Zara's chest.

He felt the urge to tell the nurse. Maybe he should give every bit of information in case it helped.

That won't help. Nothing will help. His thoughts were as cold and solid as concrete.

"Are you okay?" Mandy asked, tucking her pen into her breast pocket.

Oscar looked up and saw that she wasn't looking at him, but Marcus. He was huddled in a chair, knees tucked to his chest, eyes scrunched closed, fingers rubbing his temples.

"Oh...he's got a headache, I think," Oscar answered.

"Did he get hurt? Bang his head?" The nurse's voice was concerned as she pulled out a pen torch.

"I'm fine. I...lost my glasses. It's probably that. My head just hurts so bad..." Marcus spoke stiffly through clenched teeth.

"You'd better let us have a look at you. Are you sure you weren't taking anything?"

"*Oscar!*" a familiar voice cut through the room, lancing straight into his heart.

Oscar turned. Walking in the entrance was Zara's family.

Zara's mother rushed forward. He realised for the first time that she was the very image of Zara's future. A warm round face, sparkling hazel eyes, full of emotion and determination. *Full of love*. Time had given her fine lines in the corners of her eyes and mouth, her hair a practical dark bob.

"I'm sorry, I..." Oscar started, and then her arms were wrapping around him. She squeezed him tight, and in that moment, he was sure that they were the only thing holding him together.

Over Aanya Chatterji's shoulder, Oscar's eyes met with Zara's father's. Rohit was a sober faced man, whose severity was deepened by his grey streaked, side-parted hair and well-groomed moustache. Right now, he looked lost. Like he wasn't sure what emotion he should show. What he could let out.

Zara's little brother Hashim was huddled underneath one of his father's arms. Oscar wasn't sure that his heart could grow any more swollen, and then, standing a little distance behind them, he saw her grandmother.

Nani Anjali should have looked frail. Her thick hair was a steely grey, bound at the nape of her neck. Her face was a map of deep wrinkles, charting the long journey of her life, punctuated with eyes so dark brown they were almost black. Her back was straight, chin proud, and her posture steady, barely leaning on the stout cane she held. Her dark eyes fixed on his, sharp and wise.

"I'm sorry," Oscar breathed into Zara's mother's hair.

She took his shoulders and gently held him out in front of her, inspecting him with eyes brimming with tears, searching his face for answers. "What happened?"

Oscar struggled for words. Lying felt wrong, but he found his mouth regurgitating the words the nurse had given him. "They think it might be her heart. That it made her collapse..."

"Zara has a strong heart," Nani Anjali said sharply from where she stood, her voice reedy but firm.

Oscar was trying to find words to give back when a voice cut in.

"Mr. and Mrs. Chatterji?" It was the nurse again, Mandy. "Can you come through to the resus room, please?" Her eyes travelled across all of them, lingering on Nani Anjali and little Hashim. "It might be best if all of you come."

Zara's mother let out a sob, releasing Oscar abruptly. She bustled to Mandy, and the rest of the family followed, the sound of Grandma Anjali's cane steady and rhythmic. Her small dark eyes lingered on Oscar's, and he felt like she could see his shame. *His lies*. When he looked back up, she was disappearing out of sight down the corridor.

Oscar dropped down in the seat next to Marcus. "Are you okay?" he asked weakly. The rusty hilt of the sword dug into the bare skin of his hip. He adjusted slightly but did not move it. Part of him was grateful for the distraction of the discomfort.

Marcus grunted miserably.

"Zara. They asked them to all go through. I...I don't think it's good." Oscar's voice cracked.

Marcus grunted again, lower in what sounded like agreement.

There was a click-clacking noise, and for a second, Oscar thought that Nani Anjali was coming back, then realised she would need to use two canes for it to make that sound. Either that or...

Oscar looked up and saw Doctor Ocampo approaching, her angular face even more severe than usual. The black dress she wore looked more suited to a cocktail party than an emergency room. It cut off at her knee, elongating her graceful form down to her ruby pumps.

She pulled to a stop by Oscar and Marcus, folding her arms tightly, dark eyes fixed on his.

"Doctor Ocampo." Oscar sounded as fragile as he felt.

"I am sorry." The clipped words sounded odd from her. An apology with a fist.

Oscar shook his head, confused.

"Your friend. Zara. She..." Doctor Ocampo shifted on her feet, heels clicking gently. "I was here assessing an admission. I heard her name get called in by the ambulance crew, so I checked in. She's...it's not good." One of Ocampo's thin eyebrows twitched with the apparent effort of sustained kindness.

Oscar stared at her numbly. No words would come.

"I thought it best I tell you since we are...familiar." She cleared her throat. "They have done everything that they can. Zara...will not survive."

The words were like a solid kick to the chest, though he had surely been expecting them.

"Her heart is not able to keep beating alone much longer. It seems that all of her organs have gone into failure. There is nothing they can do. So, they are withdrawing care."

The pressure on Oscar's chest increased like a tightening vice. He leaned forward, forcing himself to keep breathing.

"I understand that this is...difficult," Doctor Ocampo was saying, her voice sounded tinny in his roaring ears.

Oscar struggled to his feet, and the room spun around him. His breath came in short, shallow bursts. *I need to get away from here. From this. I need to get outside.*

"I think it's best if you sit down." Ocampo's hand was on his shoulder. "Perhaps if you come with me to my office. We can get you a drink of tea, and have a quiet talk, call someone to collect you."

Oscar wrenched free of her grip. "I need air." He forced the words from his mouth, looking up to meet Ocampo's eyes, which regarded him with guarded disdain.

A handsome young man in scrubs, with short hair and a scruffy dark beard, approached Doctor Ocampo, giving Oscar a curious look. "Are you the one with the headache?" Oscar pointed weakly at Marcus and moved as quickly as he could to the closest door, staggering out of the painful lights bearing down on him.

He heard Ocampo's heels moving to follow him as he staggered away. He then saw Rami, Zara's cousin, come through the doors. He looked handsome in his uniform. His face was a mask of worry as he rushed past Oscar, intercepting Doctor Ocampo, questions spilling out of him. He didn't even notice Oscar slipping by.

The night air gripped Oscar like an icy fist. He got as far as he could before he fell to his knees on the concrete, head spinning. He took a gasping breath, squeezing his eyes closed tight. *This can't be real. This can't be real.*

He slumped against a stone column, head still spinning. Blinking, he realised that the door had not been the front door to the street, but the exit to the darkened ambulance bay. Two paramedics were looking at him. One looked like she might approach until her colleague touched her shoulder and shook his head, and both retreated into the hospital. *Are those the paramedics that had worked on Zara?* For some reason, he couldn't remember their faces. All he could remember was Zara, her eyes closed and face slack. The tape covering her lips and cheeks to hold the tube in place.

Oscar's breath writhed in his chest like it couldn't decide if it wanted to get in or out.

Tipping his head back, he closed his eyes.

A few moments passed before he felt a hand gently touch his shoulder. He opened his eyes, expecting to see Marcus, or perhaps Doctor Ocampo. Instead, he saw eyes brimming with concern.

"Oscar," Dmitri whispered sadly.

He was himself again. Or the self that Oscar was used to, at least. Relief prickled over Oscar, barely penetrating the thick shell of misery around him, but there all the same. Tears started to leak from his eyes, and he scrubbed them away with dirty palms.

Dmitri dropped to his knees beside him, reaching out with bloodied hands. Oscar put a hand on Dmitri's chest, keeping him at bay. No. If Dmitri held him now, he might lose himself.

As long as he didn't cry now, he might never have to shed these tears.

Maybe somehow that might make this all less real.

When their parents didn't come back, he had cried for days, and it didn't do any good. "Crying won't change anything," Paige told him, over and over. *She was right.*

Denying the tears now felt good. Like he had one choice at least.

"Are you okay?" Dmitri asked softly.

Oscar shook his head slowly. "I'm fine." His voice was hollow. "I have to be. Zara's family…"

Blinking, Oscar realised that beneath Dmitri's coat, his clothes were stiff with blood on one side, and his arm hung limp. The sharp metallic smell of blood mixed with that heavy charred scent and something deeper. An almost feral musk that was not wholly unpleasant. How was Dmitri even walking with the injuries Oscar watched him get? He had said that he healed fast, but *this* seemed impossible. His face was as it had been before again, painfully handsome and sculpted, his eyes filled with sympathy.

"I'm sorry," Dmitri whispered.

"You…know?" Oscar sniffled.

Dmitri nodded, his eyes searching Oscar's. "What did the Bean-Nighe say to you?"

"What? It…doesn't matter." Oscar sniffed. "She said she saw nothing for Zara. Is this…is this why? Is the Bean-Nighe…evil?"

"The Bean-Nighe is not evil. She just...*is*. She cannot see beyond death."

"She could have warned us," Oscar snarled, rubbing his nose with the back of his hand. "We could have stopped it."

"Some things are set, Oscar. Like a domino that will always fall, whether it happens at the start of the sequence or the end." Dmitri spoke with infuriating calm. "But please, what did the Bean-Nighe say about you?"

"Why?" Oscar demanded, pushing Dmitri away. "Why does that matter?"

"It matters," Dmitri insisted firmly. "I have suspected for a long time that there is something at that cemetery. Something that could be very dangerous."

"Because that's not set? Because you'll try harder to save me than you did my best friend?"

Dmitri flinched like Oscar's words were fists "Oscar, I—"

"I could have stopped her," Oscar spat. "I could have saved Zara...but I didn't know what to do. I couldn't decide. So, was it the monster who set those dominos falling, or was it me?"

Dmitri shook his head sadly. "It is not your fault, Oscar. You should not have to decide."

"I can't do anything right. I can't even *decide* to help," Oscar said numbly.

"You decided to come to my house. You decided to stay with me..." Dmitri reached out with a hand caked in blood and dirt.

"And who says that was the right decision? I wish none of this had ever happened. I just...I just want Zara here." Oscar's voice was empty.

Dmitri froze, drawing his hand back in and resting it on his knee. "It was...my failure, Oscar. Not yours. When the Gwyllgi attacked, I could have done more. Should have done more. But I was afraid."

"Afraid of the big dog?" Oscar's anger bubbled inside him. It felt unfamiliar and good. It felt good to feel anything other than *this.* "Like you don't have one of your own at home? Like you aren't..." Oscar shook his head angrily, swallowing. "I saw you. I saw what you turned into. Why would you be scared of *that thing*!?"

Dmitri's face stiffened. His voice was low and wounded when he replied. "I was scared, Oscar, of you seeing me as what I am. That you would see me as a monster. I was scared because of *this.* That you would see me only as the thing I have spent so long trying to distance myself from. I am trying to be more. Be better. If you only think of me as that..." Dmitri trailed off, closing his eyes. "Because of that...I failed. And I nearly lost you."

"What are you saying?" Oscar said flatly.

"I...think I have to choose."

"Between?"

"Between protecting you and...having you."

"And I get no choice?" Oscar's brittle laugh sounded cruel even to his own ears.

"Oscar, we cannot be together if you are not safe," Dmitri replied softly.

"I just...I can't take this. I can't take any of this. I'm not strong like Zara or smart like Marcus. I can't..."

Dmitri sank back, cursing softly. "I should have told you when we saw the fetch. I should have done things differently."

The fetch? That...doppelgänger?

"What?"

Dmitri swallowed visibly. "The fetch. They appear in the form of those marked for certain death. They only manifest in the appearance of those whose time is close. They usually lash out at those close to the person, but not normally so physically, so it was unusual."

"What?" Oscar repeated, little more than a rasp.

Dmitri's pale eyes met his, filled with sadness.

"You knew?" Oscar snarled.

Dmitri looked away.

"You knew and didn't tell me? You knew my best friend was going to die, and you did nothing? You lead us *into* danger?" Oscar spat.

"Oscar, even if we hadn't been there, Zara's fate was set. There was nothing I could have done."

"Go," Oscar demanded, using the word like a blade to sever them apart.

"Oscar, I have to—"

"GO!" Oscar screamed, his voice cracking.

Dmitri looked at him in surprise, standing and stepping back.

"GET AWAY FROM ME!" Oscar shouted.

One of the paramedics that had been outside before re-emerged at the entranceway. "Is everything alright?"

"Oscar, please," Dmitri begged.

Oscar felt tears threatening to escape his eyes again, tears of impotent rage and bottomless misery. He blinked them away angrily. "I wish I'd never met you." The words came out as little more than a sob.

Dmitri's face sagged, and he stepped back.

With one last look, he turned and disappeared into the night.

25

THE WRONG CHOICE

Walking into the apartment felt surreal.

It was like he hadn't been home in weeks. *Longer*. But it hadn't even been a day since he last woke up here.

The curtains were still open, and the moonlight cast a dull glow through the windows. Oscar flipped the switch, and there was a flash as the bulb sparked and failed, leaving him in darkness. He didn't even sigh as he closed the door, letting the latch click shut.

His phone buzzed in his pocket. It wasn't the first time tonight, but it was the first time he had the heart to look at it.

When he got back into the hospital, Marcus had been taken to the assessment unit. Nurse Mandy said he'd been admitted for investigations. Oscar didn't know what to do. He felt so alone, and that was a darkness all too familiar. Leaving the hospital had felt wrong, but he couldn't face seeing Zara's family again.

His phone screen lit up, telling him he had a voicemail. No surprise, given the seventeen missed calls. *All from Paige*.

Oscar moved to the large, comfortable chair by the window and slumped into it. He didn't bother to take off his jacket before he closed his eyes and put the phone to his ear.

"Jesus, Oscar. Please call me and let me know everything is okay. I'm sorry about the flat. I've spoken with a friend; they're going to come and take some pictures next week, so if you could make sure it's cleaned up, that would be..." She trailed off and sighed. "Listen, Oscar. I know this is rough. Things aren't going as well as they could be here, and I really need the cash. I know you have great friends. Maybe you could move in with Zara for a while? She always seemed to get you. But...take your time, yeah?" There was a moment of total silence; he thought she had hung up. "I love you, little bro."

The line disconnected, and Oscar's arm slumped into his lap like a dead weight.

His heart ached impossibly. The freshly healed wound from his disagreement with Zara had been torn open into an eviscerating endless pain. He knew the tears wouldn't come now. It was too late for that.

This is all too much.

He just felt numb. Beyond exhaustion, and...

Empty.

When Oscar opened his eyes, *she* was standing there.

Long black hair hanging down to her knees, dark eyes watching him calmly.

Oscar jumped, clumsily staggering up from the chair and grabbing for the rusted hilt at his hip. He snatched it out, the coarse metal grazing his flesh, and clutched it in both hands before him.

The girl's eyes regarded it with something between interest and pity, head tilted. "Come with me. If you do, you can make sure your other friends don't end up like her." The cruel words sounded beyond strange in her soft voice.

Oscar's teeth clenched, and he squeezed the rusted hilt until it dug into his palms painfully. "You lied. Everything about you is a lie, and you...you..." He couldn't finish.

The awful little girl blinked at him.

"How many people have you hurt?" Oscar swallowed; his

hands were shaking uncontrollably. Anger and fear battled in his chest. "How many people have you killed by pretending to be...*this*? By pretending to be hurt and alone? I...cared about you. I thought you were alone like me, but instead...you just make other people alone. Zara just wanted to help you, and you took her away. Why should I believe anything you say?"

"You can protect them all." Nina looked up at him, smiling sweetly. "If you don't come...well, more people will die. Just like her."

The words echoed in Oscar's mind, and then, his breath left him all at once; whatever spark of a fight he had left in him snuffed out. *I can't take any more.* Closing his eyes, he lowered the rusty handle and waited.

This is it then...the end.

He expected to feel an icy tendril of darkness spear into his chest.

But...

Nothing.

When he opened his eyes, the thing in the shape of a little girl was still watching him placidly.

"You promise nobody else will be hurt?" Oscar asked, voice shaking.

Nina nodded, smiling broadly.

"Okay." Oscar swallowed, forcing the useless hilt back under his belt. "What do I need to do?"

Nina lifted up her small hand and opened her fingers. Inside was a perfect replica, carved from wood.

A duck with three feet?

No.

A three-footed duck.

❦ IV ❧

DEATH, AND OTHER
BEGINNINGS

❧ 26 ❧

THE PLIGHT OF THE
LIVING DEAD

Oscar Tundale was dead.

He wasn't sure how he had died or why he was able to wonder about it at all. But he knew with profound certainty that it had happened.

He had felt it. Every part of his being split apart. Separated like he was some dusty stain on the earth's fabric that had been beaten loose, cast into fragile motes that hung in the air before dispersing.

Now darkness engulfed whatever remained of him, and he drowned in it like an ocean.

All he had done was touch the three-footed duck.

Oscar gasped a ragged breath.

His heart hammered in his chest like it needed to escape. *That* didn't seem right. Would that happen if he was dead? He moved jerkily, his fist catching on something cold and rough. His knuckles scraped against it, and sweet pain blossomed there. *Pain?*

He wasn't dead!

Dead people didn't need to breathe. Dead people didn't feel pain!

Probably.

He made a mental note to ask Dmitri if zombies were something he should be concerned about, but thoughts of Dmitri were quickly chased off with stabbing memories of his anguished face the last Oscar had seen him.

I wish I'd never met you.

Regret. Sadness. Confusion. All of it welled from the raw gash of the wound those words had left in the space that had been briefly inhabited by the warm feeling Dmitri had given him in his chest. They were quickly followed by hysteria.

Maybe I should have broken up with him after I didn't need rescuing from.. wherever I am now.

Oscar wriggled in the darkness, panic building in him at the closeness of it all. Each hurried beat of his heart hammered the realisation deeper into his core.

He was trapped, but he wasn't dead.

Not yet.

Oscar was becoming overwhelmingly conscious of the way the stone pressed in around him, cramping his limbs in a way that made him desperate to thrash out in the stale, thin and rotten air around him. He tried to force the building panic down. He wriggled his arms, managing to get his hands close to his chest, and then pushed up.

He pushed and pushed as hard as he could until a futile broken cry escaped his throat.

The stone didn't move an inch.

The panic grew stronger and began to overflow. He closed his eyes and tried to steady his ragged breathing. What should he do?

What would Zara do?

The thought was like being dipped in ice water. His body and mind grew numb. The fear that had threatened to overwhelm him succumbed to the greater beast of his exhausted misery.

Hands shaking, Oscar reached up again, this time his fingers methodically tracing their way around the stone, feeling for gaps and breaks around its edges. Before tonight, he wouldn't have had the first idea where he was, but after the events that had unfolded in the cemetery, Oscar was almost certain that he was in a tomb.

Twice in one night? Really?

His thoughts were coming more clearly now. He remembered touching the three-footed duck. He remembered that Nina—the thing they had called Nina—told him to.

To make sure nobody else got hurt.

But at what price?

He hadn't thought to ask what would happen to him; he hadn't expected the small carved duck to put him in a grave. He needed help, and there was no one left. Dmitri was gone, Marcus was in the hospital, and Zara was...

He was all alone.

Unless...

Oscar carefully shifted his weight, wriggling cold fingers into the pockets of his trousers and feeling the welcome shape of his phone. It took him a few tries to get it to the narrow gap between his face and the coarse stone above him. Eventually, he managed to grip it awkwardly and tried to thumb the screen to life. *Nothing.*

He pressed the power button. A moment later the screen awoke in blinding light, forcing him to narrow his eyes, though he dared not look away.

"Come on, come on, come on," Oscar whispered, jiggling his legs in anticipation. The battery cell was empty and flashing, and the signal bar didn't even appear on the screen, which was practically touching his nose, but he quickly thumbed through the screen until the name he was looking for appeared.

Marcus.

He desperately keyed HELP and thumbed send. He thought

about sending it to more people, maybe all of his contacts, but before the thought took purchase, the screen blinked to darkness.

Oscar let out a steady breath and pushed the dead phone back into his pocket.

Nothing else to do now, except lie here...or try to get out.

Oscar bit his lip.

He had to try.

Didn't he?

"Come on, Oscar." He breathed carefully, moving his hands back to the coarse stone above. This time he managed to raise his knees a little too, bracing them against the roof of the coffin. *My coffin.*

The rusty hilt from the Bean-Nighe dug into his hip. *Useless.*

Oscar took another deep breath and pushed as hard as he could. Harder and harder until a cry escaped him again, and his strength gave out. As he lay panting, tears began to leak from his eyes and he sniffed, refusing to let them take hold of him. After everything that had happened...

This is it.

Oscar slumped, closing his eyes and breathing in the damp stale air.

And then, something moved.

The stone above him was moving. But not up. Across.

With a deep scraping sound, moonlight streamed in as grit and fine dust rained onto his face, forcing him to raise his hands to cover his eyes. *Marcus?* It couldn't be, not that fast; he'd only just sent the message.

"Oh, Oscar, I'm so happy to see you!" Her voice was sweet as a knife dripping with honey.

He opened his mouth to speak but ended up spluttering from the mouthful of grainy mulch that showered onto his face. He rubbed his eyes, trying to catch sight of his rescuer, but her pale sinuous arm was already melting into the shadows.

"Who are you?" Oscar croaked, forcing himself up and wriggling out of the narrow gap. His voice was hoarse and thick with confusion. "What's happening?"

Her voice chuckled softly from the shadows, and flecks danced in the edges of Oscar's vision. His eyes could barely move fast enough to track them, but he blinked them away furiously. He staggered clumsily, trying to look everywhere at once. He had been right; this place was definitely familiar.

It was the cemetery.

Oscar heard a strangely familiar clicking on the cobblestones and spun toward it.

"Imagine finding you here," Doctor Ocampo said, the cold moonlight dancing across her angular features as she stepped from the darkness. "We have a lot of work to do."

27

THE OTHER SIDE OF THE COIN

D r. Lyn Ocampo looked different in the moonlight.
Different from how Oscar had ever seen her before.

It wasn't that she wore different clothes or had a different face. She was still the same beautiful ice sculpture of a woman. Same sharp features and black silken locks. What was unusual, Oscar realised, was her smile.

He had never seen her smile before, and now he knew why. For most people, a smile lit up their faces. Offered a glimpse of their inner self. The best smile was kind, guileless, and bright, with no care for how it crinkled eyes or showed imperfect teeth.

Lyn Ocampo had a cruel smile. It hardened her eyes to obsidian hammer points and made her angular features sharp as razors. She seemed at ease in the cold night air, though she wore only the same fitted black dress he had seen her in earlier that night.

Oscar staggered back in surprise, and Ocampo chuckled softly at his flailing arms. The way her predatory gaze followed him keenly, he couldn't help but feel like a clumsy mouse that had wandered into a serpent's den.

"It's nice to finally meet you, Oscar. Properly at least." The softness of her voice might not have sounded dangerous if not for that smile.

"D-Doctor Ocampo," Oscar stuttered.

"I know all about *you*, of course. All about your...*history*." She smiled languidly, the words practically dripping from her mouth with false syrupy sweetness. "I know you better than you know yourself. Well enough to tell you that there is irony in your tale. For such an insignificant soul to hold such lofty purpose."

"How...how did I get here?" Oscar asked. It looked like the same cemetery as before, but he wasn't altogether certain that he would be able to tell one cemetery from another.

Ocampo smiled. "The three-footed duck. Quite a marvellous thing. I'm not sure if any actually remain alive, but a small idol bathed in their blood gains the ability to transport one to a corresponding rune. It takes time to recharge, of course. No wonder they were hunted to extinction. I imagine your primitive mind might consider it a wormhole of sorts, but in truth, it is closer to an aperture in function."

Oscar shook his head, confused.

"I see you're not following, so I won't waste my breath." Ocampo sighed, offering him another sickly smile instead.

"Is it...like a parallax?" Oscar asked. It hadn't felt like that, not like passing through the cemetery's wall. It had felt closer to when he had been swallowed by darkness after meeting the Bean-Nighe. As if he had been unravelled and then stitched back together in an instant.

Ocampo's eyebrow twitched, irritated by his use of the word. "It is not," she answered crisply.

There was a flickering behind her, and Nina appeared. Or the thing that was shaped like the little girl, at least. *Acheri*, Dmitri had named it.

The thing that had killed Zara.

Oscar felt an absurd urge to cry out, to warn Doctor Ocampo, even though he knew what the truth must be.

217

Doctor Ocampo looked at Nina with an approximation of fondness. "Well done," she purred, then leaned down to whisper something to the girl-shaped monster. The acheri looked at Oscar and smiled broadly before moving to the open area of ground between them. She dropped swiftly to her knees and began to trace her finger on the cracked flagstones. To a passerby, she might have looked like a playing child, drawing out lines to play hopscotch, but her small fingers traced unseen lines over and over with uncanny accuracy.

"Doctor Ocampo," Oscar breathed.

"Oscar." Ocampo's tone and face grew serious. "You should know, you serve an extraordinary function. A noble end. You are quite unique for a human. A golden calf amongst a listless herd of cattle. Your value is great, even if your innards are just the same. You should be proud."

That jagged smile flashed again as Ocampo folded her arms. "I spent decades tracing your line to find you. It was not easy. It is quite fortunate you worked in a hospital, as that has been my domain for many years." Oscar looked at her with his eyes full of questions, and Ocampo shrugged and smiled wickedly, flashing now pointed teeth. "Convenience food."

Oscar's stomach rolled at the thought.

"I had, over the years, built the preconception that when I found you that you would be exceptional in some way. Not less than average." Her eyes scanned him with familiar disdain. "It bothers me that you should be important. Be *needed*." She shook her head.

"What...what do you mean?" Oscar asked. He began to edge away ever so slightly, stepping behind a gravestone to put distance and an obstacle between them. Maybe if he could just get away? Maybe he could...

"Your blood. Your body. Every cell in the otherwise useless clump of structures that forms what you are. You are the key to restoring balance and healing the world." She smiled, her fingers tracing their way across her quivering lip in excitement. "The *worlds*."

Oscar froze.

"It is only right you know the gift you nobly give before you give it. You're a special human, Oscar, and you deserve the truth."

"The truth?" Oscar echoed.

Healing...the worlds?

Ocampo's eyes glittered with amusement.

"Your ancestor, James Tundale, had an unfortunate meeting with one of my kind and was dragged across the barrier between worlds. He caught a glimpse of the other world. The fuel of Dante's tales...what some of your people may wrongly call *Hell*."

Her mouth curled with contempt for the word. "Humans. So quick to fear what you do not understand and call what is different *wrong*," she spat. "The other is just like this place, but not. The yin to its yang, the weight that provides balance. Believe it or not, humans even know its name. *Theia*. They named it Orpheus at first, but one of my kind set that right. Your scientists believe that Theia was a planet that collided with Earth four and a half billion years ago, resulting in the world as it is now. The truth is far simpler. Theia and Earth are one. Two sides of the same coin. This is something that, unfortunately, your kind are growing closer to discovering, finding scars in the veil, and wondering at a parallel universe. James Tundale was not the first and certainly not the last of your kind to go there, but he was very unique in one sense." That cruel jagged smile returned. "He got back out."

Oscar shook his head numbly.

"Can you imagine? A human! Though, he was not left unscathed. The other was forced into his body and mind deeper than he knew. Driven into his cells like overwhelming irradiation. His blood carried a flicker of the shadow. A seed of the *Antumbra*." She looked up at the moon, its pale light bathing her sharp features as she basked in it. "He did not live many years longer. But he did live long enough to sow his oats. And that potential passed down through generations as a torch to bear. A perfect seed waiting for the right loam to sprout." Her eyes opened. Their whites were a golden yellow now. "You are the product of centuries of genetic incubation, Oscar. The cells in your body are a vessel for that seed. I can practically taste it coming from you. The touch of Theia vibrates against your human cells, calling to be harvested. Your essence sings."

Oscar shook his head. *Sings?*

Hadn't Dmitri said something similar?

And the Bean-Nighe. What had she said?

He remembered her mysterious smile, those white round lidless eyes fixed upon him.

Hello, Cricket.

"Oscar, your human life is short, even if you let it drag on for as long as it can. You have the gift of being able to fulfil a great end. *Your purpose*. You are about to become the catalyst for the greatest event in the history of both worlds. You should be so very proud to have this opportunity."

"What...what are you talking about?"

Ocampo's mouth twitched with irritation. "I just told you that your blood carries a flicker of the Antumbra. The worlds are separated by an impenetrable wall, the veil, but you will serve as the key to the greatest parallax on the planet. It will open the door to a world of divine beauty and power...*my* world."

Oscar swallowed. "Hell?"

She smiled. "Theia. Oscar, you must know that *this* world is already what anyone would consider Hell. For both your kind and mine. Humans are rotting and destroying this world beyond repair, whilst my kind withers as a consequence. Our worlds are an echo of each other's, separate yet co-dependent. Energy cannot be created or destroyed, only transferred or transformed. A law of physics shared by one of my kind, of course, but touted by yours. The origin and destination of energy are sometimes unknown. The missing piece of the puzzle is that there is a place beyond your reckoning that shares the same fabric where energy is shared. There is no light without dark, no creation without destruction. Theia has starved for too long, strangled by the self-mutilation of your kind on this place." Her mouth twisted in contempt. "But there has always been a solution. To merge both worlds. To make both into one as it was truly meant to be. Whole. And *you* can be the one to do it."

Oscar's mouth worked wordlessly. This was...too much. There was no way he could let this happen. His eyes scanned his surroundings, desperately searching for some clue of what to do, a direction to run, *anything*.

"It is what *this* planet needs. Your kind are killing this world, and if they succeed, *ours* will be destroyed in turn. We must restore balance. You must understand that, Oscar."

Oscar shook his head, pointing at the girl who still traced shapes on the ground. "She...she said no one else would be hurt. If the worlds become one...and monsters come here...everyone will be killed."

Ocampo tutted. "Not at all. Not all of my kind feed on flesh and blood. Many feed on *other* things. Fear, waste...even pleasure. Our worlds *need* each other to survive, and this is the only way for both to be saved. I can even guarantee the safety of some few of your choosing."

"Why? Why are you even talking to me? Why not just force me to do what you want?"

Ocampo smiled. "Finally. The question that matters most, I was beginning to think you wouldn't even ask." She took a step toward Oscar, and he took another clumsy step back, almost losing his footing. Her smile broadened, showing her sharp teeth. "The sacrifice must be made willingly."

Oscar's tongue stuck to the roof of his mouth. Willingly? That meant he could stop this.

"If you do this, you save both worlds. Your friends and family can be safe. And if you don't...well, let's just say that your friends and family...and countless others will be far less than safe." Her face split in a wicked grin. "I will ensure their ends are far more violent and painful than Zara's. I will make a gift of their entrails and torn faces, heaped in a pile with the eye of the one you hold dearest on top like a cherry. Perhaps I will have you eat it. Push you into the depths of madness before I bend you to my will."

Oscar's stomach clenched, cold horror thrumming through his bones. "How do I know I can even believe you?"

Ocampo shrugged, smirking. "You don't. But I'm sure you can believe that if you don't do this, I will make everyone you have ever loved suffer to their last breath." She licked her lips. The tongue that slid from between her jagged teeth was black and pointed.

Oscar's fingernails dug into his palms painfully, and he felt the muscle in his jaw twitch. Ocampo watched him patiently, and the girl-shaped monster continued tracing shapes on the ground between them.

"I...I don't know," Oscar stammered.

I have to get away from here. Away from her...and warn everyone.

Ocampo scowled impatiently, her voice sharpening once more. "You have a simple choice, Oscar. Save the worlds, and give everyone you love a chance to live or have their carcasses piled upon you until you do it anyway."

Oscar thought he was going to throw up. If he ran, would she just start...killing people? Could she do that?

Yes. He knew with cold certainty that she could and would.

He just needed to buy time.

Perhaps against all hope, Marcus had gotten his message and knew where he was. Maybe he could make this all stop somehow. Maybe...

"Is it a deal?" Ocampo asked, leaning forward with her hands on her hips, eyes shining in the night.

Oscar's heart hammered. What would he say? He needed to stall, even if he was going to run. "O...Okay—" he began.

In the space between them, where Nina traced, shapes began to glow in faint coiling patterns, like the moonlight itself was being reflected from within the stones. The earth began to hum beneath his feet, its vibrations ringing through his bones.

Ocampo's eyes widened in pleasure, and a wicked grin split her face. "The deal is made," she said rapturously.

Oscar's heart dropped like a stone.

"Wait...what?" He hadn't meant to say that, and he was about to say more, to ask more...but something was happening.

The world was ending.

TAXONOMY OF MONSTERS: THE HOMINUM
(HOMO SAPIENS)

"A terrible gnawing, proliferating breed infesting their sickly host, desperate to obliterate it, each other, and themselves. To quell their voracious appetite for annihilation, they have created fabled 'Monsters' to romanticise. I do not know what ill met encounters fated these creations to so masterfully skirt the truth, but there is indeed some truth to be found. A shadow of a whisper of the truth, but a truth nonetheless."

— EXCERPT: THE REVENANT'S ARCANUM

28

THE SAPPING STONE

The girl-shaped monster stepped back, the patterns she had been tracing on the ground glowing brighter than before. All at once, the humming in the earth stopped. Oscar felt odd when the shiver running through his bones disappeared, leaving a deep stillness like the ringing silence after a scream. The bright coiling patterns dimmed. Darker and darker, they dropped to an inky black, a nest of coiling serpents made of midnight. Then darker still.

And then the earth began to bulge.

The flagstones should have cracked and split. Instead, they *stretched*, smoothing and softening until they formed, cube-like, into what looked like a small table.

Or an altar.

The shapes that the acheri had been tracing, the squirming eels of darkness, had stilled into interlocking patterns. They throbbed, blacker than obsidian. It was hard for him to pull his eyes away from their pulsing; even in stillness, they looked as if they moved. It was as if Oscar could feel them. Feel their pull on him. They were...*hungry.*

Oscar blinked, his head swimming, and his heart filled with a deep, forbidding dread.

"The contract has been made," Ocampo breathed, reaching out to trace her shaking fingertips across the stone.

Oscar swallowed. His tongue stuck to the roof of his mouth.

The world is ending...because I messed up. Because I said the wrong thing at the wrong time...

"I didn't mean that. I was about to say——"

Ocampo's mouth twisted in disgust. "The contract is made, fool." She took a slow breath, and her features softened. "But I will show you some small respect. You may speak *one* name, and I shall do my best to ensure that they live."

Oscar's knees threatened to give out, and his lip trembled.

Ocampo began to tap her heel impatiently.

Should I still try and run? Is it too late? Should I...should I name someone?

Marcus? Paige?

Oscar's mind reeled, remembering the hospital and Zara's family. Zara's little brother? How could he choose any one person over any other? Even if he chose someone that *he* loved, what about everybody else? Breath shallow and harsh, Oscar's eyes desperately searched around him, as if the gravestones would provide the answer.

They did.

"Dmitri," he murmured.

"Ha!" Ocampo barked loudly, the cruel smile returning to her thin lips. "A wasted name. I knew I smelled that pathetic mongrel on you. He must have felt the song in your bones, too. I suppose it could be enticing in a way. But really, Oscar, you were special for a human; if you were going to bond with one of our kind, you could have done better. You shouldn't just let any old beastling spray their muck up you."

"Get away from him." The voice was like molten iron.

Standing not far from them, amongst the tombstones, one

arm hanging limp, hair matted in blood, and pale eyes burning with fury was Dmitri.

Doctor Ocampo laughed softly. "What sorry state is this coming to join our fun? I thought I smelled you on the human, but I should have sensed the stench of dog coming closer." The smile slid from her face, and her golden eyes narrowed. "Is it not enough that I tolerated your presence in this world at all? Do you have any idea what I am? And now I imagine you wish to challenge me?" She smiled, showing those razor-sharp teeth.

"I should have known you were not human," Dmitri growled.

Ocampo scoffed. "We don't have time to discuss your ignorance. You are less than nothing beside me. You may be one of my kind, but you were born in this world." She waved her finger chidingly, and Oscar saw that her fingers were tipped with wicked black claws now. "Tell me, whelp, have you ever even seen one born pure of Theia?"

Shock crossed Dmitri's features for a moment, but then he stiffened, face becoming a mask of grim resolve. His eyes locked on Oscar's for a moment, and he spoke. "I'm sorry, Oscar, I have made my choice. I...I'm not too scared to be what I am to protect you."

He bared his teeth in a snarl as he turned to face Doctor Ocampo.

As he stepped forward, his body twisted and bulged...and the monster that lived inside of him burst out of his skin.

THE RESTLESS SOUL

How such a thing had been contained inside Dmitri seemed impossible. It was massive. It must have been at least eight feet, from tail to...*snout?*

Dmitri's handsome face had stretched into a wolf-like muzzle. Pale grey eyes transformed into glowing embers, smooth human muscle to a rippling lean form resting on all fours, powerful haunches ready to pounce. Inky dark scales down the creature's flanks; the rest of its body was coated in sleek black fur but for a row of thick, scaly spines that ran the length of his back. The spikes grew ever finer as they travelled down, flowing to the tip of the tail lashing behind him.

The thing that had been living inside Dmitri met Oscar's eyes. He was...*beautiful.*

"Fascinating." Doctor Ocampo's voice was silken steel. "It must be near a century since I saw one of your kind. What is it the fools called you? *Pterolycus?* Zburător? How this world has paled your shine. You are nothing compared to your sires. *Much* smaller for one. I will cleanse this mockery that insults your kind."

The girl-shaped monster twitched beside her, moving toward Dmitri with a fiendish smile, but Ocampo held up a pale hand. "Watch the human."

The thing that had been Dmitri, the zburător as Ocampo had called it, snarled, a low rumbling sound that vibrated deep in Oscar's chest.

In a flash of dark fur, muscles, and teeth, Dmitri pounced. Ocampo moved, spilling like a serpent to the side and striking out with terrifying speed. Her body twisted and grew even as she did, pale skin taking on a sickly grey tinge, clothes straining as she brought her joined hands together with the side of the giant beast. There was a *whoomph*, and Dmitri was thrown through the air, colliding with the side of the nearest mausoleum with a deafening crash of crumbling stone.

"Pathetic." Ocampo sneered, as more stone and debris from the shattered building tumbled onto Dmitri. "I walked between the realms before you were ever imagined." Her hair lashed around her face, now even more angular and striking. Unnaturally prominent ridges ran down her cheekbones, and her teeth bared in a shark like smile. "I have gone by names you have never heard, and some few you may have. *Kumiho. Leyak. Black Annis. Manananggal.*" Her lips curled around the last word, making it succulent, like sucking the juice from ripe fruit. "Why bother defending this human? Even a mewling pissant like you must sense it. Sense the thrum of the shadow in his blood. He is how the balance shall be restored, and the worlds shall finally be rejoined."

The zburător struggled to stand, rising with difficulty from the rubble and ruin.

"It would usually give me no pleasure to slaughter one of my own," Ocampo said, "but in this case, I will make an—"

The night lit up in a torrent of searing flame. It burst from Dmitri's jaws and engulfed Ocampo. Heat blossomed across

Oscar's cheeks, though he was nowhere near close enough to be burned. He fell back, shielding his face. Grit and cobbles chafed his palms as he scrambled away and cowered against a mossy gravestone.

A hand grabbed his wrist. Stunned, Oscar turned, looking into the darkness and finding Marcus, crouching wide-eyed beside him.

Oscar's heart soared. "Marcus!"

"We need to go," Marcus urged.

The air became colder around them, and the hair on Oscar's arms stood on end.

The little girl, Nina, stood beside them. Her head cocked to one side, and an amused smile appeared on her face, eyes pools of darkness. "Oh, you mustn't leave. We need to play." She giggled and opened her mouth as if to shriek, but it opened and opened, spilling shadows that burst from within her, engulfing her until a maelstrom of thick, inky tendrils lashed forth.

Marcus threw something that smashed by the clump of swelling darkness. There was an ear-shattering sound, like thousands of birds screaming, and the cloud of heaving darkness recoiled, spasming and flickering.

"Something Dmitri gave me to slow her down," Marcus said, looking even more surprised than Oscar felt. "It won't stop her; we need to go."

The night dimmed as the searing plume of flames stopped.

Oscar spared a glance back at Dmitri, hopeful that Ocampo might be a sizzling ruin, but saw that his jaws were closed for a different reason. He was muzzled. Ocampo's marble pale arms latched around his jaw, her face wild with the pleasure of battle. Oscar gawked at her naked body, clothes burned away completely. Her lithe, powerful limbs now crested with blade-sharp bones at their joints. Twin spikes at her elbows, barbs at her wrists, two blades like crescents at her shoulders.

"Oscar!" Marcus pleaded.

"No," Oscar breathed. "We need to help him."

His hands fumbled at his waist, finding the rusty hilt and pulling it free. *What am I doing? I don't stand a chance...*

Oscar heard Marcus let out a shriek and saw that he had made *another* mistake.

Too slow.

The little girl that was a mass of deadly shadows flickered close. "I said I wanted to play!" the mockery of a childish voice screeched.

Marcus desperately fumbled for his pockets, perhaps trying to pull out another bottle of whatever Dmitri had given him. But a dark tendril was already snaking out and reaching for him. "No!" Oscar cried.

Marcus fell back, arms raised, eyes wide with horror as the writhing shadows shot a dark tendril at his chest.

Not again. Not like Zara.

"NO!" Oscar lunged at her with the rusted hilt on instinct.

"GET IT, OSCAR!" Marcus cried. "STAB HER WITH THE THING!"

Oscar squeezed his eyes closed desperately. *Please. Please. Not Marcus. You can't take him from me, too.*

Icy cold enveloped his hands like he had driven them into the depths of a frozen lake.

And then...*silence*.

Oscar gasped a ragged breath and dared to open his eyes.

The girl that they had called Nina stared back at him. A little girl once more, albeit with a face whiter than snow and eyes like large dark smudges. Her mouth was wide in surprise, staring at the rusted hilt flush with her chest.

She burst into a fine pale mist, evaporating into the night.

In his hands, Oscar saw...

Impossible.

The hilt was still clutched in his white-knuckled grip in both hands, rust coarse against his palms. Coming forth from it, only a little longer than his thumb and far too small to match the hilt itself, was a blade. Not a blade of steel or even stone, but of a pale flickering mist. Like a beam of faltering moonlight clinging to the air at the end of the hilt, forming a short, broad stub of a blade.

Oscar dropped it in surprise, and the blade faded into nothingness as the hilt clattered onto the ground.

"Oscar!" Marcus gasped, looking amazed. "You did it!"

There was a crash behind them, and a something sailed overhead. The massive zburător plummeted, its body thundering into the ground with bone-crushing force, shattering several tombstones in the process.

"Dmitri!" Oscar breathed, moving toward the fallen zburător. Something snagged him roughly by the collar.

"Disgusting!" Ocampo hissed. "That one of your kind dares end one of mine. DISGUSTING."

She flung him like a rag doll, and he collided with solid rock. Blinding crushing pain engulfed Oscar's body. His ears rung with it, his vision flashed white, and the air in his lungs was expelled by the force. The sharp metallic taste in his mouth told him he must have bitten his tongue, but he was more concerned with trying to breathe. A hoarse breath mercifully inflated his lungs on his third try, as he blinked dazedly.

"Oscar!" he heard Marcus cry out, voice distant and tinny, as though there were worlds between them.

Oscar was trying to force more air into his lungs when he felt something grip the back of his jacket and lift him as though he weighed nothing.

"Enough of this," Ocampo snarled.

Oscar stared at her groggily and saw what barely looked like Doctor Ocampo anymore. She was taller than any human, her bare body scaled, mottled grey, and taut with powerful sinuous muscles. A week ago, he did not think he could have been more terrified of her, but even now, he saw this as her truth. This form suited her in a way the other could never. It gave the true majesty to her power that only her eyes had whispered of before.

"It is time," she growled, golden eyes drilling into his.

"Oscar!" Marcus howled again, and Oscar heard another vial shatter beside them. Ocampo spared a moment to jeer at his friend before dropping Oscar. His head bounced painfully as he collided with stone. Stone that was mercifully *warm* somehow. But when Oscar tried to move, he found that he could not. He struggled to twist his body away from it, but he was *stuck*. Turning his head, Oscar saw the dark pulse of interlocking shapes beneath him. The dark serpentine pattern throbbed hungrily against him, and his heart sunk.

"It is not a quick end, from what I understand," Ocampo mused darkly as he struggled to twist his head to look in the direction of her voice. "The veil cannot be broken quickly. If the realms come crashing together all at once, both would be obliterated. First, gateways will open, but it will not be long before the veil begins to tear and the worlds begin to bleed into one another. Look...it is already happening."

Oscar blinked, his eyes searching for whatever she spoke of. His head felt so heavy, he could barely lift it at all. But then, he saw it. Between the mausoleum she had partially ruined by throwing Dmitri into, and the one beside it. The air was...*shimmering*.

"Soon, Theia will get her fangs into this place. My kind are coming. First, with the lowest of the Shadowlings, barely formed into beings. But soon, more will feel the breach and begin to cross over. The energy from Theia will nourish me, imbue me to what I once was...a being far beyond even this."

"Get away from him, you bitch!" a voice said, hard and cold as the night.

Ocampo turned, face flashing with irritation. "What do you—"

A huge, pale fist sculpted from light collided with Ocampo,

blasting her back with violent explosive force. Oscar struggled to lift his head to see what had happened.

A round face with eyes the colour of freshly fallen autumn leaves appeared before him.

Zara grinned. "Hey, Booboo, what's up? I guess you really liked the cemetery, huh?"

INTERLUDE THE THIRD: THE
WANDERING EYES

B arloh had been there when the blue lights pierced the darkness. He had watched them load the girl into the back. He'd dealt with his fair share of emergency calls in the past. Screaming loved ones begging for help down the receiver, describing what was happening as though it would make any difference. Even if he hadn't spent countless hours flicking through images of crime scenes and autopsies, he would have known the girl was as good as dead. It wasn't just the size of the response team; it was the grim mechanical way in which they handled her. Just going through the motions. Even the pale guy with the mopey face and the kid, *Marcus*, knew it. He saw their faces as they were guided into the back of a police car. Numb. Like the moment when flesh has been sliced—fast and deep—and for just a fraction of a second, the body is too shocked to even bleed. They knew they had been cut, the damage was done, but for just one impossibly long heartbeat, they were frozen. Soon they would react. Soon they would fall apart. Just like he had.

Barloh itched to go home, get online, and spill everything he knew into the hungry void of the internet right then. He knew no matter who tried to hide his words, there would always be a trace.

But there was a problem. He still didn't have his *proof*. As the flashing lights pulled away, he realised that amongst it all, Tza was nowhere to be seen. Something about that guy made his skin crawl. He knew he needed more, and figured *Marcus* may be the answer, so he rushed back to his car and followed the lights to the hospital.

Barloh found a tattered newspaper on one of the chairs in the emergency waiting room. He was pretending to flick through this whilst he watched. The skinny pale guy looked ready to throw up, and *Marcus* cradled his head in his hands. Then the girl's family arrived. He felt a pang of emotion when he saw what he guessed were her parents. The ghosts of old daydreams danced across his mind, daydreams where his parents had mourned *him* like this girl's would mourn her. Daydreams where they both lived and moved on, and he hadn't had to lose them. Avenge them.

No.

Focus.

A stern-faced doctor came out and started to talk to the pale guy. He eyed her appraisingly, lip curling. She would *definitely* be hot if she smiled more. She looked like she was far more likely to want to step on your skull with one of those high heels, though. *Maybe that wouldn't be so bad.*

A couple of minutes later, the pale kid freaked out and bolted. *Fight or flight.* Barloh grunted. He kept his seat as the hot doctor got waylaid by a newly arrived brown-skinned police officer, built like a bull, and led him away. He watched as *Marcus* got briefly prodded and probed before being led away by another doctor.

Then Barloh followed.

Not too close, of course. He followed them down the hall, close enough that people passing thought he was with the kid, but far enough that they didn't see him following.

Funny thing with places like hospitals. If you acted like you were supposed to be there, no one ever challenged you.

As he followed, he passed a room full of people in uniforms

and the girl's family. The guy in the police uniform was there. He must have been one of the girl's relatives too. Despite his thick neck and stubborn jaw, his face was streaked with tears. In fact, *all* the family were sobbing.

Barloh felt a prickle of smug vindication. He'd been right. She wasn't going to make it.

There were only a few doctors and nurses in the room, all looking deflated. One was detaching the breathing tube from the girl's mouth, and others were already leaving the room through a door at the back until just one remained.

Barloh loitered near the door, the private and personal moment too intensely magnetic for his perverse curiosity to resist. Maybe they'd say what had happened to her...

"We will give you a few moments to say goodbye," the older looking nurse who remained said. She had a severe bob and a face that looked unaccustomed to such gentle words.

The woman that Barloh guessed was the girl's mother burst into tears. Wretched, body shaking tears like she was letting something awful out of herself.

When all the medical staff had finally left the room, the old woman spoke. To say she looked fit to be blown away by a breeze, her voice was hard as nails. "It is time," she said.

Barloh figured they were talking about the girl dying, and he was about to move on, but then...

"Are...are you sure," the her mother sobbed. "You have carried it for so long."

"W...what?" the burly police officer said, blinking away his tears. "I'm supposed to be next in line. I'm supposed to—"

"It is time," the old woman simply repeated, her eyes flashing dangerously at the bullish young man. He spluttered into silence, a snuffed flame. "The burden has been mine for long enough. At least this way, some good may also come of passing it on."

Barloh got closer, peering through the door as the old woman laid her hands on the girl's slack round face.

The lights flickered in the room, the hall, even the atrium behind him. Barloh leaned closer to watch, mouth hanging open. The old woman stiffened, then sagged, like she had set down armfuls of heavy baggage. Her body slumped. If she had just looked old before, now she looked ancient. Frail and weak. Her body hadn't changed, but something about her was completely different. She swayed, and the girl's mother stepped forward to support her.

Barloh frowned. *What the fuck was that?*

Suddenly, the girl—*the dead girl*—gasped a deep breath, her eyes shooting open.

"Oh, thank you! Oh, my girl!" the father cried, stepping forward, tears streaming down his face as he clung to his daughter.

There was a shout, and the medical staff were all suddenly rushing back into the room. So many uniformed bodies that Barloh was forced to back away, slinking back into the corridor for fear of being questioned. His heart pounded angrily in his chest.

Monsters. More fucking monsters. Everywhere he looked.

He stalked down the hall, his head spinning. He had to find where they had taken *Marcus*. He wasn't sure what exactly his plan was. Questioning the kid face to face wasn't exactly his wheelhouse, but maybe he could overhear what happened. All he knew was he needed *more*, and this was the best place to get it.

"Excuse me, sir, can I help you?" a young dark-skinned nurse wearing a headscarf asked, surprising him.

"Oh..." Barloh cleared his throat, abruptly aware of his state, brushing previously unseen crumbs from his stained shirt. "I just got a call. My...stepson is here. He was having a problem with his headaches?"

The young nurse gave him a long appraising look, eyes narrowing slightly. "What's your stepson's name?" she asked, pursing her lips.

"Marcus," Barloh answered quickly, praying the girl would leave him alone.

"Taminah, they need you to put a cannula in someone in bay two!" a voice called from down the hall, causing the young nurse to look away for a moment.

Barloh shifted to one side, gesturing for her to pass.

"You want the MAU," the nurse replied quickly, looking harassed and already geared toward her next task. "Down the hall, second door on the left." And then she was moving away with someone already pestering her to do something else.

"Thank you," Barloh said softly, smiling.

Thank God for underfunded health services.

He followed the nurse's directions. Fortunately, he saw no staff around, all busy in the bed spaces. The Nurse's station hummed with the headachy glow of halogen lights. He leaned over to peer at the large screen mounted on the wall. *Room 5: WILLIAMS, M.* Barloh grinned and tucked his hands in his pockets, sauntering through the unit, eyes scanning numbers by doors. He found cubicle five and peered through the small slotted window.

The first thing he saw was the nurse.

She was standing not far from the door with a vague and dreamy look on her face, staring into space. The kid, *Marcus*, was lying on a gurney. His mouth was moving, but Barloh couldn't quite see who he was talking to. He moved closer, peering through the window to try and get a better look.

He caught a flash of dark coat and jet-black hair. Barloh's stomach flipped. *Tza.* He recognised the man from earlier. He was handing the kid something. A phone? The screen lit up, and the kid looked shocked. Their conversation was more animated now. Tza disappeared from view, and the kid got up and followed on unsteady legs. Barloh leaned, pressing his face to the glass.

There was another door at the back of the cubicle.

They were gone.

He gave it to the count of five and followed them as quietly as he could.

The nurse didn't even flinch when Barloh passed her, and he had a heady turn for a moment. The room had a strange sharp and smoky smell. His vision blurred at the edges, and his step faltered. *What the fuck is that?* He growled and pushed forward.

Barloh staggered through the corridors, struggling to keep up, his vision swimming. Tza was clearly in a rush, despite Marcus obviously being sick. He thought he'd lost them in the atrium when he heard a yell that made him back up against a wall as someone darted past him, almost knocking him flat in their haste.

Barloh gasped as the girl who had just had a tube pulled out of her throat to die minutes ago ran past him.

"Zara!" Marcus cried out, grabbing her in a fierce hug. "You're okay?! How?"

The girl answered him, but the words were lost to Barloh over the ambient sound of voices and movement around them. But something else had caught his attention. He stared, fuzzy vision fixed on Tza. He looked different somehow, his hair no longer neat but slightly wild, and his body largely obscured by his dark buttoned up coat. This was the first time he had gotten a clear view of his face. A face Barloh knew. He would never forget. The scar covering the back of his hand burned like it had been yesterday.

After all these years...

"Spring-heeled Jack," Barloh whispered.

THE MOUTH THAT SPITS MIDNIGHT

"How? You died," Oscar breathed.

Zara shrugged. "Only for a few seconds technically, barely even counts." She reached down and took hold of Oscar's wrist. "Apparently my body didn't have the energy to go on living...but it turns out Nani had a secret. I kind of got my inheritance early. Well, Rami's inheritance, to be exact." She pulled, trying to lift him from the altar.

Oscar was stuck fast.

Worse, as she pulled, he felt a dragging sensation deep inside his chest. Like the stone was trying to hold onto him from the inside out. Zara pulled harder, and the force deepened, like being squeezed by a concrete fist. He cried out in pain and surprise.

"Oscar!" Zara stopped pulling. "It's the stone? It's like it's holding on to you."

The contract has been made.

Oscar groaned in agreement, blinking up at his friend as his lip quivered. "Zara, I..."

Over her shoulder, the darkness throbbed between the mausoleums, a silvery shimmer around its edge.

Oscar swallowed, nodding weakly at the shimmering air. "She

did something. I made some kind of deal. It was an accident. I think...I think the world is ending."

"How did you make a deal like that by accident?" Zara's eyes bulged. "It doesn't exactly sound like a fucking pyramid scheme, Os."

"I...don't know, I'm sorry." Tears threatened to blur his vision; he blinked them away. "I thought you were dead."

Zara reached down to grip him in a clumsy embrace.

Oscar might have lost himself in that moment, but the gateway, somehow darker than even the darkest night, *leaked*. From the tear in the sky that sucked in the moonlight...something was coming out.

The *something* was not really anything that he had ever seen before, but still very familiar. They were not quite fully formed things, more the suggestion of them. Hazy, shadow-like shapes of darkness that seemed to need you to concentrate to be sure that you could really see them at all without your eyes sliding off.

The more that Oscar stared, the more that he recognised them very clearly.

Flecks.

Only these ones weren't going away when he looked at them. In fact, they seemed to be getting clearer, their forms pulsing in time with the gateway as if it were their beating heart.

The largest was perhaps as tall as his waist, and each was as different as could be. Their shapes were a cruel mockery of familiar creatures. Or rather, *a combination of them*. The elongated shadow of a boar with a crocodile's jaws and a long tail tipped with barbs writhing menacingly. A fat slug with small moth-like wings on its back, too small to ever lift its swollen body from the ground. A prowling shape with the grace of a panther, but a head closer to some kind of lizard and wide clawed feet...

"Zara," Oscar breathed.

Zara stood, following his gaze and moaning, "Oh...that's not good."

There was a rumble, the sound of falling stone, and Oscar struggled to twist his head to find its origin. Doctor Ocampo rose from the rubble of the wrecked mausoleum she had landed in. Dark oily blood matted one side of her now wild hair. "*You*," she hissed.

"I thought I told you to back off," Zara growled, raising her fists.

Ocampo's wild-eyed smile was positively horrific with her pointed teeth and bloodied skull. "Now, that *is* fascinating. I always knew you had potential. A *Ghatotkacha*. I thought I felt something at the hospital, but I would never have imagined that this was what it was. How did you come by this power? A relative? What is her name?"

Zara narrowed her eyes "Sorry, Nani warned me that you were a sharp-toothed bitch when I woke up. She also told me to tell you that you should never have made it out of Nepal—whatever that means."

Doctor Ocampo hissed, fury in her golden eyes. "Perhaps I can get you to tell me what it is like to die twice. Then I will share your last words with the old woman as I rip out her organs."

A shadow from the gateway scuttled to her side. The largest yet. Vast legs like a spider jointed with thick bony segments carrying a spiky body like a sea-urchin. Ocampo raised her arm and gripped one of the thing's legs. Rather than struggle, it shifted into her, breaking apart and clinging to her pale limb affectionately. Others joined, bounding toward her pale form and curling around her body.

She started to laugh. "My current form in this realm is but a simulacrum of my potential, worn thin by my years here. The wider the gate becomes, the more powerful I shall be. If I dipped even a finger through that gateway, I could crush you without a thought." She laughed again as a serpent with a head like a lion coiled around her waist. She stretched like a basking lizard, only as she stretched, the coiling shadows clothed her like a living gown of darkness across her marbled skin.

Other things were coming out of the gateway now. *More of them*. What looked like a pack of hyenas with jaws full of sabre like teeth stalking around the other flecks.

"Sweet little Shadowlings," Ocampo cooed affectionately. "We shall tear this world apart...starting here."

"Ugh," Zara grunted. "I can't believe I had a crush on you."

Marcus ran to stand beside Zara, his eyes wide as saucers. "I'm glad you're alive, Zara, but...wait, are you...glowing?"

Oscar looked at Zara, but she didn't look any different to him. Was Marcus seeing something he couldn't?

"End them," Ocampo hissed.

Several of the flecks moved on her command, a flurry of bounding, slithering and undulating death.

Marcus snatched at his pocket, and Oscar caught a glimpse of a small vial as he tossed it. But the shadows moved quicker than his throw, and the pack split around the shattering glass and reformed just as quick. They were nearly upon them when Zara stepped forward.

The panther-like fleck bounded ahead with snapping crocodilian jaws. Zara thrust out her clenched hand, and there was a flash like bright moonlight. A large translucent fist encased her own, at least five times the size. The blow connected with such force, it blasted the panther fleck's body into motes. Oscar opened his mouth to shout out in alarm, to warn her of the writhing mass coming at her from the left, but she was already stepping into a short kick. A massive, unearthly, glowing foot stomped forward to crush that and another fleck close beside it into nothingness.

The other flecks seemed to take alarm from their own being destroyed. Shrill and ugly cries like scraping cutlery on a clean plate went up in the night as more came forward like a pack.

They surrounded Zara, vast jaws nipping at her heels, jumping back when she lashed out.

"Zara!" Oscar cried. As he did, the deep pulling in his chest intensified. He gasped, his head swimming from the sapping pain. When he opened his eyes, Zara was still surrounded.

But the dark tear in the night...it was bigger. *Darker*. His eyes dragged inexorably toward it like a circling drain.

More things were coming.

Lots more.

And they looked even worse.

THE SHATTERING DARK

Zara jumped forward, bringing down both hands together. A glowing blow like a massive hammer scattered several of the flecks and blasted three more into oblivion. Oscar felt the vibration of the strike shuddering through the altar.

Two broke away from the pack, skittering away from Zara.

Toward Marcus.

Marcus let out a shout of surprise, reaching into his pocket and casting a handful of glass at them. One of the creatures was caught up in the liquid. Thick tentacles thrashed angrily around its spiny body, letting out a guttural cry. Even their noises sounded more solid now.

Marcus threw again, but it went wide, smashing uselessly on the cobblestones.

His glasses. He can't see without his glasses.

Numb panic flooded Oscar as the remaining fleck, one of the hyenas with massive fangs and a jagged tail, swerved and continued racing onward menacingly.

Fast.

Too fast.

"Marcus!" Oscar screamed. Marcus fell back toward the altar with a yell, hands snatching at his pockets.

There was a flash of movement. Something large leapt over Oscar and the altar with a snarl, its massive body covered in dark shaggy fur. *Yes.* Oscar's heart lifted.

Their saviour landed on the beast and grabbed its throat in its massive jaws, shaking it quickly into motes of nothingness.

"Ed!" Oscar gasped.

The mimick-dog wagged his tail happily.

"Oh...I guess we're even now, huh?" Marcus panted, pulling out another vial from his pocket.

Ed let out a deep bark.

Ahead, Zara stamped again, the ghostly extension of a limb thumping the earth and blasting another shadow to smithereens.

Ocampo was watching, swaying in the shadows, golden eyes flashing hate. Observing Zara as she danced from shape to shape with a grace Oscar had never seen from her before.

Oscar felt a rush of excitement. *Maybe they can do this, maybe they can...*

But then the gate throbbed again.

The stone beneath him pulled, hungry to take everything that made him with crushing force. Oscar howled in agony.

More shadows rushed out of the gateway. More robust and solid than before. Oscar could practically see the hairs on them, the scales and spines, and they were starting to take on dull colours. Their eyes were filled with livid ecstasy, and their over-sized jaws snapped hungrily at Zara, dripping in darkness. They converged on her. She desperately slapped three away with a massive pale palm, but there were too many.

Ocampo began to laugh softly in the darkness.

Two of the shadow beasts were already on Zara, pulling at her clothes. A massive ant-like thing with dragonfly wings and pincer-like jaws bit her, and Oscar saw the skin on her arm break. As her blood started to flow, the others stalking around her rose in a frenzy. She cried out as three more leapt on her.

"Ed, help Zara!" Oscar begged.

Ed bounded forward, tearing one of the flecks in two with massive jaws. But more turned on him, their dark teeth snapping at his legs. Ed wheeled around, catching one of their heads in his jaws and crushing it. More and more of the beasts converged on him, and Ed and Zara disappeared under a writhing swarm of darkness. *There are too many.*

"She could have grown to be strong...but such poor control of her powers. Barely a newborn," Ocampo mused from where she now sat upon a mass of shadowy forms arranged beneath her like a throne.

Oscar caught a flash of movement as something substantial moved through the gateway. He twisted his head but wasn't quick enough to see whatever had passed through. Clenching his teeth, he waited for the inevitable pull at his core. But it didn't come.

Whatever passed through was big. *Too big.* He swallowed.

Ocampo stretched on her throne of shadow, dark veins webbing her mottled flesh.

"Come on, Zara!" Marcus bellowed, throwing a handful of glass vials at the writhing mass of flecks. Oscar saw tears streaking his friend's face. The vials shattered, catching a few flecks at the edges and setting them shrieking and spasming. "That's all I have," Marcus panted, hopelessly.

It's not enough.

It's not...

The teeming mass of flecks that had piled on Zara seemed to retract for a moment, and then swell. A burst of glowing light broke them apart, and the monsters scattered, several breaking apart in the air from the sheer force of it.

Zara struggled to her feet.

A bright glow like armour withdrew into her body, like a

flexing muscle relaxing. Her clothes were torn, her skin scratched and bloody. Her eyes were full of rage.

The blast had caught most of the beasts on Ed, and he twisted, gripping the throat of the last fleck and tearing it open as he limped to his feet.

"Bravo," Ocampo jeered. "You certainly *do* have some potential. Quite a beautiful specimen dwells within you. Centuries old. I don't suppose you'd be interested in joining the correct side? You are one of us now, after all." She stood, raising her arms. The flecks that had formed her throne moved with her, their bodies breaking into a dark mist and swelling around her. It flowed like a vast cape, solidifying and lifting her smoothly from the ground and several feet into the air.

"No, thanks." Zara squared her shoulders and spat on the ground. "I'll stick with the winning side."

Ocampo laughed softly, licking her lips with her dark pointed tongue. "I don't favour your odds."

Oscar felt the altar starting to pull at him again. Worse this time. "No!" he cried out, his vision blurring. *It's getting stronger. I...I can't take much more.* It was trying to tear every fibre of his being apart and soak it up, pushing itself between his joints, his bones, his muscles, every one of his cells with agonising, inexorable force. He didn't even realise he was screaming until the agony started to subside.

"Oscar!" Marcus sobbed. He was clinging to Oscar's hand, tears flowing freely down his face.

The gateway was bleeding darkness now. Dripping it. There was a heavy thumping, like a pulse. Or like...something trying to break through. *Knock knock.*

"It is time," Ocampo crooned. The tendrils attached to her throbbed as more of the flecks started to feed into them, and she arched her back in pleasure. Thicker tendrils of darkness coiled around her body and limbs. When she opened her eyes again, they were as black as the gateway itself.

She cast an arm, and a volley of dark spikes broke free from her, lancing through the air like spears at Zara. Zara leapt back, not with athleticism but power, a burst of light at her boots carrying her several feet away where she landed heavily. The spears struck the ground where she had been standing a moment before, driving deep into the earth before they melted back into the darkness. Zara staggered unsteadily, readying herself for another volley.

"You are no match for me. There's still too much human in you," Ocampo sneered.

Zara grunted. "Maybe." She wiped a hand across her mouth. "But maybe I don't need to be."

Ocampo cocked her head curiously, a dark vein in her temple throbbed.

"Maybe I just needed to buy some time for *him*." Zara grinned, wiping blood from her mouth with the back of her hand. The heavy otherworldly banging sounded through the gateway once more, and it began to darken.

"What are you talking about?" Ocampo snapped, her eyes flashing around, searching for something.

No. For someone.

Zara laughed, and Ocampo's eyes bulged with fury, the dark tendrils that lifted her throbbing and bulging.

And then something passed through the gateway.

A massive form with all the loping grace of an alpha predator.

Dmitri.

Or what had been Dmitri.

He was vast, stalking forward with regal power on massive paws from the gateway, eyes flickering with endless black flames. The zburător's fur looked longer, fuller, flickering with shadow. At first, Oscar thought that shadows were swarming around his back, like they did Ocampo's, but as the colossal beast flexed its thick muscle, great black wings, dark and leathery as a bat's, unfurled from his back.

Ocampo snarled a fierce grin full of malice. "Interesting," she purred. In a twist and push of lashing darkness, she spilt through the air toward him. She thrust both her arms out, and a shower of dark tendrils lashed forth like a rain of arrows.

Dmitri dropped back on his haunches and let loose a billowing torrent of blinding flame, searing the darkness from the sky. Oscar had to close his eyes because of the brightness and heat. When he opened them again, there was no sign of the darkness that Ocampo had cast.

Ocampo let out a furious cry, rolling through the air, and descended upon him, colliding with such force that the stone beneath the zburător's paws shattered.

Impossibly, the blow did not break him in two. Instead, there was a low rumbling growl, and the thing that had been inside Dmitri raised its head slowly. It almost looked like it was smiling.

Faster than Oscar thought possible, the zburător swiped viciously with a paw, forcing Ocampo to dance away. She bounded back in a wave of darkness, landing with a snarl. "You are nothing," she spat, thrusting her arms with a feral roar. All the remaining flecks swarmed toward her, feeding into her darkness.

The altar started to tug at Oscar again, and he cried out. His heart faltered in his chest.

This is it. I can't take another one...

"Oscar," Zara panted, coming close and pulling at him once more. The leeching stone only pulled harder, pulled deep inside him in a place he had never felt before, and he let out a scream.

"Stop!" he panted. "It...it's killing me..."

Dmitri tumbled across the cemetery, rolling with Ocampo and her massive cloak of shadows.

"Stop," Oscar begged. "Just...make it stop. Please." Maybe there was only one way to make all this stop. *Maybe...maybe I have to die before the stone takes all of me.*

"Oscar," Zara moaned, a tear rolling down her face. Her bloodied hand touched his cheek.

"If you kill me...maybe the gate will close. Maybe everything will be okay." Oscar's voice was weak. Hollow.

"No," Zara sobbed.

"Wait...break it!" Marcus said, grabbing onto her shoulder. "Break the fucking stone!"

Zara blinked, looking shocked for a moment, and then her eyes lit up. "Oscar...hold on. This might...sting a little," she warned, stepping back.

"What?" Oscar moaned weakly.

"But I guess we don't have much to lose at this point, Booboo."

Zara stepped forward, and with one massive stomp, her ethereal foot connected with the altar. An enormous thud shook Oscar to his core, jarring him back to consciousness.

The world blurred around him, and when his focus came back, he realised he was still on the altar.

"Hold on, Oscar," Zara shouted. Her voice sounded further away now.

The stone was dragging on Oscar, worse than ever before, deep and hungry and desperate. Rushing to finish devouring the dregs of him.

Oscar heard heavy footsteps running toward him and opened his eyes to see Zara soaring through the air, her feet glowing with energy, like a human missile directed toward the altar.

There was a colossal crash, and Oscar shattered into a thousand pieces.

❧ 33 ❧

SPRING-HEELED JACK

The first thing Oscar became aware of was his head. It was thick and aching but cradled on something soft. A lap, he realised. Blinking, he saw Marcus looking down at him, eyes wide with concern.

The next thing he realised was that he was all in one piece and not a thousand. He was sure of this because every single part of him hurt. He was particularly aware of a hard lump of what felt like jagged stone poking into his lower back. A wet snuffling in his palm led him to Ed, as small a doberman as he had ever seen, ears flattened to his head and shivering.

Finally, beyond the rubble and ruin, beyond Zara, who stood watching with her back to him—back straight and fists clenched —was the dark wound hanging in the air.

It wasn't bleeding shadows anymore.

The altar. Zara shattered the altar.

The darkness, the throbbing pitch that split the air, shivered and then collapsed in on itself. A churning mass of inky worms rapidly consuming themselves before disappearing altogether.

There was a blood-curdling scream filled with endless fury and murder.

It brought Oscar all the way back to his senses at once. Gasping, he tried to push himself upright but found he was far too weak to manage it.

"I've got you, buddy," Marcus said, hitching him up under his arms so that he could see.

Ocampo was still fighting.

Her cloak of shadows lashed around her in the night, pushing her up from the ground and sending her tumbling through the air with horrifying grace. Oscar blinked. The shadows were definitely fainter than before. Her eyes livid gold again, not black.

"You fool!" Ocampo shrieked into the night. "Do you not know what you are? What you have done?"

A mass of dark fur, muscle, and fangs rocketed through the sky. Massive beating wings carried the zburător at a terrifying speed; Oscar caught only a glimpse of burning eyes and flashing teeth. Ocampo spilled to the side, landing smoothly as her attacker's beating wings carried him into the night, sending a blanket of dust into the air in its wake.

"This means nothing; there are other doors!" She spat, cackling wildly, her voice on the edge of hysteria.

Reaching out her arms, Ocampo *pulled*. The darkness that had coiled itself to her was drawn in, soaking into her body. Dark veins webbed her flesh again, and when she opened her eyes, they were like oil slicks in her pale face once more. "What remains should be more than enough to finish you."

Dmitri sailed through the air again, it was as if the very night itself struck at her with claws and teeth. Ocampo was not prepared to dodge this time, but she didn't need to. One pale sinuous arm lashed out, snatching at the zburător, sending him tumbling from the air. He landed with an earth-shaking crash, rolling, before catching himself on massive paws and skidding to an upright halt.

"I will destroy all of you but the one that matters. Find a new world-parallax," she shouted. "I felt it. Though the veil was only bridged for a short time, Theia has taken its grip on this world." A wicked rapturous grin split her face.

The zburător pounced, but Ocampo was too fast. She swayed to one side, casting out her arm. Blades of darkness sprung free, lancing through the air.

"Dmitri!" Oscar cried.

In a beat of vast leathery wings, he banked to the side, but not before some of the shards of darkness split his scaled flank, crimson blood flowing freely. He landed roughly, growling, back leg moving gingerly.

"It's not enough," Oscar breathed.

Ocampo smiled darkly. "Come, little one. Let us end this."

"'ERE LOOK OUT THE BLEEDIN' WAY," a croaking voice bellowed from nowhere.

A massive shape bounded out of darkness, crested with a small mossy lump. Oscar's jaw dropped.

The Gwyllgi.

The monstrous fleshy monster sailed through the air, eyes like scorching furnaces. Gax was mounted on its back like a tiny lumpy lord riding into battle.

Ocampo spun, face slack with surprise.

The Gwyllgi's dripping jaws snatched at her, and Ocampo rolled to one side, narrowly avoiding its clutches.

But she didn't have time to move fast enough from the other teeth that came from the dark. The set of jaws that took her across one shoulder, snatching her viciously.

She hissed angrily, twisting in Dmitri's grip, savagely thrashing at his muzzle as he shook her. "I will destroy you, wretched fool," she snarled. "I will destroy you all!"

The Gwyllgi leapt over, teeth closing around her legs, pulling at her like a chew toy.

Surprisingly, Ocampo fought on, limbs thrashing furiously, dark shadows coiling from her flesh, driving at Dmitri and the Gwyllgi, leaving deep gouges in their flesh.

"I'll be right back," Zara said darkly, stepping forward.

Oscar opened his mouth to reply, but Zara leapt into the air with a burst of brightness at her feet. As she came down, Oscar saw the angle of her fall aligned perfectly with the thrashing shape of Ocampo. Zara raised a hand into the air as she descended. A massive ghostly fist came to life around her own, and she brought it down with crushing force across Ocampo's middle.

There was a sickening wet crunch as the doctor came apart.

Oscar closed his eyes and shivered as he saw the Gwyllgi gobbling something down that looked like a leg.

When he opened his eyes again, Zara was walking back, her face a steely mask.

Over her shoulder, Dmitri let out a searing cloud of fire over Ocampo's remains that seemed to go on forever.

"Are you okay?" Zara asked, pressing her fingers to his wrist. "We need to get you to hospital. You're so pale...and your pulse is weak."

"That's just me," Oscar croaked weakly, wincing at the pain that blossomed in his chest when he almost laughed.

Zara grinned, leaned down, and took both his hands in hers gently. "That looks like a broken rib laugh to me, Booboo. Go easy on the comedy."

"You...have powers now?" Oscar asked, looking up at his friend.

"Well..."

"She is the vessel of an ancient magical ghost!" Marcus cut in excitedly.

Zara scowled. "It's not...well, that sounds quite cool, I guess. Even if it's not technically accurate."

"Hell yes!" Marcus beamed.

"How did you find me?" Oscar croaked weakly.

"Marcus got your message. Dmitri had a hunch that this place would be where you were." Zara paused and wrinkled her nose. "When we got here, he seemed to find you by scent, Os. I won't say it wasn't creepy...but now that we're here, I can see how he managed it."

Oscar almost laughed again but winced instead at the warning pain in his ribs. He definitely *did* need a shower, but he might never have been so glad that he hadn't had one.

There was a wet *pop* nearby.

"I'll consider me debt repaid then," Gax announced, clearing his throat theatrically. "For leavin' you before. I know you're a sensitive sort, you 'umans."

"Gax!" Marcus grinned. "You were amazing! How did you get the Gwyllgi?!"

"Turns out 'e could sense someone was gearin' up to breach the vale. That's why 'e was particularly not fond of your mate 'ere." He nodded toward Oscar. "Could smell the potential of 'im. Reason 'es got a reputation as the Guardian of the underworld 'innit." The Bugge shrugged his small shoulders, wide nostrils flaring. "Ole Beanie 'ad a chat wiv 'im. When 'e got back and were acting right n' proper, I led 'im 'ere. Looks like we were too late for part one, but just in time for the curtains."

"Better late than never," Marcus agreed.

"Oh." Gax cleared his throat, his squat body standing straighter. "Looks like there's someone wants to make sure yer okay." He shuffled back.

Oscar turned his head and saw the vast form of the zburător. *Dmitri*. His dark wings were tucked tight onto his back, his glowing eyes downcast, flickering with light, as he padded slowly forward on massive paws. He held his head low, nose practically scraping the ground, breath steaming in the night.

"Holy shit," Marcus breathed.

The zburător dropped down onto his front, letting out a low whining sound, his face dripping blood from several deep gouges.

"I...I'm okay," Oscar said weakly, blinking. His heart hammered in his chest.

The zburător's eyes fixed on his, and for a moment, he could see Dmitri there, grey swirling behind the burning flames like ash. Before he knew what he was doing, Oscar raised a hand toward him.

"Oscar," Zara murmured.

The massive thing's wolf-like head lifted, slow and tentative, touching gently against Oscar's palm. The fur of his muzzle was smooth and silky as Oscar's fingers rested upon it. Oscar smiled.

Amongst the tombstones, the Gwllygi let out a rumbling howl, seemingly finished with its meal. It fixed the group with a burning stare for a moment and dipped its head to the zburător before springing into the night.

"Dmitri," Oscar breathed. "I'm...I'm sorry. Thank you for coming, I...I..." Oscar swallowed.

The zburător moved away, shuffling back before it rose. Oscar thought he saw wetness in its eyes. In one smooth move, like flowing darkness, it spun and leapt into the night sky.

Oscar's breath felt forced and ragged as he stared into the darkness after it. *After him.*

"Will he...will he stay like that?" Zara asked softly.

"Not sure, lass," Gax rumbled. "'e crossed over. Not sure what it'll do to 'im, but probably nothin' good."

Then Oscar heard a low wailing in the night.

Sirens.

Of course, there was no way that all that noise and destruction would go unnoticed.

"Gax, can you help get us out of here?" Zara said quickly. "I don't think the police will be too pleased to find us here again tonight."

Gax smiled broadly. "Aye. But you'll 'ave to carry that lovesick lump."

TAXONOMY OF MONSTERS: THE PRETA
(ESURIITT EXSPIRAVIT)

"They shall hunger in death as they did in life. Consumed by compulsivity, jealousy, and greed. They will never be sated. In death, their hunger will be as corrupted as they, and even viler than their sin. They will hunger for human waste. For oozing wounds or rotting filth. And in the most unfortunate of cases, they shall hunger for flesh."

— ON CORRUPTED SOULS: ARTHUR'S NOTES ON THE BEYOND

34

THE HEILIGENSCHEIN

"Oh, Oscar!" Paige groaned. Oscar held the phone away, expecting a tirade of colourful abuse. "I've been so worried about you, you bloody idiot. Are you alright?"

He almost dropped the phone in shock.

Oscar blinked. "I'm...fine. I'm sorry I didn't call. There's been...a lot happened."

"Oh? Like what?"

Oscar swallowed, his eyes wandering to the table, where the not-so-useless rusted hilt sat propped up against his backpack. "Nothing big, really." Well. Nothing since *that* night almost three weeks ago. Not only had he not been able to make the pale blade appear again, no matter how hard he tried, he had barely even left this room.

After the events in the cemetery, they had managed to get Oscar to some steps down the street before they called for help. Marcus told the ambulance crew that Oscar had taken a bad tumble on a night-time walk for insomnia. Zara left before they arrived, not wanting to explain her torn clothes and already healing wounds.

As far as Oscar was concerned, three broken ribs and a lot

of bruising was getting off pretty light when a magic rock had tried to suck you in to open a gateway to hell. But it wasn't the physical injuries that were so bad. He was drained almost completely of energy, like the glowing wick of a burned out candle.

Marcus and Zara had insisted on him moving in with them, for the time being at least. Marcus had even given up his own room for Oscar to rest in; he would have protested, but at the time, he was barely strong enough to peel an orange. Given her own recent hospitalisation, Zara had no problems getting signed off from work to watch over him. On more than one occasion she had needed to help Oscar into the shower, achieving new heights of what Marcus called 'friendship goals'.

"Oscar, about the flat..."

"Were the pictures okay?" he interrupted.

"They were...great actually," Paige admitted. "The place looked immaculate. It should be going up for sale today."

"Good." Oscar forced a smile like she might see his facial expression through the phone. He had spent all of his meagre savings on a cleaner to get it that way. "I can have my stuff out whenever."

"Thank you. I'm so sorry. I really need the money, Os. The market's strong at the moment, so it should sell fast, and with how long we've had the place, you should have no problem getting your own little place with your half."

Oscar opened his mouth, but no words came out. He cleared his throat and tried again. "My half?"

"Of course." Paige sounded surprised. "We didn't have much left from Mum and Dad, so the flat was our inheritance. Wait...did you think I was just going to take the money and run?"

Oscar struggled for a response.

"Oh, God," Paige said quietly. "You *did*, didn't you?"

Oscar managed only an awkward, flabbergasted noise.

"Os...I know I haven't been the best to you. It's been...hard. I wasn't ready to become a parent, and we just had to figure things out. But...I wouldn't do that to you."

Oscar swallowed.

"Are you there?"

"Yeah."

A stiff silence hung on the line for a moment. Oscar was just beginning to wonder if Paige had hung up when she spoke again. Her voice was small and uncertain with a gentleness they were both unaccustomed to. "Are you happy?"

The words hammered into Oscar's gut, leaving him winded. "I'm...okay," he managed weakly.

Am I? Sleep wasn't easy to come by. Every night he woke up several times. His body as paralysed as it had been on the altar that tried to drink his life away. Sometimes his bed *was* the altar, feasting on him to open the gateway to Theia. Sometimes it had a voice and whispered to him and laughed. He'd wake up tangled in sheets and soaked in sweat, heart hammering in his chest.

He hadn't told anyone. He didn't want to be any more trouble than he already was and tried to focus on the fact that at least Zara was fine, even if she seemed to be struggling with some of her new...special features. Marcus had been out a lot and seemed quieter than usual, but...

"Are you...seeing anyone?" Paige ventured.

Oscar's stomach flipped. "No," he said quickly.

Too quickly.

"Oh," Paige replied slyly. "Boy trouble. I know it well."

Oscar felt his heart lurch. This was a side of his life that he and Paige had rarely discussed, and it wasn't as though these were exactly *normal* conditions.

He hadn't heard from or seen Dmitri since the zburător fled into the night. With little else to do other than recover, his mind had constantly been running every moment they had shared on a loop. Every touch, kiss, whisper, and look. He was beginning to congratulate himself when he made it through even a minute without thinking about him, only to realise he had just undone his good work.

Frustratingly, the wedge of Oscar's anger—which he had driven between himself and the memory of how happy Dmitri made him feel—seemed to be fading faster than the good feelings themselves. It didn't help that every time Oscar brought it up, wanting to somehow get the feelings out, Zara and Marcus redirected the conversation at any cost.

"Not anymore," Oscar answered sadly.

"A break-up?"

Oscar grunted.

"Don't worry. When it doesn't work out, it's for a good reason. Just be grateful that it didn't go on any longer and waste more of your time. If it's anything like my break-ups, it's one hundred percent his fault anyway."

The words needled Oscar. *Waste more time? How long had it even lasted? A night? Two?* He didn't have much to compare it to, other than Rami, but two days was short even by Oscar's standards.

Dmitri had just felt like so...*so much more*. The sheer weight of it. The intensity in his eyes and the things he said. Oscar's skin raised in goosebumps every time he remembered those eyes on him, glowing or grey. He wished he could ask Dmitri what he could see. What it was that fascinated him so because, whatever it was, it wasn't anything Oscar could find in the mirror. No matter how hard he tried.

"You'll be fine, Oscar. You have to be, don't you," Paige said brightly. It wasn't a question.

"Yeah." He brushed a tear from his cheek. "Of course."

35

THE IMPOSTER

A few days later, Oscar managed to get himself out of bed early.

He was slowly getting stronger, like some final parts of himself were snapping back into place. His ribs still hurt, but only when he reminded them with a cough, sneeze, or any other sudden movement.

Walking to the bathroom still sometimes left his legs shaking and head spinning, but he had been gradually decreasing the long periods of bed rest, under Zara's watchful eye.

But today was going to be different.

Today he had managed to get up and showered before the others woke up. His hair was brushed, and the scruffy fuzz on his face shaved. He considered making breakfast, but then remembered his last attempt at porridge—or heaven forbid, a boiled egg. Instead, he settled for putting a couple of boxes of cereal on the table with bowls and spoons. All through this, Marcus snored loudly on the nearby sofa bed, one long leg sticking out of the covers at a strange angle.

Oscar was just taking a seat at the table when Zara emerged from her bedroom, wearing an oversized T-shirt and joggers. Her teal streaked hair spilt from its messy knot, and she rubbed at her eyes tiredly. "Oscar?"

Oscar smiled.

"What? What's going on?" Marcus sat bolt upright, eyes still closed.

"Oscar has been possessed by an evil demon, and he's acting weird." Zara yawned.

"Oh." Marcus fell back into the sheets. "Just mash him up with your ghost hands a bit." He gestured vaguely.

"Maybe later," Zara agreed sleepily. "And stop saying ghost. It's more of a spirit."

"Potato tomato," Marcus mumbled into his pillow.

Zara pulled out a chair and sat down, still eyeing Oscar suspiciously. "What brings this on, Booboo?"

"You two have both been looking after me for almost a month. You've waited on me hand and foot, and I wanted to start doing something nice to help."

Zara's eyebrow raised. "You nearly died."

"You *did* die."

"I'm going to die if you two carry on." Marcus clambered out of bed, duvet cocooning around his shoulders. "Oscar, please tell me you didn't cook."

"No, I...just got cereal out."

"Oh, thank God." Marcus stumbled sleepily over to a chair and dropped onto it. "I can't deal with any Oscar cooking at this time of day."

Oscar felt his cheeks heat.

"Thank you, Oscar," Zara said sharply, nudging Marcus.

"Oh, yeah...thank you, Oscar." Marcus winked, reaching for the most sugar-loaded colourful cereal.

Oscar cleared his throat. "I was going to start looking at new places to buy...for when the money from the flat comes through, I mean."

Marcus whistled. "Party at Oscar's house."

Zara looked troubled. "I'm not sure, Oscar. It seems a little soon. You're only just getting stronger. You've lost weight, and I swear you've been rendered unconscious way more times than anyone should in the last month."

"I can't stay here forever," Oscar said.

"You could stay at my parents' house." Marcus grinned helpfully. "They have a spare room. If you can stand constant prying and smothering adoration, that is."

Oscar smiled. "I think that's unique to you."

Marcus shrugged. "I guess. The only child and all that. Not my fault I'm so bloody adorable." He crunched a mouthful of cereal. "I'm at work today, but I can help you look this weekend."

"That would be great." Oscar smiled and helped himself to some chocolate puffs.

Zara's frown deepened and concentrated itself into a deep crease between her eyebrows.

"So, uh...Marcus. Have you seen Dmitri at work?" Oscar finally asked, trying to sound as casual as he could manage.

Silence.

All chewing and movement stopped. Oscar watched Zara's and Marcus' eyes briefly connect and shift away just as quick.

"Ummmm..." Marcus swallowed a mouthful of half-chewed multicoloured sugary loops with what looked like great discomfort. "Nope. Absolutely not."

Oscar leaned forward, suspicious. "What's going on? Why do you both look like that?"

"Well..." Marcus stalled, his eyes seeking Zara's nervously.

"Dmitri has taken a leave of absence. He hasn't been to work since...that night," Zara said.

Oscar's skin prickled. "Oh." He pushed his cereal around in the bowl, watching the milk stain with colour.

"He's totally fine, though, he just—" Marcus was cut off by a loud thump. "OW! Did you just spirit kick me?!"

"Nope. That was a normal kick," Zara warned sharply. "You do not want a spirit kick. The last person I spirit smacked—"

"You yeeted into bits. Yes, I saw." Marcus scowled dramatically.

"What's going on?" Oscar asked again, voice firmer now.

"Zara is keeping Dmitri secrets," Marcus said grumpily. "She's scared you're going to go all doolally after his snack-pack again."

Zara shot Marcus a dangerous look before meeting Oscar's eyes. She sighed. "Dmitri is fine. He just needed...some time away is all."

"How do you know?" Oscar asked, his stomach clenched like a rock.

"Because I spoke to him," Zara admitted stiffly.

"When?" Oscar demanded.

She sighed, unknotting her hair and ruffling it out with her fingers. "Every goddamned day since it happened, Oscar. He won't leave me alone."

"Why?" Oscar's voice shook.

Zara gave him a measured look. "Because he is worried. He wants to know how you are. If you're better, stronger, eating. How many times you bloody smiled. It's...a lot."

Oscar sagged, his heart lurching in his chest.

"Speaking of old Wolf-face, how are you feeling, Os? Especially hungry? Would you say you...*craved* those choccie-puffs?"

"Marcus," Zara growled, "will you stop it with that? He is not pregnant."

"You don't know that, Zara," Marcus said sourly. "It could happen. I've read fanfic."

Zara ignored him. "Oscar. Dmitri told me that he knew what the Bean-Nighe would see. Or wouldn't as the case may be. What the fetch meant."

Oscar looked at her, remembering those words. Remembering what he said to Dmitri after he heard them.

"I won't say that he was right to keep it from us, but I do see his point. This was the way it was meant to be. If he had tried to deviate the path...I might not have been so lucky. Nani might not have been able to get to me in time. He asked me to keep his...inquiries after your health between us. He doesn't want to upset you, so he asked me to make sure nothing else happened. He is worried that there may be another Ocampo incident, and that's why I'm worried about you leaving. I need to be able to keep an eye on you, Os. We can't have any more little monster girls snatching you."

Oscar chewed his lip. They still assumed Nina had taken him, and he just could not bring himself to tell them the truth. That he had given up. That in that moment, after everything that had happened, he didn't have the strength to fight anymore. And now, with every day that passed since that night, that fact grew darker and heavier in his heart. It had sunk so deep into him that he knew that he could never tell them the truth.

"Sounds like Batwolf has it bad," Marcus mused, swallowing another mouthful of cereal and grinning broadly. "I had no idea you were such a monster-fucker, Os."

"Ugh. How long have you been sitting on that one?" Zara groaned.

Marcus shrugged. "Since the cemetery."

"Oscar..." Zara shifted uncomfortably in her seat. "I think you should talk to him. Not just because I'm sick of him calling me every day, but I think you need to."

"Okay," Oscar said softly, his body flooding with gratitude. This was it. This is what he wanted, and now Zara had suggested it even before he had gotten a chance to ask.

Zara smiled.

"I want to go today."

Marcus laughed loudly, and the worried crease between Zara's eyebrows reformed. "Okay, but I'm coming with you."

"Tell Ed I said hi," Marcus said.

Zara raised an eyebrow. "Oh, you're friends with the head-biting dog now?"

Marcus shrugged. "He stopped that other thing from biting my head in the cemetery, and I reckon that one was going to bite way harder."

❧ 36 ❧

THE RIGHT WRONG CHOICE

T he beginning of winter whispered in the air, making hushed promises of cold days to come. The cabbie dropped them off on the roadside not far from the pathway to the old house. Something had changed. Had the hedges been trimmed back? It looked less wild and overgrown.

"It looks...different," Oscar noted aloud.

Zara grunted, taking his hand tightly as they walked up the path. "Not different enough. This is deja-too-much for me."

Oscar grinned anxiously. "At least it can't go as badly as last time."

"Nothing goes as badly when Marcus isn't involved." Zara smirked.

They rounded the corner, and Oscar paused, looking up at one hundred and thirty-eight Kinmount street. It had definitely changed, and not just because Dmitri's sleek black car was already parked outside this time.

"Oh yeah," Zara said, "Dmitri said he was getting some work done. Pretty impressive for a month. It's still creepy as fuck, though."

It was, but there were new, clean windows, and some of the

moss and vines had been stripped back, exposing dark red brick beneath. When they reached the door, Oscar ran his finger along the ornate knocker of dark, twisted iron that hung on the fresh dark wood of the new door.

"You do it," Zara said softly, squeezing his hand. "This is all you."

The door opened before he ever had a chance.

Ed scrabbled out, a fluffy pomeranian, eyes wild with glee and so excited that his legs could barely hold him up. Oscar smiled as Ed pawed his shins, wondering if his ribs would hurt if he leaned down to fuss him, but his thoughts were interrupted by the other figure that emerged.

Dmitri hung back, his black hair tied back neatly and pale eyes shining anxiously. "Oscar." His tongue wrapped around Oscar's name the way it liked to. Like it wanted to hold onto it for safe keeping.

Oscar felt like everything inside him might turn to liquid and leave him an oozing person puddle on the ground. That was a feeling he almost hadn't missed.

"Hi Dmitri." Oscar's voice came out hoarse.

Dmitri's eyes flashed at Zara. "This is too much. He is not strong enough to be out like this."

"I'm fine," Oscar said quickly, a flash of defensiveness giving his voice strength. "Zara is taking care of me."

Zara shot Dmitri a sullen look. "Maybe if someone invited him in, he could sit down rather than stand out in the cold."

Dmitri's cheeks immediately flushed pink. "Please, come in." Was he...nervous?

"I don't think I need to be here for this." Zara squeezed Oscar's hand again before disentangling their fingers.

Oscar's face dropped. She was going to leave him. Now? He chewed the thought over. Maybe it was better this way. He met her eyes and gave her a nod.

"Of course. I will bring him back to you. After we have

talked." Dmitri bowed his head meekly to Zara in a show of defer-
ence that made Oscar's eyebrows shoot up in surprise.

Zara shrugged. "If it comes to that." She smirked ominously,
then leaned over and kissed Oscar's cheek. "Oh, I know you know
this, Dmitri, but if you upset Oscar...well, let's just say I might
develop more stompy punchy feelings for that pretty little face of
yours." Her eyes twinkled. "You're not the only one around here
with powers anymore. Maybe you're on *my* territory now."

Dmitri grunted. "Point taken. Also, speaking of territory..."
He stepped back out of sight behind the door for a moment and
returned with an old looking vase with faint swirling blue patterns
clutched in both hands. His face was a mask of neutrality. "I
believe you marked this as yours? You should take it."

Zara made a choking sound and had no choice but to accept it
as Dmitri pushed it into her hands. Her chin lifted, and Oscar
thought he saw a flash of amusement in her narrowed eyes before
she spun and retreated back down the stairs. "Remember!" she
said loudly. "Stompy punchy feelings!"

Dmitri watched with the ghost of a smile as she stalked down
the driveway, then his eyes found their way back to Oscar.
"Please," he said, "come in."

"WOULD YOU LIKE TEA?" Dmitri asked as he led Oscar down the
hallway, Ed skipping merrily beside him.

"Dmitri...the house. It's changed so much." Oscar's head
twisted around, trying to take everything in. The walls were a
crisp, clean white, the smell of fresh paint still thick in the air.
The floorboards looked to have been completely replaced, stained
the colour of warm honey. Everything looked as fresh and clean as
the owner himself, smooth-shaven and hair neatly knotted. It was
impossible to compare this to the place it had been just weeks
ago. If the house had been the carcass of some long-dead beast

then, now it was alive again, fresh and thriving. But most of all, it was *warm*. So warm Oscar had to wriggle his old pea coat off almost immediately.

"Do you like it?" Dmitri asked quickly, turning to seek his response with an eager gaze.

Oscar chewed his lip. "It...it's nice."

Dmitri's handsome face split in a wide smile, and for the first time, Oscar saw that not *all* was quite as it had been before.

Dmitri's mouth was full of dog sharp teeth.

Seeing Oscar's stare, Dmitri's expression changed quickly, brows knitting and lips sealing tightly. "Tea?" he repeated weakly.

"No. Thank you," Oscar said numbly, looking Dmitri over once more. Was he taller now too? His shoulders seemed broader...

"Please, come and sit down." Dmitri led the way into what Oscar remembered as the dark room where he had first seen Ed's eyes shining. Now it was bright and airy, with two oxblood chesterfields set to either side. The walls and floor were as pristine as the hallway, and the only other piece of furniture was a rustic looking coffee table of dark wood.

"Are you sure you don't want tea?" Dmitri asked, gesturing to the nearest sofa. "It's not my...herbal tea. I have quite a few food supplies in the house now."

"No, thank you." Oscar moved quickly toward the sofa, conscious that his knees were beginning to shake. Dmitri moved awkwardly, stepping back to give him space and clumsily knocking the coffee table as he moved.

"Are you...bigger?" Oscar asked, sinking down onto the sofa.

"Yes. It is a result of...a side effect..." He cleared his throat. "Changing is quick. Turning back, not so much. And I never changed quite like that before. When I passed through the gateway, it made me...*more*. I was not sure I would be able to change back at all." He sunk onto the opposite couch.

"Your teeth..."

Dmitri blushed. "Normally they would have changed back long ago. I suspect that this may be permanent. Other than that, most things are...normal."

Oscar chewed his lip thoughtfully. "Normal, huh? I don't know if I know what that is anymore."

Dmitri smiled wanly. "I don't think I ever did."

Oscar watched him for a moment. The other man was seemingly content to sit in silence, watching him. Oscar shifted uncomfortably under his gaze. That look again. It made his skin rise in goosebumps despite the warmth. Finally, Oscar cleared his throat. "Dmitri, I came here to apologise for the way I spoke to you. You were doing your best and what you thought was right. You saved my life, not only that night but probably more times than I can imagine." Oscar dared a glance and found Dmitri listening, rapt. "I won't pretend I have forgiven you. Zara is my best friend. Even if what you did was the right thing, it hurts that you kept something like that from me."

Dmitri's eyes shone, but he nodded silently.

"I want to forgive you. It's just...everything is so much right now. There's so much I don't understand, so much that has happened." Oscar stopped, taking a moment to gather himself.

"Are you okay?" Dmitri asked softly, leaning forward.

Oscar took a steady breath, and then a second and third, before he continued.

"My best friend died," he said slowly, letting the words hang out there. "Monsters are real. My best friend died, but now she's fine and has superpowers. And I'm some kind of cursed human who is the key to opening a hell dimension. And the guy I like...he's a giant...wolf bat dragon man."

"Zburător," Dmitri offered quietly.

"Yeah, that." Oscar slumped back. "How can I...how was I supposed to be prepared for any of that? How am I supposed to manage these things?"

"I'd say that you've been doing a pretty amazing job so far," Dmitri said, clearly struggling to stop himself from grinning.

"Why are you smiling?" Oscar said, irritated.

Dmitri attempted to make his face look serious. "I'm sorry, I just...please go on."

"The only thing stranger to me than all of this happening is it *not* happening anymore, so now I have time to think about what the hell happened, and...Dmitri, I swear to God, why are you still smiling?"

"I'm sorry." Dmitri struggled to school his face, thick brows knitting in consternation. "It's just...you said...that you like me."

Oscar sighed. "You're like a thousand years old, and suddenly you act like a teenager."

"Getting warmer on the age." The corner of Dmitri's mouth curled in the hint of a smile, flashing just the hint of a pointed tooth.

Oscar narrowed his eyes, not sure if he was joking or not, but Dmitri's expression gave nothing away.

"In truth, you make me feel like a teenager," Dmitri admitted. "It has been a very long time since I allowed myself to care for anyone. I have met countless humans over the years that I have been alive. Had more lovers than you can imagine."

"Oh my God, really? This isn't a good start..."

"I have bandied words with poets, swung blades with warriors, and traded whispers with coveted concubines. But never, in all my years, have I met anyone like you. So, this feels...new. It makes *me* feel new."

"I'm just normal." Oscar shook his head. "Worse than normal. I'm just...nothing. I nearly ended the world because I couldn't even say the right thing."

"Oscar...may I hold your hand?" Dmitri asked.

It was an absurd request, but given the earnestness in Dmitri's eyes, Oscar found himself nodding almost immediately. Dmitri stood and moved to sit beside him, leaning over and taking his hand in his own warm grip. His gaze trained on Oscar's, and Oscar found that he could not break it. "Oscar. You are a good person. A far better person than I would ever have been if I had been born human. You have flaws, but every one of your cracks just shows the light that you have inside."

Oscar blinked.

"This...*us*...I should never have pursued you. I do not deserve you," Dmitri said fiercely.

If Oscar's heart had soared at any words Dmitri had spoken before, now it plummeted. Careened like a lead weight into the pit of his guts.

"I also did not dare to leave you alone. At least not before. But now that Zara has obtained her power, I can leave you be. I can go and search for other gateways to keep this place safe. To keep you safe without hurting you anymore."

Oscar felt a deep aching within his chest where his heart used to be, and his breath felt shaky.

"I should have already gone, but I delayed. I wanted to see you once more and have this conversation."

Oscar shook his head slowly, pulling his hand free of Dmitri's. His voice was strangled. "What are you talking about?"

"The gateway. The world-parallax. Ocampo succeeded. Since that night, darkness has spread across the world like a metastasising tumour. That small leak of power awoke more world-parallaxes, weakened more places in the veil. Ones that have lain dormant for longer than ages. I have contacts who have informed me of several potential starting points. It will take months, maybe even years of research..."

"You're...leaving?" Oscar swallowed.

Dmitri's eyes slid away from his. "Oscar, I want you to take this house."

Oscar stared at him blankly. "What?"

"Before...before we were together, it was a ruin, just as I was. You breathed life into me, Oscar. This house belongs to you. Zara said you needed a place to live and I hoped this may, in part, go toward repairing some of the damage that I have done to you and yours. I have some legal contacts, and I signed the papers transferring this property to your name. Highly illegal, but the right thing to do is sometimes wrong. I am truly sorry, Oscar. For everything."

Brittle silence hung in the air.

Oscar's voice, stiff with rage, shattered it.

"You can't do that."

Dmitri's eyes widened in surprise "I-"

"*You*...after everything. The things you said. Everything that happened...you think you can just give me a house and wave goodbye, and I'm supposed to be happy?"

Dmitri blinked, mouth gaping, showing the tips of his pointed teeth.

"Do you think I could bear to be here? Haunting this place whilst you ran off, never to be seen again?" Oscar laughed bitterly; he felt tears stinging his eyes. He wiped them away roughly. "No. I don't want it. And fuck you for trying to make that happen."

"Oscar..." Dmitri said, looking torn.

"When you looked at me before, I felt special. Now I just wish I was special because then maybe then you would want to stay. I should have known you would just want to get away from me."

"I don't want to go," Dmitri breathed.

Oscar shook his head, tears welling in his eyes. "Then why?" He got shakily to his feet. He didn't know if he wanted to walk away or toward Dmitri, he just knew his body was so full of frustration and energy it had to go somewhere. His body, however, didn't quite agree, and his legs shook unsteadily beneath him like a newborn foal.

Dmitri was on his feet quickly, close to Oscar, eyes brimming with concern. Before, he had barely been a head taller, but now Oscar's eyes were level with his chest.

"Oscar...what is it that *you* want?" Dmitri pressed. "All of these things that have happened. They have happened *to* you. I don't want to be a thing that happens to you, I..."

"I don't want to be weak anymore," Oscar growled, prodding a finger against Dmitri's chest. For all the effect it had, he may as well have jabbed his finger against a wall. "I don't have any powers or abilities...just weakness. I'm not good at making decisions, but...I don't want you to go."

"Oscar," Dmitri whispered.

"Like you said, the right thing to do is sometimes wrong. For once, I know what I want to do, and I...I want to be with you. I don't want to be left behind again. I *can't* be left behind again. Not like Zara almost left me. Not like Paige...not like my parents..." Oscar's voice cracked. He sniffed, rubbing tears away from his eyes. He straightened his back and lifted his chin, forcing as much strength and pride into his voice as he could manage, even if it shook with emotion. "I don't want you to go, Dmitri. And I don't want to be apart from you. I want you to look at me the way you do. I want it every day. I want you to keep making me feel the way you do. I...I love you."

Oscar's words had barely left his mouth when Dmitri's lips were upon them. Gentle and tender, he kissed away whatever else Oscar might say, whatever he was going to think. Oscar melted into his arms, embracing Dmitri's warmth as the larger man gently pulled him to his tiptoes so their mouths could better meet.

A sharp tooth caught Oscar's lip, and he yelped in surprise, pulling away, and touching his fingertips to his mouth instinctively to check for blood.

"I'm sorry," Dmitri said quickly, blushing.

Oscar sniffled and smiled. "I guess it comes with the territory."

Dmitri took him gently into his arms again. "I don't think I could have left you," he said tiredly. "I am so glad, iubite."

"You called me that before," Oscar sniffled. "At the graveyard. What does it mean?"

Dmitri smiled. "It means 'beloved'. It means my heart was yours from before you could ever know."

Oscar wiped more tears away from his eyes; they just wouldn't seem to stop.

Dmitri cradled his face, kissing them away. "You're crying," he whispered. "Are you okay?"

Oscar sniffed again. "Of course."

"Oscar...I am glad you told me what you want. But please...let me in." He cradled his face, eye to eye as he whispered. "I see you, Oscar. You are surrounded by people who love you, yet you struggle to manage everything on your own. You are not alone, and you do not have to deal with everything yourself, Oscar. We're all here. It's...it's okay for you to need help. I'm here, and I...I see you."

Oscar came apart.

Everything that had been knotted within him for the last few weeks, for so much longer, unravelled.

Tears came faster and harder than he could control, and he let out a sob. He cried in a way he couldn't remember crying since he was a child, and maybe not even then.

"I'm here, iubite," Dmitri whispered into Oscar's hair as he held him. "I'm here, and we are together. And if anyone ever tries to keep us apart, I will pull the moon from the sky to guide my way back. I would tear the earth in two to find you."

VITA POST MORTEM: VENI,
VIDI...VICI

Barloh had been watching.

He had huddled behind one of the mausoleums, phone in hand recording everything that happened. He had recorded as the strange shadow creatures had burst out of the tear in the sky. As the monster-woman was ripped apart. He had gotten it all. Gotten the truth.

Finally. After all these years.

When it was all over, sirens began to sing in the distance. Marcus, the girl that died, and the weird pale guy—whatever they all were now—had fled. He knew now that they were all clearly just as much monsters as Tza. As Spring-heeled Jack.

His fingers curled into fists, the scarred skin on his right hand and wrist pulling painfully the way it always did, like a glove three sizes too small. Seeing what Spring-heeled Jack really was...the searing pain felt today just like it had that first day.

The years after the Thames incident had been hard.

Mostly for his mother.

They had sent her for therapy, barraged them with diagnoses, medications, and social workers. It wasn't her fault, and he never blamed her. It was *their* fault. The monsters.

Harry had been sent to the therapist too, but he kept his mouth shut. He saw the way they looked at his mother when she talked about the woman living in the river. About drowning in water coming from her own lungs and flame-eyed monster men. It was too much for her. Too much for her to do anything else with it crowding her mind. Too much for her to even eat and sleep.

Too much for her to take care of him.

It had been a toss-up between who would be taken away first.

It was her.

She almost seemed relieved when they took her. She hugged him weakly and then sagged into the wheelchair, a distant smile upon her face. He had been alone ever since. Not necessarily on his own, but *alone*.

He'd been sent to live with his aunt and uncle.

They weren't bad people, but they weren't good either. *They weren't his parents*. His sweet mother and mischievous father.

Harry hated the monsters for what they had done. He hated the river woman for killing his father, and just as much, he hated the wild-haired demon who had burned his hand trying to scare her away. His hand still ached most days, even though it was as healed as it would ever be. The skin felt tight, and most of the pain was nerve damage, the doctors said. They called him lucky.

Lucky.

At night he would sit in his room and read books that he had gotten from the library. Books that made his aunt angry when she found them, made her take him to the priest to be blessed for his demonic obsession.

Harry started to track disappearances and strange news, falling asleep in school because he spent his nights learning about monsters. He eventually learned what it was that they had seen.

Jenny Greenteeth and *Spring-heeled Jack*.

Each day and night revealed more and more of the truth about the world to him, and once his eyes were open, it was impossible to close them again. Each detention or spanking was trivial.

Laughable even. He never cared how much trouble he got into because he was succeeding.

Years later, he had found others like him on the internet, where he had ceased to be Harry Barlow, and become just *Barloh*. Where he had become part of something bigger, and found ways that he could accomplish in his greatest ambition. No, his *purpose*.

To prove that his mother was telling the truth.

To prove that monsters were real.

And then destroy them.

Now, he had his proof. He had the footage of Spring-heeled Jack, as big as a van, pouncing around and tearing into the woman with a cloak made of darkness. He knew that he had to get online to share it; he couldn't give this up to the papers. They'd monopolise it, crawl after the rights. He needed to make this *his*.

His mind raced with ideas. He would be the world's foremost authority on monsters. He'd have scholarships, interviews on national television, he'd consult the government. *This was it.*

But he needed more.

People would claim that the video was a hoax. Edited. He needed...*samples*.

He'd seen Spring-heeled Jack bleeding. Seen the woman with grey skin dripping in darkness torn in two and burned to a cinder. He knew there must be something left.

His pockets were already full of pieces of the stone that the pale kid had been lying on; that seemed to be significant. It had a bleached white appearance though he could have sworn earlier that it had weird black patterns on it. Either way, he tried to collect as many of those pieces as possible whilst the sirens got ever closer. Then he decided to go looking for whatever was left of the woman.

It took him a few minutes to find what looked like one of her arms. It was so thick with blistered char it was barely recognisable. He started to consider how he was going to transport them without getting that shit all over him when he heard it.

A whisper.

At first, he thought it was the wind in the trees, but then he heard it again.

"*Hello.*" It was faint and low. It made the hair on the back of his neck stand on end.

His eyes darted around the broken tombstones. Something moved in the shadows.

He squinted, trying to see it better even as he tensed, ready to run.

There was nothing.

That was to say, there was only a shadow. *More* shadow to be exact. *Deeper.* Shadow so dark, it stood out in the other shadows like they were the brightest daylight.

"*Hello, friend,*" they whispered. "*It seems that we have much in common, you and I.*"

Harry opened his mouth to scream, but the darkness was already forcing its way inside.

THE LESSER KNOWN MONSTERS SERIES
CONTINUES, IN....
THE BONE GATE
RORYMICHAELSON.COM

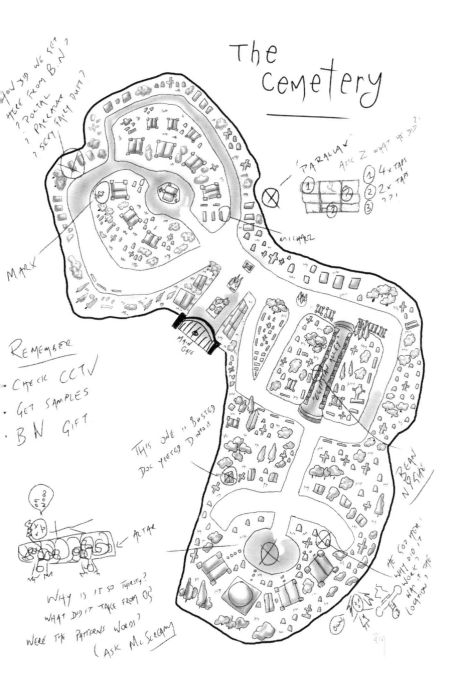

ACKNOWLEDGMENTS

When I first wrote LESSER KNOWN MONSTERS, I had no intention of sharing it. It was a secret and special thing, just for me. Now that you hold it in your hands, I think it's nice for you to know that, because it tells you how close to my heart this journey started. So, thank you for taking (or at least beginning) this wild ride with me. It means more to me than you can ever know. I hope you enjoyed this iridescent and ridiculous shard of my strange and hopeful soul.

I have so many people to thank.

Ash, who somehow convinced me to send her my excitable unpunctuated rambling about queer romance and monsters. Jayme, who may love these books even more than I do, and has been the series' biggest cheerleader, injector of rocket fuel, and champion on all fronts. I will always be grateful for the courage and confidence you both gave to me to help share these stories.

Charlie Knight, my editor: thank you for your kindness, ferocity, passion, and inspiration. Without you, these books would have made a lot less sense, and had about two thousand fewer commas. Dean Cole, my cover designer: thank you for endless patience and tolerance of my copious and wandering requests. Axel Toth (Urban Knight Art), thank you for seeing my characters and bringing them to life with your incredible illustrations. All of you are held dearly in the dark beating heart of the LESSER KNOWN MONSTERS series, and there is nothing you can do to escape it...

I've had such an incredible amount of support for the series from so many wonderful readers and amazing authors, including

Shimaira, Halo, Drew, Mario, Chris, Gabe, M.E, Lou, Addy, Katherine, Gideon, and Tizom. Thank you to Matt and Queer Lit for their passionate support of my books. All your time and kindness has made every day since sharing this story a little brighter for me.

Finally, thank you to my partner, who tolerated countless hours of me working on a secretive project on my laptop, with no idea what I was doing. Thank you for your patience and respect, and your love, which without I might not know what to write about at all.

ABOUT THE AUTHOR

Rory Michaelson is always doing too many things, and rarely the ones that they ought to be. The Lesser Known Monsters series includes Rory's debut novel and short story collection. They were born and raised in the UK, love stories in all forms, and are easily bribed with cookies.

You can follow Rory on Twitter (and other social media platforms) for shenanigans @RoryMichaelson, or subscribe to their newsletter at RoryMichaelson.com.

ALSO BY RORY MICHAELSON

The Lesser Known Monsters Series

Lesser Known Monsters

The Bone Gate

The Torn Earth

The Little Book of Lesser Known Monsters

"Go on then, bugger off!"